Making sure that my mother thinks that I'm having a good time at camp is probably more important than actually having a good time at camp. I'm used to not having a good time at things that involve interacting with other people. I've long resigned myself to a lifetime of avoiding unnecessary social situations at all costs and, if forced to go, standing in the corner awkwardly while more exciting people talk around me. My mother, on the other hand, has *hopes* for me. She wants me to put myself out there and have some normal teenage experiences with "kids my age." I mean, that's why everyone goes to camp, right? I'm not sure how to explain to her that "normal experiences with kids my age" at wilderness therapy camp means living with a roommate who has brought an arsenal of banned items, across the hall from someone who is probably a sociopath.//

Praise for *Four Weeks, Five People*

"Readers looking for contemporary fiction that thoughtfully tackles the challenges inherent to psychological and emotional disorders will easily connect with this book."

—*Booklist*

"First-time novelist Yu does a good job of presenting the therapy process, capturing the words therapists use and realistically describing the uncertain arc of recovery.... Moving and of interest to teens experiencing similar stresses."

—*Kirkus Reviews*

"An amazing story about the power of friendship and the struggles that too often go unspoken."

—*Seventeen*

Also by Jennifer Yu

Imagine Us Happy

JENNIFER YU

FOUR WEEKS, FIVE PEOPLE

seventeen FICTION
FROM HARLEQUIN TEEN

Recycling programs
for this product may
not exist in your area.

ISBN-13: 978-1-335-46887-1

Four Weeks, Five People

Copyright © 2018 by Jennifer Yu

This edition published by arrangement with Harlequin Books S.A.

For questions and comments about the quality of this book, please contact us
at CustomerService@Harlequin.com.

Printed in U.S.A.

For my parents,

Qifeng Yu & Mingzhu Chen,

to whom I owe countless novels' worth of thanks.

MOVE-IN

STELLA

A FEW WORDS of advice for those attending Camp Ugunduzi for the first time:

Contrary to what the brochure may have told your parents, siblings, grandparents, estranged uncles, teachers, psychiatrists, well-meaning friends, not-so-well-meaning friends, and other people of distant relation who "care about you" and have therefore shipped you to the middle of upstate New York (read: out of their lives) for one month of summer while everyone else just goes kayaking and eats hot dogs, you will probably not discover a way to change your life at this camp.

In fact, despite being at a camp named Ugunduzi—the Swahili word for "discovery," because nothing says *profound* quite like Google Translate—you are unlikely to discover very much here. Things like...

Yourself.

The meaning of life.

Love.

What it means to be human

...will generally not be found during your time here. You're actually fairly unlikely to discover anything other than 1) approximately ten new mosquito bites a day on body parts you didn't know existed, and 2) at least fifty ways to hide alcohol from the counselors.

But hey, don't let me get you down. Your parents are excited. Your grandparents are excited. Your therapist is less excited because she's missing out on four weeks of checks, but still excited because *this experience* could be *the next step* to a *healthy lifestyle*. Your friends are the most excited of all, because they think a month of trust-building exercises in the woods is going to get them the "old you" back—you know, the one who did fun, stupid things with them, like go to the mall and giggle at every cute boy that walked by, or prank-call strangers at 3:00 a.m. while high off sleep-deprivation and Ben and Jerry's. The one they grew up with, before the monsters under your bed found their way into your head and Lunchables turned into a stackable pile of pills and Truth or Dare started feeling like a confessional.

Believe me, I don't want to ruin this for you. I know how it feels—like everyone else is so full of hope and excitement they're counting on this camp more than you are. And I know that even though you yelled at your mom to stop counting down the days way back in April, and even though you rolled your eyes when you promised your psychiatrist you'd *immerse yourself*, and even though you told your friends it was just some "bullshit summer camp for psychos," you're also excited. Because you kind of want the old you back, too.

CAMP

19 83

UGUNDUZI

Camp Ugunduzi is an experimental four-week therapeutic wilderness program for teenagers ages 15–17 who may be experiencing a variety of mental health issues, including depression, anxiety, self-destructive behavior, antisocial behavior, and other mood disorders. Founded in 2010 by Dr. Ash Palmer, Ugunduzi operates upon the principal that teenagers struggling with emotional illness deserve a summer camp that is as recreational as it is therapeutic—one that taps into the natural healing power of the wild without the risks and potential dangers of similar boot camp programs. Over the course of the program, campers are introduced to the four basic tenets of Ugunduzi: (1) understanding and accepting the past, (2) forming authentic relationships, (3) celebrating personal success, and (4) forgiving personal failure.

Ugunduzi should not be used as a substitute for inpatient treatment in the case of serious psychotic symptoms such as hallucinations, persistent delusions, or suicidal behavior.

→

CAMP RULES

- The main principle of Camp Ugunduzi is respect. Campers are expected to treat others, the property, and themselves with respect at all times.

- Horseplay, roughhousing, and physical altercations between campers are strictly prohibited.

- All forms of alcohol and drugs that have not been prescribed are strictly prohibited.

- All foul language is strictly prohibited.

- Campers must remain in the main camp area during individual time. They may not go on hikes unsupervised during this time.

- Campers must remain in their rooms after the day ends. There will be bed checks every two hours over the course of the night.

- Camper participation is required at all individual and group therapy sessions.

- Use of the TV is restricted to designated movie-viewing times on weekends.

- If, at any point during a group session, a camper feels triggered or emotionally threatened by the discussion, he or she may signal to leave and take a five-minute break.

- These materials are prohibited and should be turned in to the counselors at the beginning of camp: cell phones, other electronics, spiral-bound notebooks, hair straighteners and curlers, earrings, mechanical pencils, keys, blades and knives.

- Razors, nail clippers, and hair scissors must remain in lockers at all times when not in the shower.

- Body checks will be performed every Friday.

- Campers will be weighed every Wednesday.

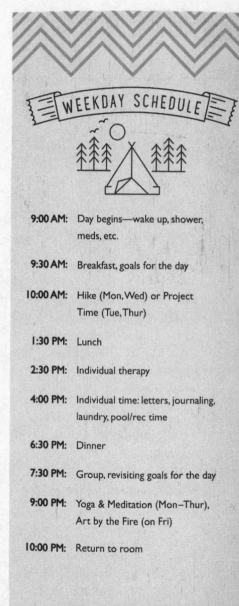

WEEKDAY SCHEDULE

9:00 AM: Day begins—wake up, shower, meds, etc.

9:30 AM: Breakfast, goals for the day

10:00 AM: Hike (Mon, Wed) or Project Time (Tue, Thur)

1:30 PM: Lunch

2:30 PM: Individual therapy

4:00 PM: Individual time: letters, journaling, laundry, pool/rec time

6:30 PM: Dinner

7:30 PM: Group, revisiting goals for the day

9:00 PM: Yoga & Meditation (Mon–Thur), Art by the Fire (on Fri)

10:00 PM: Return to room

WEEKEND SCHEDULE

10:00 AM: Day begins—wake up, shower, meds, etc.

10:30 AM: Breakfast, goals for the day

11:00 AM: Individual time

1:30 PM: Lunch

2:30 PM: Yoga & Meditation

5:00 PM: Individual time

6:30 PM: Dinner

7:30 PM: Group, revisiting goals for the day

9:00 PM: Individual time

12:00 AM: Return to room

CLARISA

MY MOM ASKS me how I'm feeling seven times on the way to camp. We have just left the house. She manages to merge safely onto the freeway before she looks over at me, eyebrows furrowed, and lets the words escape: "How are you feeling, honey?" She has been dying to ask this ever since we pulled out of the driveway, I know, and I feel bad for not being able to give her the answer she wants. But I also know that if I say anything resembling the truth—even if it's something perfectly normal, like "a little nervous," or "kind of apprehensive," or, God forbid, "I'm kind of scared"—we will talk about it for the next three hours, until we get to camp. We will talk about it until we have rehashed every single conversation we have ever had about "stepping out of my comfort zone" or "trying something new." We will talk about it until the sound of her voice makes me want to collapse and I have to put my head between my hands and count, very carefully, over and over again, just to get my heart rate back down. //

"I'm fine," I say, and turn my gaze to the mile markers flying by outside the window. 23 (bad). 24 (bad). 25 (good).

There's something comforting in the numbers. There's something stable and predictable and real. There always has been. //

I know it's unfair for me to blow off her concern like this, but it's hard to feel sympathy when I know that she knows exactly how I feel. How many times have I told her that the point of not having friends is that there's never anyone dragging me out of the house to places I never wanted to go to in the first place? Or that I'm perfectly happy to stay in my room all summer rereading the *Harry Potter* series from start to finish for the twelfth time? I don't know how much fun she expects me to have at this camp, but I can pretty much guarantee that it's not going to be as much fun as Harry Potter discovering a whole other, magical world. And learning the true meaning of family for the first time in his life. And, oh, yeah, defeating Lord Voldemort, like, six times. The only problem is, I don't think my mom considers living vicariously to qualify as, well, actual "living." //

"You doing okay?" my mom says when she can't stand the quiet any longer. "Do you want some water? There's some in the backseat." 26 (bad). 27 (*really* bad). 28 (good). "I'm fine, Mom," I say. //

Mile 45. "Are you sure you don't want anything to drink? Or eat? Are you feeling okay? You barely ate anything this morning." *Stop*, I want to say. *I barely ate anything this morning because it was 6:00 a.m. and I could barely muster up the motor function to walk to the table.* //

Mile 57. "Clarisa?" "I'm fine." We are an hour into the drive and a familiar note of concern has entered my mom's voice. Outside, the buildings of New York City have dissolved into endless forests of deciduous trees. They cling to each other, branches locked together, roots trawling the dirt for space. I count the number of trees in every overcrowded cluster we drive by and feel the numbers fill my head, pushing the anxiety away: eight trees, ten trees, seven trees. //

"Drink some water, Clarisa," my mom says. "You're probably dehydrated. I don't want you to get sick—" "—six, four, twelve, four, six," I interrupt. "What?" she says. "The trees," I respond. "They cluster together—I was counting them." //

My mom bites her lip, her knuckles white on the steering wheel. I watch her blink rapidly—one, two, three. I feel bad for her, I really do. "You're going to get dehydrated before camp even starts," she says, starting to sound desperate. "I'm *fine*," I repeat. *Eight, nine, four*— "What the heck, Mom!" //

My mom takes one hand off the wheel and reaches into the backseat, trying to feel her way to the water bottles. We are going sixty miles an hour on a busy highway, and I can practically see her saying, "Screw it all," for the sake of getting me a flipping *water bottle*. "Mom!" I shout. I reach into the backseat and grab a water bottle myself before she can get us both killed. "What the heck are you doing? Are you trying to kill me before we even make it to camp?" The sheer terror in my voice must get to her, because my mom snaps her arm back, replaces her hand on the steering wheel, and takes a deep breath. //

"I just don't want you to be dehydrated," she says, so controlled that it's almost scary. Her eyes are blazing. "This is not about me being dehydrated, and you know it!" I respond. "Honey, stop," my mom says. "Aren't you excited for camp?" I stare at her for a second. She is fighting so hard. //

"Honey? How are you feeling?" I can feel the still-unopened water bottle in my hand. There's a part of me that wants to squeeze it until the plastic crumples under my grip and water bursts everywhere. Instead, I turn around and look back out the window—back to the mile markers, back to the trees. Back to the numbers. I can practically hear the fight go out. //

Sixty-six miles later, my mom finally breaks the silence. "I'm sorry I snapped at you," she says. She sounds exhausted. "Are you okay?" I tell her I'm glad she asked. I mean it, too. There is nothing comfortable about silence between two people who have too much to say to each other to speak. //

It's not long until the first sign for the camp appears. *Camp Ugunduzi*, it says, *Next exit*. My mom's breath and mine catch at the same time. I put my hand on her arm, partially to reassure her, and partially to stop myself from shaking. "You packed sunscreen, right?" she says. "And bug spray? And Band-Aids?" //

"It's going to be fine, Mom," I say. But that's another one of those things that neither of us really knows how to believe. So instead of talking, we just sit and watch as the camp grounds come into view. First there's the main housing building, directly ahead of the parking lot, painted a hideous shade of bright yellow that makes it impossible to miss. Behind it, a lake unfurls, water sparkling in the sunlight. There are picnic tables scattered across the grass in front of the building and a volleyball court in the distance. And then we're parked, unmoving, and I should be getting out of the car, I should be grabbing my suitcase from the trunk, I should be doing *something*, for goodness' sake, but all I can think of is my mother's voice, her question echoing in my head over and over and over again. //

Are you okay? Are you okay? Are you okay? Are you okay? Are you okay? Are you okay? And just like that, I can't breathe. //

"Um, Mom," I say. My voice comes out shrill and uneven, which of course makes me feel even worse. "Oh, honey," my mom says. She looks so touched. "Don't be nervous. Ashley has sent someone here every year since they started the program and never had a bad experience, and Dr. Manning says the Zoloft should be kicking in over the next two weeks, too, so there's nothing to—" "That's not it," I say. //

I close my eyes. "I need you—" I start, before a wave of panic rises in my chest and crushes the sentence. "I need you to…to ask me again." "What?" she says. *Breathe*, I tell myself. And then again. And again, and again, and again, and again, and again. //

"I just need you to ask me again," I say through gritted teeth. "How I am. You asked six times, so I just— Could you please ask one more time?" I can feel the tears starting to well up in my eyes. *Pathetic*, I think. Camp hasn't even started and I'm already breaking down. //

I look over at my mom, who has frozen with one hand on the door handle. An expression on her face I know all too well. "We're here," she says, voice brutally calm. "How are you feeling?" I open my eyes, finish the rest of my water bottle, open the car door, and step out. I do not bother replying. She knows the answer just as well as I do. //

MASON

MY PARENTS, IN typically self-absorbed fashion, think that this is their fault.

You should hear them talking to each other about it when they think I have music playing through my headphones, or am sleeping in my room, or have gotten so absorbed in my phone that I've lost cochlear function. "We shouldn't have spoiled him so much as a kid," they say. "We shouldn't have raised him in this neighborhood, it's too gentrified, there's too *much* here—it's made him entitled." Then comes the long pause when my mother looks at my father with sad, guilty eyes, and my father looks back at her, crossing and uncrossing his arms over the dinner table and wishing he had an answer.

"There's nothing we could have done, Amy," he always says.

There's nothing we could have done.

They've been relying on that phrase for a while. In the fourth grade, when Brian Whitaker tried to steal my lunch box and I took a pair of scissors from the art corner and quietly destroyed his in return. *There's nothing we could have done.* In eighth grade, when I called Jenny Winters a slut in gym class and she had a conniption of epic proportions even though, let's face it, I was just the only one brave enough to say out loud what everyone else was thinking. *There's nothing we could have done.* In sophomore year, when Peter Chu called me a faggot and opened his locker the next morning to find his stuff covered with fifth-period AP Biology's supply of dead frogs. *There's nothing we could have done.* It took a four-hour meeting with half of the administration to sort that one out, and the only way our bumbling pushover of a principal would let me stay at the high school was if my parents agreed to send me to a therapist for a serious psychological evaluation.

It wasn't long until we were sitting in some over-air-conditioned, underdecorated therapist's office in downtown Bethesda, listening to some psychiatric hack spout an endless stream of nonsense. It took only three words for all of my parents' worst fears to be confirmed.

Narcissistic Personality Disorder.

Narcissistic Personality Disorder.

"Narcissistic personality disorder?" my mom repeated.

"That's not even a real thing, Mom," I said. But she was already starting to fall apart, and I knew she wasn't listening to me. In fact, I knew exactly where her mind was as she looked over to my father, teary and frantic, for reassurance.

There's nothing we could have done.

They're trying, of course. In one of the least self-aware moves two remarkably not self-aware people have ever made, they are now trying to undo what they see as the negative externalities of wealth by sending me to a twenty-thousand-dollar summer camp.

So here we are, staring at each other in the room I'm about to be imprisoned in for a month. I watch as my mom takes her hand off my suitcase and then puts it back, unable to decide whether or not she's ready to leave. "Mason," she says, and takes a deep breath. This is my mother's *holding-back-tears voice*, which means that it's time to rearrange my face into a sympathetic, pained expression. "Mason, promise me you'll take advantage of this opportunity."

"I promise," I say, looking into her eyes. I walk toward her, place a hand on her shoulder, then draw her in for a hug. By the time we pull apart, she is dabbing at her eyes. This is a *good thing*, I say to myself. I am doing a good thing. My mom will go home and convince herself that she's found the perfect program for me and that when I come home in a month, I'll be a totally different person. Then she'll drink tea and actually be able to fall asleep without worrying about me for once. I won't have to deal with a lecture that I've heard a thousand times already, and my father can feel manly and important, since he's footing the bill for this stupid camp. Besides, what else am I supposed to say? "Mom, everyone else at this camp is going to be a dipshit and there is no reason for me to be here. But if you're going to make me come, the least you can do is hurry up and leave me in peace." She doesn't deserve the anxiety and I don't deserve the fallout.

So I hug her, and I smile in the way that I know reminds her of my father, and I take the suitcase. "I got this," I say. I move it to the side of the room, where there's a pile of bags starting to form, and then walk back and shake my father's hand.

"Be good, son," he says.

"Yes, sir," I say, and flash him a grin.

"All right, Amy," he says, squeezing my mother's hand and guiding her past the suitcase. They leave hand in hand—my mother teary, my father stoic. I see them exchange a look as they walk out the door.

There's nothing we could have done.

ANDREW

IT STARTED KIND of as a joke.

I'm in this band, right? It's called The Eureka Moment. And I know every single kid in every single band ever says this, but we're actually pretty good. Jake is a killer guitarist, Aidan has been playing drums since before he could walk, Sam doesn't get pissed about no one *actually* giving a shit about bass (way more important than skill when it comes to bassists, to be honest), and I have a good enough voice to get away with having pretty average guitar skills and even more average hair.

We weren't very well-known for most of our time together. The first two years, we played a lot in garages and not a lot anywhere else. It was fun, obviously, but still, we dreamed about making it big just like any other band, you know? It wasn't just the fame or the money—kind of the whole deal. The lifestyle, I guess. The image. I remember we'd spend hours looking at pictures of grungy lead singers with bands dressed in all black and ripped-up cigarette jeans that only anorexics and addicts can fit into. *Heroin chic*, it was called.

I don't know how it happened, really, but I think we all kind of ended up adopting that look, thinking it would make us more popular. I mean, girls dig that shit, right? And then it turned into this stupid game, where whoever spent the most time smoking and the least amount of time eating "won." There was never really any prize. I guess the satisfaction was enough. It was one of those jokes that everyone takes a little too seriously. We probably dropped a hundred pounds between the four of us in a few months.

The problem is that it worked. People were into us. Or maybe they weren't *into us*, really, but they were at least *interested* in us. They gave us a chance, is what I'm saying. Our Twitter followers doubled. Girls started tagging us in Facebook photos their parents probably wouldn't be thrilled about. The local newspaper picked up a couple stories about us. More and more people started coming to shows.

We never really talked about the game after we got more popular. I think the other guys just sort of realized it was stupid, quit, and went back to eating absolute crap and calling it "bulking." You know, normal sixteen-year-old guy stuff.

But I couldn't get it out of my head. I think maybe it affected me more than anyone else. I'm the lead singer, I guess, so people noticed my appearance more than some of the other guys. Smoking anything I could get my hands on and not eating and buying jeans I couldn't afford and shouldn't have been able to fit into and watching my cheekbones get more and more noticeable—I felt good about it. It was like accomplishing something, like becoming someone I wanted to be. And then, gradually, it pretty much became all I was. I mean, my friends were totally freaked out. My band mates hung around because we played together, but even they thought I was taking the whole thing a bit too far. The only people who really wanted to spend any time with me anymore by the time The Incident rolled around were people who dug the band but didn't actually know anything about me as a person.

I'm not going to say that I don't have a problem, because that would be kind of ridiculous at this point. I mean, I'm here, right? Camp Ugunduzi. I came willingly. I said okay when my parents suggested it and told them I would work on my issues and meant it. I'm not even angry about the fact that we're in the middle of nowhere. Or that they took our phones away. Or that we're not going to have internet and I'm not going to be able to jam with the guys for, like, four weeks. I'll take that if it means I can bring myself to eat a burger and fries when I get back.

And it's not like it's not nice here. They've gathered all the campers on the grass by the lake so that the director can give some kind of speech before we break into our groups, and I have to admit, it's pretty much just as beautiful as the brochure promised it would be. This is the kind of place artists go when they need quiet inspiration. When they're sick of playing distorted power chords all day long and want to do something acoustic, something peaceful. I sit down on the grass, head filled with melodies and choruses and wishing I had brought my notebook out with me so that I could get it all down before they disappear. Inspiration is like that. There, and then, all of a sudden, gone.

By the time the director finally joins us, there's about fifty people out on the grass. Some of them have formed small clusters and are talking to each other, but most people, like me, are just sort of staring into the distance. And then there's this deafening screeching that I'd recognize anywhere as microphone feedback. For a second, it's almost like I'm back in Aidan's basement, plugging in all the amps and messing around with mics before a show. It's a sound I've grown weirdly fond of, considering how awful it sounds. But then the director starts talking, and I snap out of it.

"Welcome to Camp Ugunduzi," he says. "My name is Dr. Ash Palmer, and I'm the director here."

The first thing I notice about this man is that everything about him is gray. Gray hair, gray eyes, gray suit. Even his voice, which is low and deep and gravelly, makes me think of the color gray.

"I could not be more thrilled to be starting the fifth year of our wonderful pilot program with you," Dr. Palmer says. Which sounds great and all, except it would be impossible for this guy to look any *less* thrilled. Seriously. Dr. Palmer looks like one of those dudes who is literally not capable of smiling.

"Unfortunately, my position as director means that, for the most part, I won't be seeing much of you over the course of the next few weeks. With that in mind, I thought long and hard about what I wanted to say this afternoon.

"Foreboding warnings against misbehavior and disobedience seemed like a bad way to begin what I hope—and I certainly know you all hope—will be a positive experience. Attempts to find some sort of grand, overarching teaching message that would apply to a group as complex and diverse as you seemed infantilizing, not to mention destined to fail. And the usual cliché words of encouragement—well, I'm sure you're all sick of hearing those."

At this point, I'm pretty confused. I mean, is he trying to be nice? Is he trying to be strict? Is he trying to intimidate us? Does anyone know? I look around the circle. Based on the looks on everyone else's faces, the answer is definitely not.

"So I thought I would leave my opening dramatics to this, and leave the rest to our terrific, incredible staff," Dr. Palmer continues. "For many of you, Camp Ugunduzi is a land of unknown. You may feel apprehensive, unsure, perhaps even scared, about what the next few weeks will entail. For others, it is a place where you've come to identify and address your problems. Your time here may hold many challenges, but you've come determined to confront them as best you can. Whatever role Camp Ugunduzi may play in each of your individual lives, I hope that for all of you it means an opportunity. To heal. To change. And, ultimately, to grow."

Dr. Palmer does one last sweeping look across everyone gathered outside. Then he nods. "With that, I take my leave. You should now find your way to your group leaders, who are stationed around the area with signs with their group number on them."

I stand up and start walking toward the woman standing next to the water with a giant 1L sign. Then I watch as everyone else finds their own group: clusters form around the 1R sign, then 2L, then 2R, then 3L, and so on until all ten signs are surrounded by five or six campers. But even as I look around, trying to take everything in at once, my head is still on Dr. Palmer, in his gray suit, giving his speech in his gray, gray voice. It was nothing unusual, I know. I shouldn't even be thinking about it. Just standard stuff that you'd expect to hear on the first day of camp—about how we're going to grow, and change, and help each other solve all of our problems and whatever else. It's stuff that should make me excited actually—because this is why my parents sent me. Because this is why I came.

But the thing is, there's a part of me that's scared. There's a part of me that doesn't want to grow, or change, or let anyone help me get through this stupid problem. Because sometimes it feels like it's everything I have. Or everything I even am. And sometimes, like the nights before shows and the moments after eating something I know I really shouldn't have and when I'm counting my ribs as I'm lying in bed, I can't think of who I'd be without it.

BEN

Here is the exposition:

```
FADE IN:
EXT. CAMP UGUNDUZI MAIN GROUNDS—DAY
A field of grass.
The sun is shining. The air is warm. There is
no noise other than the chirping of birds, the
rustle of leaves in the wind, the occasional
crack of branches from the forest in the dis-
tance. All is calm. All is beautiful. All is
perfect. Well, except—
PAN to reveal the UGUNDUZI 1L BLOCK: five un-
happy campers standing in a circle and looking
like they're facing certain death. One of them,
lanky with brown hair and green eyes, grimaces.
```

BEN (V.O.)

```
Yeah, so that's me.
This isn't as weird as it seems.
Think about watching a movie. Think about
```

the feeling you get when you're actually in the theater, watching stuff happen on-screen. You're invested, right? You want to know what happens. You like the characters, or you hate them, or you want them to hook up, or you want one of them to kill the other, or you want everyone to kill everyone else because they're all imbeciles (I call this last one the Michael Bay effect). The point is, you care about them as if they're real humans. You react emotionally to the things they do as if they're real humans. But at the same time, you know, in your mind, that they're not *actually* real humans. You know that in half an hour, or an hour, or two hours, or way too *many* hours (Michael Bay effect again here), the lights are going to come back on, and the universe you've just been lost in for however long is going to disappear, and all of the people you just rooted for or cheered against or lusted after are going to vaporize, too. And so, while you care, there's always a part of you that's holding back. And sometimes, that part of you is strong enough to drown out everything else you're feeling in a sea of indifference.

That's what moments like this feel like. People always say that dissociation is when things don't feel "real," and I used to say that, too. But then I realized—that's not true. I know that I'm standing outside in the middle of a state park in upstate New York, and that I'm with four other people, and that we're all furiously avoiding eye contact with each other while waiting for the adults to start talking and tell us what to do, and that I would do *anything* to disappear and be somewhere else right now. Life doesn't get much realer than that.

What it *does* feel like is that, at any moment, the lights will come on and the credits will play and I'll be put out of my troubled, awkward, unavoidably *real* misery. Sure, I'm so panicked that I can barely breathe right now, but just wait until the act-two turn! And yeah, I'm positive that everyone can already tell how terrified and pathetic I am, but I'm sure it'll all get sorted out in the closing pages of act three. Whatever mortifying thing I'm about to do or say, however much I feel like I'd rather be alone in a hole in the ground than have to talk to everyone standing here and make a total idiot of myself, even if it's so bad that I feel like I can never justify getting out of bed again—none of it matters, not *really*. The girl glowering at the grass will exist to the left; the boy to my right will disappear off-screen. It'll all be okay. Because that's just how movies *are*.

Here is the rising action:

I've barely had a moment to look around the circle at the other campers before one of the counselors steps forward, a shit-eating grin splitting his face. JOSH (fifties), as his name-tag reads, looks like what would happen if Zach Galifianakis and Seth Rogen had a love child, and then that love child was raised in an Amish family that didn't believe in things like haircuts, and hygiene, and shaving. Bearded, potbellied, decked out in a T-shirt and sunglasses too small for his face, Josh's presence is enough to halt the panic threatening to suffocate me—if only because it's been replaced by a wave of disbelief.

JOSH

(booming, still grinning)
So, there's this blind man, right? And he walks into a bar. And then a table. And then a chair.

Josh beams at us like he's just told the funniest joke in the world. No one laughs. Not even JESSIE (forties), the other counselor holding our group's sign, cracks a smile.

JOSH

Okay okay okay okay. Let me try another one. My friend Sal once told me that time flies like an arrow. I told him, I don't know about that, Sal, but I do know that fruit flies like a banana.

The ASIAN GIRL standing next to me shifts uncomfortably. She's pretty but looks TERRIFIED to be here. Entire body tensed. Fists clenched. Eyes squeezed shut.

BEN (V.O.)

Let's just say that I can relate.

A DARK-HAIRED BOY standing directly across the circle from me blows his bangs out of his eyes and squints at Josh like he's an apparition. He's unhealthily thin—gaunt, in fact—but the long hair, bad posture, and black clothes combine to give off an aura of DISAFFECTED COOLNESS.

BEN (V.O.)

Let's just say that I can*not* relate.

Josh, who apparently has materialized straight out of a Coen Brothers film, continues to grin encouragingly at us.

BEN (V.O.)

The thing is, there are days when I would think that every single stupid joke that Josh is making right now is absolutely hilarious. Days when I'm the kind of person who thinks that every single thing *period* is hilarious. And I wish that today could be one of those days, if only to make this situation a little less unbearably awkward. But it's not one of those days, and I'm not that kind of guy right now, so I guess all I have to be thankful for in this moment is that it's not one of those *other* days—when it feels like the world is collapsing in on my chest no matter what I do or where I go, when no joke would get me to laugh no matter *how* funny it was.

JOSH

No? No? All right, I got one more for you guys. This one's about pizza. Everyone loves pizza! But maybe I shouldn't tell it. It's pretty chees—

CAMPER

(over)
For Christ's sake, Josh. Does that shit ever work?
Everyone turns around to look at the ANGRY GIRL who's just interrupted—including the two counselors.

JESSIE

Watch your language, Stella.

STELLA

Ugh, are you *serious*? What are we, in kindergarten?

JESSIE

No foul language. Camp rule #4. You should know that, Stella, we've been over this.

★ ★ ★

Stella looks like she wants to argue, but—

STELLA

All right, fine.

She turns back to Josh.

STELLA

Does that *stuff* ever work, Josh? Seriously, those jokes haven't gotten funnier since you used the exact same ones last year.

JOSH

Ah, Stella. If only I could have your wit.

STELLA

Yeah? I'll trade you for emotional health.

Josh seems legitimately unfazed. If anything, he looks *thrilled* that someone's actually talking to him. Stella stares back evenly, clearly unimpressed by the compliment.

BEN (V.O.)

Having seen every camp movie made since 1950, including the entirety of *Wet Hot American Summer*, I feel fairly qualified to make the assessment that Stella is the girl that every guy here falls in love with by the end of camp. First off, she's apparently already been at camp before, so she actually knows what's going on. And second, she's kind of a bitch, which, according to every rom-com ever made, is the number-one way to attract people with emotional problems and low self-esteem.

I resolve to spend as little time with her as possible.

JOSH

Well, anyway. All of this is just to say—WELCOME, friends! It is so, so good to see all of you. And on such a beautiful day, too—isn't it? Nothing gets the positive energy flowing like fresh air filling your lungs on a beautiful day. Except maybe some good old-fashioned classic rock. The Doors, anyone? Jethro Tull?

Josh looks around the circle hopefully, but no one says anything. I start to feel like we're being hazed. I mean, I've never actually *been* hazed, but I have seen *Animal House*, and I'm assuming that movie wasn't added to the National Film Registry for nothing.

JOSH

Oh, well. Regardless, I could not be more excited to be beginning our journey together. I can only hope it will be as rewarding, as wondrous, as *transformative*, as my journey has been since starting at Camp Ugunduzi its first summer four years ago. Today, my spiritually embattled campers, we begin anew.

Josh beams and turns to face Jessie. I look around and am relieved to find that no one else appears to have any idea what he's talking about, either.

JOSH

And now—Jessie? Would you care to bestow some of your wisdom upon our campers?

Jessie—short brown hair, glasses—ignores Josh's wink and steps forward, smiling tightly. It's the kind of smile that's only one ill-advised statement away from becoming a frown. Jessie, it's pretty obvious, is not going to start her opening remarks with a lineup of corny jokes.

JESSIE

Thank you, Josh. And thank you for your, ah, encouraging words.

She pauses for a minute. If Josh can sense any irony behind her words, his face doesn't show it.

JESSIE

Like Josh, I am thrilled to welcome you to Camp Ugunduzi. I am confident that you will

find the next weeks to be productive and sup-
portive, and that when we part four weeks from
today, we will all be better for our time here.

I encourage you to use Josh and myself as re-
sources in whatever way you need. We are here
to help. We are here to educate. We are here to
be a support system. Please never feel afraid
to use it.

Jessie pauses, readjusts her glasses.

JESSIE

On the other hand, we are not here to be your
best friends. We will not turn a blind eye to
misbehavior or any dangerous, illicit activity. We are here to keep you safe and healthy.
Is that clear?

No response. Jessie tries again, the question sounding considerably more like a demand
this time.

JESSIE

Is that clear?

This time, we all get the memo. A chorus of
dutiful *yeses* fills the air. But no one looks
particularly happy about it. Jessie's an obvious reminder that as hard as we might try to
pretend, this isn't exactly the kind of camp

you go to when you want to have a summer of fun and games.

JESSIE

Excellent. Now we can proceed to the introductions that matter—yours. Stella, will you start us off?

Not really a question. Stella glares at Jessie, who looks back calmly. There's clearly history there. A beat. Two beats. Three beats.

STELLA

("fuck you")
I'd love to. What exactly do you want me to say?

JESSIE

Oh, nothing out of the ordinary. Why don't we do—name, age, hometown, what brings you to Camp Ugunduzi. Anything else I'm missing, Josh?

JOSH

Mmm. Happy place.
Confusion flickers briefly over Jessie's stern expression. Stella buries her face in her hands.

JESSIE

Sorry?

JOSH

Happy place. Where is your happy place? The place where you feel most at home. At one with yourself. In line with the rest of the uni-verse. At peace—

JESSIE

Right. Happy place. Of course. Go ahead, Stella.

STELLA

I'm Stella. Seventeen. From Wethersfield, Con-necticut. My happy place is… Well, it's defi-nitely not here, I can tell you guys that much.

JESSIE / JOSH

Stella! / Hmm.

JESSIE

Is this really the note you want to start camp on, Stella?

STELLA

Well, I didn't really want to start camp on any sort of note, thanks very much. Or at all. But since no one asked me, I guess this is the note we're all stuck—

                        JOSH

Hmmmmmm.

Josh's voice is so deep and mellow and pleas-
ant that both Stella and Jessie stop arguing.

                        JOSH

If you could be anywhere else right now in
the universe—feel free not to limit yourself
to this world!—where would it be?

                        STELLA

Running. Well, that's not a place, but— On the
road, I guess. On the road, running.

Josh looks at Stella very seriously.

                        JOSH

Hmm.

                        JESSIE

And why you're here.

                        STELLA

And why I'm here.
Deep breath.

STELLA

I don't know. I used to be this normal, happy-go-lucky kid. But then at some point I couldn't remember the last time I felt normal or happy-go-lucky. I couldn't remember the last time I even wanted to get out of bed.

For a moment, Stella looks surprised at her own honesty. Then she pulls it together and makes the bitchiest face imaginable to compensate.

STELLA

The point is, I couldn't bullsh—oops, I mean BS—about *feeling fine* well enough to get my psychologist to believe me. Whatever. You go.

Stella turns to the BLOND GUY next to her, who is tall and blue-eyed and tan in a way that makes me hate him instantly.

ANNOYINGLY ATTRACTIVE TEEN

Mason. I'm seventeen, and I'm from Bethesda, Maryland. My parents are idiots, is basically why I'm here. My happy place is...a land...governed...by rationality.

He pauses every few words, an obvious (not to mention incredibly irritating) effect meant to demonstrate how *profound* he is. I watch Stella's eyes get narrower and narrower until they're barely even slits.

MASON

Somewhere where people use logic instead of succumbing to blind emotion.

Mason sighs, as if the burden of being the lone rational agent in a dumb, emotional world is heavy on his shoulders indeed.

MASON

So, sure as hell not in that world. Oops, sorry, that might have been a little aggressive.

BEN (V.O.)

Mason is so into himself that it's terrifying. Mason is Patrick Bateman in training. Oh, and if cinematic precedence means anything in the real world, it's that Mason is *so* going to hook up with Stella by the end of Week 3.

Mason shrugs, then looks over at me, expectant. I realize, suddenly, that I am standing next to Mason, that the camera has panned left and I am on-screen with absolutely zero lines written and a captive audience. I take a deep breath and swallow hard.

Here is the anticlimax:

BEN

I'm Ben. Sixteen. From the suburbs of New York. I guess I would say that my happy place is…being in a movie theater. You know, like, the minute the opening credits roll. Which is, uh, which is kind of like the moment you disappear from this world, into another, if you think of it that way…
And why I'm here. Uh.

BEN (V.O.)

And just like that, I'm panicking. What other personality traits do you have, Ben? Intimately acquainted only with fictional characters? Literally incapable of human interaction? Caught between an endless string of *down* days and *up* days and days when you don't feel anything at all?

Josh strokes his beard thoughtfully. Jessie raises an eyebrow. Mason looks terribly, terribly above it all. Stella makes an "And…?" face.

BEN (V.O.)

Say something say something say something—

BEN

I'm horribly emotionally unstable.

I stop.
Everyone is still looking at me.

BEN

Except for when I, like, don't feel anything at all.

Continuing expectant silence.

BEN (V.O.)

Here is a list of things I do not say:
I do not say: I am sorry. I am sorry that introduction was pointless and I am sorry I couldn't come up with anything more interesting to say because it *is* one of those times when I don't feel anything at all.

And I do not say: It's not always like this; I'm not always so far away. Sometimes life is real to me, and I'm sorry this isn't one of those days.

And I do not say: But the truth is I'm not sorry. The truth is that sometimes it is easier to not feel, to pretend we're all just actors waiting for the credits to roll and disappear forever, than to be a cocktail of feelings waiting to burst into flames. The truth is that this is one of those times.

BEN

That's it.

Here is the falling action:

BEN (V.O.)

I am trying to stay with the moment, but I am rapidly losing focus. The camera pans from one person to the next and I just can't will myself into believing that it's any different from an on-screen fight that falls flat, or a miscued pseudoromantic beat. I rewrite the lines I've already said six, seven, eight times in my head, as if the director will shout, "Cut," at any moment and I will get the chance to say them again, but better this time.

This is the moment everyone always worries about, because I could do anything—because anyone could do anything—and it would all feel equally trivial to me. Stella could punch me, I could slice my wrists open, the Asian girl currently talking could melt into the ground and disappear, and I just wouldn't care. I wouldn't care, because—

Here is the denouement:

BEN (V.O.)

I am waiting for the screen to fade to black.

STELLA

I'VE ALWAYS BEEN awful at this first-day-of-camp business.

Even in middle school, way back when "camp" was still synonymous with rope swings and tennis courts and swimming pools, I was always the girl scowling through introductions and rolling my eyes every time anyone said anything particularly stupid—which, because this was middle school and middle schoolers are uniformly idiotic, was pretty much the entire time. Now camp is synonymous with being cut off from the rest of the known universe and being yelled at by therapists who won't even let us swear, and it's even worse. The problem with the first day of camp, see, is that I'm always the only one who's realized how utterly miserable camp is going to be, and done the logical thing and just given up. Everyone else is all bright-eyed and hopeful as we *introduce ourselves* and *get to know each other* and *learn about our next four weeks at camp!* We're supposed to put in a good-faith effort to be positive and friendly, which is sort of a problem for me on account of the fact that I am not very good at positive and downright terrible at friendly.

Needless to say, I'm pretty relieved when we finally finish introductions. "Does everyone remember each other's names, or do we need to go over them again?" Jessie asks, and I have to resist the roll of my eyes and get myself yelled at again. Clarisa is the one who stammers through most of her introduction and has to be asked to speak up five times, Andrew is so skeletal that it's not exactly a mystery what *his* issue is, Mason has the most punchable facial expressions I've ever seen in my life, and Ben looks so zoned out it's like he's on a permanent acid trip. There's five of us. It's not exactly rocket science.

After Jessie is done extorting deadpan *yes*es from all of us, she and Josh walk us all to The Hull, which is what everyone calls the residential building. "The Hull" sounds like a really, really stupid nickname for a building, I know—but once you see it, everything makes sense. For starters, it's literally shaped like a ship's hull: only five floors tall, but seems to extend on and on forever from one side to the other. Second, the entire thing got painted over in a really tacky wood stain when they started Ugunduzi so that it would fit in with the whole "camp" theme, but whoever was in charge of painting the building over didn't do a very good job: the paint is completely uneven, and there are patches where it's peeling off completely to reveal the gray, occasionally mossy, occasionally moldy blocks of concrete behind it. Needless to say, the building is fucking hideous.

Each floor of The Hull is designated a number and divided into a left wing and a right wing. Our group name, 1L, means that we're housed on the first floor, on the left side. Like I said: the Ugunduzi founders may have been kindhearted and well-meaning and all that bullshit, but they sure as hell weren't very creative.

Jessie and Josh lead us into our common lounge—where there's a pool table, a bunch of sofas, and a kitchen area—and tell us that we can hang out until dinner and "bond." I, of course, would rather impale myself on the pool stick they've left unwisely unattended, but my plan to spend the time sitting by myself and making a comprehensive list of all the ways I might be able to escape is ruined when Andrew plops down on the couch next to me.

"Hey," he says, as if we're two old friends hanging out in someone's living room and catching up. It takes me a minute to realize that I am not, in fact, hallucinating.

"Hi," I say flatly.

"So…" Andrew says. He bites his lip nervously. I'm starting to get the idea that Andrew is coming to me with the hopes of getting some sort of wisdom or advice, which is sort of a bummer for him, because I have no wisdom, I have no advice, and I have no inclination to share anything of the sort with random strangers I've just met, anyway.

"So…" I say back, hoping he'll leave.

"So what's it like here?"

No dice.

"Hmm," I say. "Exhausting. Aggravating."

I give it a few more seconds of thought.

"And soul-suckingly oppressive," I add.

"No, seriously," Andrew says.

"No, seriously," I reply.

Out of the corner of my eye, I watch as Mason walks over to Ben and badgers him into playing a game of pool.

"But it's so nice!"

"Nice? Are you fucking with me right now?"

"No! All I'm saying is just— Look out the window! It's like having one of those travel brochures right outside, except it's not a travel brochure, it's *actually* what's outside—do you know what I mean?"

"We're never allowed to be together unsupervised, just in

case we accidentally end up murdering each other. The counselors do bed checks every two hours after lights-out. And every day of every week is planned with some dumb therapeutic activity that's supposed to make us confuse exhaustion with actually feeling better. I'm going to go with no. No, I don't know what you mean."

"But don't you feel kind of hopeful about it all?" Andrew says.

"Being hopeful didn't work out so well for me last year. So I've abandoned it for a better strategy."

"What's the better strategy?"

"Unadulterated apathy."

"Oh," Andrew says. He looks down at his hands. "I guess that works…"

I don't know what makes me do it. Maybe it's the fact that Andrew genuinely looks like all of his hopes and dreams have just been dashed. Maybe it's the way he starts looking out the window again, all wistful and earnest and full of *feelings*. Maybe it's that the kid just came up to me and started telling me his life story, for fuck's sake, as if we're best friends as opposed to strangers tossed into the middle of New York for a month. Whatever it is, before I can stop myself, the words come tumbling out of my mouth.

"But hey—don't be too upset. It won't be miserable, like, a *hundred* percent of the time. I'll get us drunk. And there's always The Ridge, even though no one—"

"You brought alcohol?" Andrew whispers, awestruck. His faith in humanity restored.

"Were you expecting to get through this experience sober?"

"Isn't that kind of against the rules?"

I sigh. If this kid has spent his entire life trying to avoid going against the rules, it's no wonder he wound up at Ugunduzi.

"Yeah, it is, so stop yelling about it. Look, are you in or not?"

"Like, now?"

"Yes, right now. Right now, right here, in front of Jessie and Josh standing across the room, both of whom will promptly see us and expel us from this lovely camp that our parents have pinned all their hopes and dreams on. Actually, that's not a bad idea."

Andrew looks taken aback.

"No, not now. Later, after lights-out."

I pause. Is this really something I want to do? I was planning on waiting until the end of the first week of camp to break out the alcohol, when everyone is especially miserable with the realization that they still have three more weeks of camp. But right now we all have *four* whole weeks of camp left, and isn't that even more miserable?

"Yeah, let's do later tonight," I say. "Look, you guys just have to sneak into our room. It's really easy. We literally *never* got caught last year."

"I don't really—" Andrew starts.

"All you have to do," I continue, cutting him off, "is wait until right after they finish the first bed check and then walk across the right wall of the common room to our side of the hall. Then as long as you're back before two hours, it's all fine."

"That's not what I was saying. What I was saying was—"

"Look," I say, exasperated. "All you have to do is come over. It'll be fun. And could you please stop looking like someone murdered your family pet? It's making me uncomfortable."

"All right," Andrew says. "What's the plan?"

Once I explain the camera blind spot and how foolproof the entire process is, Andrew is actually pretty down with the plan. He gets super into explaining all of the times he and his band mates snuck into various parks, or museums, or stores, which is impressive, I guess, considering it took three solid minutes to convince him to come over and drink. No, Andrew is all right. It's Clarisa who ends up being the bigger problem.

"So," I say to her when we're alone in our room after dinner. "You ready for the *initiation*?"

Clarisa looks up at me, alarmed. "Initiation?" she echoes.

I take the last pile of clothes out of my suitcase and open up the compartment at the top. There, I've hidden eight water bottles full of vodka, obtained from one of my older brother's friends through a potent combination of charm and cleavage (that is to say, ten percent charm, ninety percent cleavage), and six shot glasses.

"Stella," Clarisa says, "tell me that's water."

I grin. "It's a lot more fun than water, I promise."

Clarisa closes her eyes and takes seven deep breaths.

"Stella," she says. She puts down the poster she was in the process of taping to the wall and clasps her hands together. "Stella. Stellastellastellastellastella. That's...that's definitely not allowed."

"Astute," I say.

"Okay," she says. Her words come tumbling out, one after another. "I don't want to be, like, *the lame friend*, even though I've been the lame friend for the past fifteen years of my life. But—"

She takes another breath.

"—whatifwegetcaught?"

"We won't get caught," I say. "We never got caught last year, and no one last year knew anyone who got caught the year before. Getting caught is not a thing that happens. They never do room checks more than once every two hours, and they always do one at midnight. So between that one and 2:00 a.m., we should be fine. Oh, and I invited the guys over."

"*What?*" she says. Clarisa is one of those people who deals with heated discussions on illicit topics by lowering her voice to a furious whisper, which would be great and all, except there's no one who can hear us, anyway. "Stella, you can't just do this!"

"What is your problem? This is a nice thing!"

"I don't *like* nice things!" she whisper-shouts. "Not when they come out of nowhere and give me panic attacks!"

"Oh. Right."

I take a deep breath. "Okay. Okay, I'm sorry. I just— I already told Andrew to come over. I guess they could come and then we could ask them to leave, but— I don't know. Don't you feel like it's camp, and you want to do camp things, and not let 'your illness control your life,' or whatever? Does your psychologist say that?"

"Every psychologist says that," Clarisa says, and, well, she certainly has me there.

"Good point," I say.

"Look," she says. "It's fine. Yes. You're right. I'm supposed to be confronting my anxiety and moving out of my comfort zone, so I will *try to do this*, but I would just really appreciate some kind of warning next time you decide to carry out an entire illegal operation in our room, and also if then you didn't try to pass it off as some messed-up therapeutic exercise."

"Yeah," I say. "Yeah, you're right. I'm sorry. Look, it's quarter of twelve. We should pretend to be sleeping for when they come to check on us."

Clarisa shoots me one last dirty look and then starts taking breaths in groups of seven again. I shut off the lights and climb into bed and pretend to sleep, feeling an awful mix of guilt and resentment and annoyance. I hate it when I'm sorry.

The boys arrive fifteen minutes after the bed check. Andrew comes in first, having switched from a black V-neck and black jeans to a black T-shirt and gray shorts, which I suppose is a step up. He still looks emaciated, but there's only so much progress you can make over the course of one evening. After him comes Ben, who is actually fairly attractive, in a perpetually mussed-brown-hair and dazed-looking way. Then comes Mason, who, of course, has decided to grace our room with his presence shirtless and in boxers.

"Mason," I say. "Where the fuck are your clothes?"

"Thought I'd do everyone a favor and lose them," he says.

"Okay," I say. "You know you're not *actually* James Dean, right? I know it must be hard sometimes, to remember, but I'm surprised you haven't figured it out by now given how much time you must spend thinking about yourself."

"Feisty," he says.

"And correct," I say.

"So, what is this heralded 'camp tradition'?" Ben says. "And also, is this the kind of thing that's going to get us sent into the woods and fed only rice and beans for a week? Because I saw a documentary about wilderness boot camp once, and—"

"Yeah, that's exactly what happens," I say. Ben's eyebrows shoot up in horror. "And then they make you walk fifty miles naked." Ben's mouth drops open. "And after that, they waterboard you until you swear to never even think about breaking a camp rule ever again." Ben's expression reaches cosmic levels of dismay. "And *then*, when you've been reduced to a quivering, semiconscious puddle of obedience, they make you do lines."

"Lines?" Ben whispers.

I muster up the most solemn face I can possibly arrange under the circumstances. "Yes. You have to write 'I am a pathetic excuse for a sixteen-year-old boy who will believe anything anyone tells me' one million times, until you're not so gullible."

For a second, Ben just looks confused. But then Mason and

Andrew burst out laughing, and I guess he finally gets it, because: "Hey!" he shouts. "That was fucking mean!"

Mason holds up his hand for me to fist bump, which I calmly ignore. "I try my best," I say. "But seriously, calm down. This isn't boot camp. That's Palmer's thing, you know? He thinks all that crazy intense stuff does more harm than good. That we should have normal camp experiences just like everyone else. I think secretly he *wants* us to get together in the middle of the night and break all the rules."

"So what are we doing tonight?" Ben says, looking incredibly suspicious. "Are we going to run through the woods naked or something?"

"Or, like, a time capsule deal?" Andrew says.

"Spin the bottle?" Mason asks hopefully.

"No, no, and almost," I say. I whip the blanket off my bed to reveal the bottles. "Who wants to take the first shot with me?"

This is when I am reminded, despite my best efforts to pretend otherwise, that I am not, in fact, at a normal camp for normal people who want to engage in some perfectly normal illicit-substance-aided bonding, and am instead stranded in upstate New York with a bunch of lunatics.

"Oh, God," Ben says. "Does everyone here think they're in *Wet Hot American Summer*?"

"Uh," Andrew says.

"Fuck, yes!" Mason says. I try to restrain myself from throwing something at him.

"Clarisa?" I ask, slightly desperate.

She looks at me. "I'd love to," she says. "But then I'd have to take six more to make it an even seven, and I'm not so sure that's a great idea for my first night at camp."

I look back at Andrew, who's still staring at the bottles

with an uncertain expression on his face. "I don't think I can," he says.

"What do you mean, you don't think you can?" I say. "Aren't you the one who wanted to do this in the first place?"

He shifts and looks away from the alcohol, to the floor in front of my feet. "I wanted to bond," he says. "And, like, come over and hang out, and stuff. But drinking... Alcohol is just so *unhealthy*. It totally screws up your metabolism, and... and there are just so many calories, even in one shot, and—"

"Jesus Christ, guys," I say. "Ben. We are clearly not in *Wet Hot American Summer* because if we were, we'd all be plastered and I'd have killed Mason already. And, Andrew, I know that it feels like if you take this *one shot*—because a shot is, what, a hundred calories?—everything you've ever worked for is going to be meaningless and you've failed. But everything you've ever worked for *is* meaningless, anyway, and it's not like you've never failed before!"

"That was a terrible motivational speech," Ben says. "I recommend more political dramas."

I glare at him.

"But I'll take the shot with you."

"Yeah," Andrew says, sighing. "I guess I will, too. But not more than two."

"Fuck, ye—"

"I know you're taking the shot with me, Mason. Jesus!"

"I'm going to sit this one out," Clarisa says. "But, Stella?" She looks at me with big, sad, hopeful eyes, which means that the best course of action for me to follow right now would actually be to flee. "Make sure I do this at least once before camp gets out, okay?"

"Er," I say. "Mason will do it. Right, Mason? Don't say, 'Fuck, yes,' I swear to God."

I pour out four shots of vodka and one of water, for Clarisa.

"And so our five dissolute campers make a toast to the experiences of their future," Ben suddenly says. *"It is stupid, it is night, it is youth. It is hope, it is rashness, it is liquid courage. It is—"*

"Dude," Andrew interrupts. "What are you *talking* about?"

"Sorry," Ben says. "Do you ever think, like, if life were a movie with really dramatic voice-over, what would that voice-over be saying? You know, like, if Morgan Freeman was—"

Ben catches the expressions on our faces and cuts off. "Yeah, never mind. I think I've seen too many movies. Just ignore it."

This is why I can't pretend I'm at normal camp, I think. But I hand out the shots and raise mine, anyway. "To pretending we're at normal camp," I say.

We take the shots.

BEN

HERE'S THE PROBLEM: the first shot, the excitement of it all, the rush—it all makes me ridiculously happy. Which in turn makes me ridiculously stupid.

It's not even just the alcohol that does it—it's the entire situation. I mean, here I am, in the middle of the night, surrounded by people I barely know, after sneaking out of our room and risking CERTAIN DEATH. Well, maybe not CERTAIN DEATH, but definitely CERTAIN DISAPPOINTED LOOKS, and when you're the literal antithesis of cool, like I am, that's bad enough to make you pretty nervous.

I didn't even want to come at first. I know better than anyone that putting me in social situations with a bunch of strangers is like sending a firefighter into a forest fire with a watering can. But Andrew wouldn't shut up about "bonding" (no, thanks) and "haven't you ever done anything exciting in your life? You know, just for the thrill of it?" (definitely not) and "please don't leave me alone with Mason" (I begrudgingly gave him that last one). So here I am.

And I guess Andrew must have had a point after all, because I'm feeling surprisingly good. *Shockingly* good. Better than I've felt since watching *Fast & Furious 6* a couple of years ago and having every negative thought obliterated from my brain through sheer force of CGI. It's the first shot that does it, I think—the taste, lingering in the back of my throat, the burn that follows it all the way down my chest and into my stomach. This is why Nicholas Cage becomes an alcoholic in *Leaving Las Vegas*. I finally understand.

So I take another shot—because Stella and Mason are still going, so it can't hurt, right? And then another one—"to not letting ourselves reach Norman Bates levels of insanity"—with Andrew. And then another one—"to *motifs* in movies," I vaguely remember saying, "because they're all we can derive meaning from!"—at which point nearly everyone is in hysterics, except Clarisa, who merely looks tentatively amused. Even Stella has managed to break out a genuine smile.

"I'm done, I'm done, I have to be done," I say, and I'm so happy I can barely think straight, but then Mason fills my glass and shouts, "To not being a pussy!" and the four shots I've taken already are enough for that to actually force me into action.

The really stupid thing is that I know exactly how this ends. I've been to enough therapy sessions and sat through enough boring health classes to know that I really shouldn't drink like this, especially here, with people who now probably think I'm a total dumbass, for the first time ever. I'm not fun. I'm not anywhere near cool. I'm pretty much the last person anyone would invite to a party. In the fifteen minutes during which I am feigning sleep after we sneak back into our room, I realize that a) I have been an idiot, and b) more urgently, I need to throw up, now.

It's hard to describe the emotional sequence that follows, not least of all because I am excessively inebriated for most of it. I make it to the bathroom in time to spend the next half hour alternating between puking, feeling all the positive feelings gradually drain away from my brain, and wishing, wishing, WISHING that I could feel like I'm inside a movie again like I did on the first day of camp, that this entire disaster didn't all feel so capital-*R* Real. *I hate alcohol*, I think. *I hate alcohol, and I hate that it did this to me, and I hate myself for being stupid enough to drink even though I knew this would happen, and I hate myself for being ridiculous enough to be crying right now because of something so stupid, and I hate Stella for bringing the alcohol, and I hate Mason for calling me a pussy, and I hate myself for proving him right. I had one chance and I fucked it all up—*

"Yo," Andrew calls from outside the bathroom. "Are you okay? Dude, open the door!"

"And can you quiet down?" Mason adds. "I'm trying to sleep."

"I'm *fine*," I shout, but I must not sound particularly fine, because Andrew opens the door and barges in. *Pathetic*, I think. *He must think you're so pathetic.*

"Dude!" Andrew says. "Are you crying? Ben, what's going on?" He pours me a cup of water from the faucet and hands it to me.

"What's going on," I repeat. I take a drink from the cup and then dry heave. "What's going on? *Our dissolute camper, once so filled with hope and youthful energy, is paying the price for his impulsivity, for the belief that he could ever—* Well, I feel terrible," I say after catching the look on Andrew's face.

"You have to stop doing that," he says.

"I can't," I say. "And I drank too much."

"Yeah, that happens sometimes," he says.

"And they taught us in health class that alcohol is a depressant," I add.

"Yeah, that happens, too. But I don't think that's what that actually means. Like, I don't think alcohol actually *makes* you depressed, if you know what I'm saying. I think it just—"

"And I hate myself."

Andrew shuts up.

"Oh, God," I say. The nausea is beginning to fade now, into a constant, throbbing misery—the sense that I would be better off anywhere else, anyone else, or perhaps not at all. To make matters worse, Mason chooses this moment to walk into the bathroom, clutching—I kid you not—an issue of *Playboy*.

"I thought you were trying to sleep," I say.

"I gave up," he says.

I stare at him, speechless, before deciding that the best course of action is to pointedly ignore him.

"I shouldn't have let myself do this," I say, turning to Andrew. "People like me can't *do* drinking."

"'People like *me*'?" he says. "What does that even mean? Depressed people? People who have emotions? People who do stupid things? People like *us*, Ben. Now shut up and drink water."

"People like *us*?" Mason replies, not looking up from his magazine. "People like *you guys*, Andrew. Leave me out of it."

I stumble out of the bathroom and climb into bed, thinking that camp so far has been far, far worse than *Wet Hot American Summer*.

CLARISA

THE SUNDAY SCHEDULE says we're supposed to be up by 10:00 a.m., but waking up at a time like that is practically asking to have a terrible day. I set my alarm for 9:31 instead, and I'm feeling surprisingly well rested when it goes off. *It's going to be a good day*, I think to myself. *I'm going to get out of bed and brush my teeth. I'm going to write my mom a letter. I'm going to try to make friends.* I sit up, open my eyes, and— //

—Freeze. There are four shot glasses pushed into the back corner of the room, definitely unwashed. Pieces of paper that Ben and Mason had been scribbling on all night, now crumpled up on my desk. Somehow, Ben managed to forget his *shoes* in our room. It's not even the clutter that gets to me, which isn't as bad for me as people always think it is—it's the fact that everything is *wrong*; the sense that that's not where those things are supposed to be, not on the floor, not on my desk, no, no, no, and then I'm up and throwing away Ben's nonsensical scribblings and putting Stella's shot glasses back on her desk where they belong. Equally horrifying is the fact that it would have been *this easy* for us to get caught: the shot glasses are inconspicuous, sure, but all it would have taken was one careful walk through the room with a flashlight to notice them. And what if the counselors realized that the pair of flip-flops in the middle of the room wasn't actually mine or Stella's? //

By the time I'm done cleaning up yesterday's mess, I barely have time to finish my morning routine before we're supposed to go outside for breakfast. "You do this every morning?" Stella asks as I'm in the process of checking my covers for the fifth time. They haven't moved at all since the last time I checked them, and I *know* that they haven't, but I can't rip myself away before I've made sure. "Do you really have to?" Stella says. "Like, what's the worst thing that can happen if you don't?" "Okay, *first*," I say, spinning so that I'm facing her. I'm wasting precious time, I know, and Stella's offhand remarks aren't worth getting riled up over, but something about her tone—smug, more bemused than anything— really gets me going. //

"Yeah, I do this every morning, thanks for asking. And second, you're being pretty rude, you know that? Believe me, I don't want to be doing this any more than you want to be watching me doing it. But I just...*have* to." I stare at her, defiant. *This*, I think, is exactly why I didn't want to come to this stupid camp. It's bad enough when it's just my mom thinking that I'm a total nutcase. //

But Stella surprises me. "You're right," she says slowly, like she's just coming to the realization for the first time as she says the words. "Sorry, Clarisa. And sorry again about not checking with you before inviting the guys over last night. I guess I just didn't anticipate these things—you know—being... *problems*." "Well, that's me for you," I say. "A barrelful of un-anticipated problems." //

"That's not what I meant," Stella says. But it is. Trust me,

I've been in this situation enough times to know. "Yeah," I mutter, and grab our room keys and a jacket from my closet. The bed is fine. The room is safe. I'm ready to go to breakfast. //

I don't end up making it through very much of breakfast because Jessie comes up to our table pretty much the moment I've set my oatmeal down on the picnic table between Ben and Andrew and asks if she can see me in her office. It takes me approximately three seconds—between the time I finish processing her words and actually get up to follow her—to conclude that we've been caught, and that I am totally, totally doomed. It doesn't help that she doesn't smile at me a single time while we walk from the picnic tables outside to the counselors' offices by The Hull. By the time Jessie clears her throat to start talking, I've come up with six ways to apologize for getting roped into Stella's awful plan, all of which sound ridiculous. This is it. I am definitely getting kicked out. My stomach sinks as I imagine how disappointed my mom is going to be when she finds out that her latest plan to convert me into a normal human being, just like all the other ones, has crashed and burned. //

After a few seconds of torturous, torturous silence, Jessie finally speaks. "You started sertraline three weeks ago, correct?" she says. I stare at her for a second, unsure of how to answer. Is this a prelude to the inevitable lecture? Is she trying to terrify me before kicking me out? "Um," I say. "Yes?" //

"Are you experiencing any negative side effects? Any difficulty sleeping? Changes in appetite? Increased feelings of depression or suicidal ideation?" she asks. "No," I say. Jessie writes for a few seconds on the clipboard. I start to think that maybe I'm not totally busted, after all. //

"What about positive effects of the drug?" Jessie continues.

"Decreased anxiety, easier time focusing…?" This is when I sort of start to hate this conversation. When I start to almost wish that we *had* been caught, and that Jessie was giving me some stern lecture about "trustworthiness" and "camp values" as opposed to asking me about whether or not my meds are finally, *finally* working. Because no, they're not. And now I feel like I'm letting her down. "Not really," I admit. //

"Well, it's quite normal for sertraline to take four to six weeks to fully take effect, so I'm not too concerned yet," Jessie says. "I'll check in with you again in a couple of days and see if anything changes. In the meantime, please let me know if you start experiencing any new side effects. Is that clear?" "Yes," I say. I resist the urge to apologize even though I know she doesn't know that I've done anything wrong. Then, before she can tell me that my skirt is too short or try to fix my posture, I bolt for the door. //

When I get back to the picnic tables, most of the other fifty or so campers have come out and started eating. I make my way over to our table and slide back into my seat, only to find that my oatmeal has gone lukewarm and my biscuit has been colonized by a family of ants. "Lovely," I mutter. I push the plate away and turn to Ben. "Do you know when we're having lunch?" I ask. "Because I'm actually kind of hungry, and I can't— Oh, jeez, are you okay?" //

Ben looks *exhausted*. Half-dead. Like a different person from last night, when he seemed, well, just as energetic and happy as you'd expect someone who had taken, like, four shots of vodka in quick succession to be. "I'm fine," Ben says. He gets really into his scrambled eggs. "Did something…happen?" I ask. "I mean, last night, you seemed really happy, and now…" //

"I'm just an idiot," Ben says. "Unfortunately for me, I don't think there's really anything anyone can do about that. So, I'm fine." There's a part of me that wants to push further, if only because now everyone at the table is staring at us. But then I remember how I felt yesterday in the car when Mom wouldn't stop asking me how I was doing. And look how that turned out. So instead I say, "Okay," and turn my gaze to the camp ground around us. //

As a permanent resident of New York City, where your line of sight extends approximately fifty feet without hitting a skyscraper or a wall of smog, I'm not used to how beautiful it is here—how clean the air, how far we can see. There are mountains rising and falling in the distance, gray and jagged against the light blue of the sky. We're sitting at a cluster of picnic tables between the cabins and the volleyball court. On the other side, I can see all the way to the other side of the lake. The lake, the cabins, and the rec area are all situated in a field of grass that's almost entirely enclosed by trees. Before I can stop myself, I've forgotten all about my cereal and started counting them: *1, 2, 3, 4, 5, 6, 7. 1, 2, 3, 4, 5, 6, 7.* //

My mind goes into autopilot: start, count, stop, repeat. 7, 7, 7, 7. A part of me thinks that I can somehow count all the trees that form our perimeter—*if it's not a safe number, will they let me cut a few down?* I wonder. *1, 2, 3, 4, 5, 6, 7. 1, 2, 3, 4, 5, 6, 7. 1, 2, 3, 4, 5, 6, 7. 1, 2, 3, 4, 5, 6—* //

"Clarisa?" a voice says. "Did you get that?" I realize with a start that I've completely zoned out, and that Jessie and Josh have joined us at our table. Jessie is clearly midlecture. "The expression of sheer panic on her face would indicate that she had retreated to the warm and welcoming—often *too* welcoming, I might add—recesses of her innermost thoughts," Josh says warmly, as if that's a perfectly normal way to describe someone who isn't paying attention. "No need to worry, Clarisa. Why don't we just repeat the last part again, Jessie?" //

"I was going over our weekend policy," Jessie says, sounding significantly more annoyed than Josh does. And who can blame her? She's right—I should have been paying attention, instead of getting lost in my head like I always do. "As I was saying," Jessie repeats, "our weekends kick off every Friday night with Art by the Fire Fridays." I don't know what Art by the Fire Fridays is, but it must not be great, because Stella takes Jessie's pause as an opportunity to groan loudly. "What were you expecting?" Mason drawls. "That in the last year they'd eliminated all the therapeutic camp activities at a therapeutic camp?" //

"Stella, you clearly have a lot of opinions about Art by the Fire," Jessie says. "Would you like to explain to everyone what the principles and procedures are?" Stella scowls at Jessie but remains silent. "Thank you. And, Mason," Jessie continues. "While I appreciate your willingness to, ah, *help* us counselors out, I assure you that Josh and I can handle it. Now, on to the important part. //

"Every Friday night, all of the campers at Ugunduzi come together. We light a bonfire, we make s'mores, and everyone across all the different groups has the opportunity to share something that he or she has written. It's a great exercise. I know you'll all be amazed at the things you share with each other. It can be a poem, or a journal entry, or stray thoughts about the week—anything you feel like sharing with the group. You guys should start thinking about that and maybe even writing, if you want to perform a poem or anything like that. Any questions before we move on? //

"Great," Jessie says when no one speaks up. "After Friday night, weekends at Ugunduzi are fairly relaxed. It's always been important for Dr. Palmer and the rest of the team here for campers to have time to explore and enjoy this beautiful area on your own terms, and we want you to know that we trust you enough to let you do that. Accordingly, we've left this time relatively unrestricted—with the provision that you stay on the main grounds and remain supervised at all times, of course. Ordinarily, at this time after breakfast, you'd be able to do an approved activity of your own choice. But because it's our first full day together, we thought it would be a good idea to introduce you to your camp-long project and give you some time to start thinking about it. And so, if you'll follow me…" //

"Isn't it cute how they consider 'boxed in' and 'supervised at all times' to be 'relatively unrestricted'?" Stella mutters to me while we stand up and file into a line behind Jessie. I choke back a laugh. Not because she isn't kind of totally right, but because getting in trouble twice before it's even eleven in the morning doesn't seem like a great way to start camp. The five of us follow Jessie and Josh away from the picnic tables, in the opposite direction of The Hull, up to a small, unlabeled cabin by the water. Josh takes out a key and unlocks the door. "It's…empty," Mason says as we all step inside. "Totally empty," Andrew echoes. //

Mason's right. Not only is the cabin completely devoid of tables, couches, and decorations, but the walls are also unpainted, the windows bare and curtainless. "Exactly," Jessie says. *Solitary confinement*, I think immediately. I picture being locked in here for a full day with nothing to do or look at or sit on, with no one to talk with and nothing to listen to, free of hiking, Stella's sarcastic comments, trees, spontaneous episodes of youthful rebellions, shot glasses left lying on the floor all night… It would be like a dream come true. I resolve to get myself as committed as soon as possible. //

"It's your Camp Project," she says. "Oh, no," Stella groans. "Not *again*. Wasn't last year bad enough?" "The Camp Project," Jessie presses on, over Stella's groan, "is a Camp Ugunduzi tradition. Each team of campers every year is assigned a project that facilitates creativity, resourcefulness, and, most important, teamwork. Stella's group last year, for example, took photographs and wrote articles for a camp guidebook for their friends and their parents." //

"It was propaganda," Stella says. "Forget friends and parents—*Hitler* could have learned a thing or two from that guidebook." Mason snickers. *"This year,"* Jessie continues, her voice rising a few decibels, "we've decided to do something a little different. We've had this cabin built with the intention of turning it into a safe space for campers—a place where they could come to find peace, where they could clear their heads, to be surrounded by quiet, to reflect or write or play music. As you can see, we've left it completely undecorated. And that's where you guys come in." //

"You want us to decorate the cabin," Andrew says. He sounds extraordinarily skeptical. "You want us to make it a... 'safe...space.'" "Exactly," Jessie says. "You'll probably spend most of the first week just working together on painting it, but after that, everything is pretty much up to you. Things like what you want to put on the walls, what function you want each of the rooms to have, if any, what color scheme you want for the cabin... Just design it, and make it happen." //

"What does 'safe space' even mean?" Andrew says. "Like, toddler-safe? Like what Aidan's parents did after his baby brother was born?" "Who's Aidan?" I ask. "What if everyone else is incompetent?" Mason asks. Ben stays silent, looking like he's about to collapse from nervousness. It's a feeling that I'm all too familiar with. //

"This is a terrible idea," Stella says, cutting him off without mercy. "What if I decide that I want to kill myself by drinking a bucket of paint or stabbing myself with the nail we've just used to hang up a painting? What if we get in a fight and I kill Mason with a hammer? We are, ahem, 'depressed and troubled teenagers,'" she continues. She enunciates each of the last four words carefully, as if a psychiatrist reading from a clinical report. "We can't be trusted with chemicals or sharp objects or hammers or…or anything else, for that matter. You should probably send us back where we came from, lest this safe space become *not so safe*." //

We all stare at Stella, who looks at Jessie with a completely straight face. The problem, I think, is that no one can ever tell if she's joking or not. Jessie sighs. "No one is going to kill him- or herself. Or anyone else, for that matter. Because all of your time working on the project will be supervised, and, more importantly, because I know you all have a great deal of respect for this camp, each other, and yourselves. Despite what you try your best to convince us of, Stella," she adds. //

"I dunno, man," Mason says. "I'm pretty convinced. So convinced that you might have to remove her from the premises for this to be a safe space for me." "I'm going to remove your *balls* from the premises, Mason, I swear to—" "Stella!" Jessie says. "There is no swearing at Camp Ugunduzi. You of all people should try to set a better example for our new campers." //

Stella scowls at Jessie, but I think that just motivates her to lecture us in an even sterner tone of voice. "There's clearly no better time than the present to start building camaraderie. Remember, it's important to work together to try to integrate everyone's ideas. And I expect everyone to keep an appropriate, *positive* attitude as you work. By this Thursday, you guys should have a list of the things you need the camp to order to decorate the cabin. There are paper and pencils in the next room. Why don't you all get started?" //

So begins the first brainstorming session for Project Safe Space, or, as Stella takes to calling it half an hour in, Project Doesn't This Violate Some Sort of Labor Law? I'm not sure how to quantify the amount of progress we make over the next two hours. We decide, for example, that the color scheme will not include orange or yellow or violet, because Mason will "literally do everyone a favor and vomit on the walls," or black or gray, because, as Ben notes, "Is there any better way to encourage someone to hang themselves from the ceiling fan?" We also decide that the cabin cannot have any mirrors, as that would be insensitive to people with eating disorders ("and people with faces like Mason's," Stella adds), and duly note that "posters of some made-up inspirational Marilyn Monroe quote about loving yourself printed over a picture of the sun setting over the Appalachians" are unacceptable on account of being "bullshit, and also way too girlie." Things we do not manage to decide: what we actually want the color scheme to be, what wouldn't be horribly offensive to put on the walls, literally anything else. It's almost incredible, how much a group of five people can disagree on. I'd be impressed, if it weren't so discouraging. //

"We should get one of those four-seasons painting collections," Ben suggests. "That's literary and calming." "No," I say immediately. It is the second time I've spoken in here. Everyone turns around to look at me and I feel myself flush. "It's just— There would be four," I say. //

"No kidding," Stella says. "A four-seasons painting collection would have four paintings?" She's sprawled out on the floor of the cabin, doodling on a sheet of paper. Her nonchalance is suddenly infuriating. "Shut *up*, Stella," I say. The panic is rising up in my chest and I can feel my breath slipping away even as I say the words and I squeeze my eyes shut to try to get it to stop, but I can't; it won't—that's never worked before and it doesn't work now. The images come on too fast, too vivid—four paintings in a row, incomplete, not enough, not okay, not good, not safe, dangerous; *four*, and I can feel my brain short-circuiting; *four*, and I am watching the cabin get

FOUR WEEKS. FIVE PEOPLE

destroyed in front of my eyes; *four*, and disaster after disaster plays out in my mind, an uninterrupted sequence of catastrophes, each more real than the last. //

The roof, caving in after a snowstorm. The walls, blown over by torrential wind. The entire cabin, burning down after a candle falls or some idiot tries to smoke a cigarette indoors. Someone trapped inside, someone crushed by logs, someone burning alive, someone— *"Clarisa!"* Stella shouts. I open my eyes and realize that I'm shaking. *1*, I think automatically, counting breaths, *2, 3, 4, 5, 6, 7.* //

"Are you okay?" Ben asks. He moves over next to me and tries to put his arm around me, but I shake him off. I can't take the contact right now, and I don't deserve the comfort, anyway. "If we're going to have paintings, there have to be seven. It's the only way the cabin can be safe," I say, avoiding eye contact with everyone. There's no response. It's the only thing that's been suggested that no one argues against. //

ANDREW

DINNER IS WHEN everything gets fucked up.

Breakfast is okay. A bagel is 450 calories—around there, anyway—and I know I need to eat around there on most days, just to stay alive. Eating less than that is how The Incident ended up happening, and—well, I'd obviously like to avoid a repeat of that in the near future.

Lunch I just throw out, because there are so many people milling around the picnic area that it's easy to slip to the trash cans unnoticed, and because I've already gotten my 450 calories for the day, so what's the point? Stella gives me a sort of suspicious look as I sit back at the table, plate totally cleared, but what is she going to say? "Go get your lunch out of the trash and eat it"?

Then dinner comes around, and I discover quickly that I am totally, totally screwed. Jessie spends the entire meal sitting at our table, talking to us about how our day has gone and whether or not we're enjoying our time at camp so far. I'm so agitated that I barely have the mental focus to listen while she and Stella get into their seventh fight of the day after Stella sarcastically describes Project Safe Space as "fucking delightful, thanks for asking, Jessie." Will Jessie care if I leave dinner without eating anything? Will Jessie *notice* if I leave dinner without eating anything? The look she gives me when I try to edge off the table midway through her argument with Stella says pretty convincingly that yes, she would care, and yes, she would notice. So—and what choice do I really have here?—I force myself to eat.

It's kind of sad how quickly I stop wanting to get better. At 500 calories, "better" seems like a pretty okay thing to be. But then I get halfway through my spaghetti—+100, +200, +300, +400—and I can practically feel the carbs becoming fat and I'm thinking about all the work I've put in to get to where I am now and "better" starts sounding a lot like "disgusting." It's hard to want to get better when I'm staring down the calories in my head, I guess is what I'm trying to say.

I want to go to bed the second Jessie tells us we're done for the day. If I go to bed, then I can fall asleep, and when I wake up, it'll be morning. Back to zero. Fresh start, new beginning. But I can't. I've just eaten an entire meal, and if I take off my shirt to go to sleep, I'm going to look down and see my stomach protruding and I just— I can't. I know what it looks like, and I can't look at it right now, and I know it's there, so I can't not look at it if I do go to bed, so I sit in the lounge and watch Mason and Ben argue over whether or not movies have any value to society. I want to grab my guitar from my room and write music, but everything I write in moments like these is crap because I can't think straight, and besides, my band fulfilled its quota of sad ballads about hating yourself, like, three EPs ago.

I know something's up when Stella joins me on the couch. She's pretty much refused to talk to anyone the entire day, and I don't think I look particularly fun while drowning in my own self-hatred.

"So," she says. "You're in a band?"

"Yeah," I say.

"What's it called?" She doesn't sound genuine exactly—more like she's referencing an inside joke between the two of us that I'm too stupid to even know about, or have somehow forgotten. But she also doesn't sound completely offended at my existence, either. I take this as a good sign.

"Um, The Eureka Moment," I respond. "Because, like, we were all sitting around Aidan's basement, trying to come up with a band name, and no matter how long we brainstormed, we just couldn't think of the right one. Like, dude, we were throwing around options like Abyss Gazers and Between Bruises—it was bad. I called Aidan's suggestion some 'tween pop bullshit,' which is pretty much the worst thing you could say to a serious musician. Anyway, before Aidan could punch me, Jake was just, like, 'Guess we're still waiting on that eureka moment, huh?' and everyone realized that that was it, that that was—"

"That's cute," she says, cutting me off.

Anything else, I probably could have taken. She could have called it weird, or stupid, or even asked if we're a "real band," like every adult insisted on doing when we first started. She could have laughed out loud, for all I care. But *cute* is too much.

"It's not *cute*," I say. "It's not cute at all—we spent, like, three hours coming up with it and would've spent three more hours coming up with something better if it was something *cute*. *Cute* doesn't sell records unless you're interested in the Disney Channel crowd, which we're not—"

Suddenly, Stella grabs my hand. It takes a couple seconds for the realization to make its way to my brain. "We're not trying to be the next Jonas Broth— Dude, what are you doing?"

She pulls her hand away as quickly as she'd grabbed mine.

"Is everything okay over there?" Jessie says.

Stella rolls her eyes and gets up off the couch. "Better than okay, Jess," she says. "Andrew was just telling me about his band. They're superlegit and hard-core and not at all cute."

She's already turned away from me by the time I realize that she's slipped a piece of paper into my hand.

Our room, right after the midnight room check, it says.

Well, I think. *At least that'll be a few more hours to burn calories.*

I went on a camping trip with my band last year for Memorial Day. This was before anyone knew who we were, when we were just a few friends bothering the neighbors at weird hours of the night with music no one really understood. I still have no idea how any of us managed to convince our parents to let us go—especially after Jake's dad found the giant cooler full of forties—but somehow we did, and then there we were, just the four of us in the middle of the woods with nothing to do other than drink and fuck around on guitars and a bass you couldn't really hear and a drum box.

I think that weekend was when all of us realized that this was actually something we could picture ourselves doing together for the rest of our lives. I mean, whatever, that's really corny. But I just always figured it was one of those things that would be set to really dramatic, violin-heavy music in a documentary about our band, you know? This one night, we each had, like, three beers, and then started hiking, and then got so, so lost. It was crazy. We all thought we were going to die. We were passing around a notebook writing down goodbyes when Aidan found the map in his backpack and we realized we had walked in a giant circle and were actually five minutes away from the campsite. I blame the beer.

For some reason, tonight makes me think of that night. It's weird, because they're totally different—then, I was with my best friends in the world; tonight, I'm with four people I don't know at all. But when we walk into Stella's room and find her and Clarisa dressed in jackets and hiking boots and Stella tells us to "go back and put on real clothes—except you, Mason, you can get hypothermia if you want—because we're going on a hike," I'm kind of excited. Stella picks the lock keeping the back door shut from the outside with a hairpin, and then we walk outside and the freedom, the air, the forest—it feels familiar. It doesn't really matter that Mason won't shut up and it doesn't really matter that Stella might be the worst person in the world to follow into the woods in the middle of the night and it doesn't even matter that we might get caught. I mean, they can't exactly kick all of us out of camp.

We follow Stella away from the cabins, toward the trees. By the time we step into the forest, I can hear Clarisa breathing hard. "You all right?" I say.

"So many trees," she whispers back, as if there's someone around to hear us. "I have to count, I can't count, I have to count, I can't count, I have to—"

"Count steps," I say. "If it takes a safe number of steps to get to where we're going, then it's safe, right?"

"The *trees*," she says again, her eyes squeezed shut. "There are too many. I can't count them—"

"Look *down*, Clarisa, look at your feet," Stella says. "Step forward. Okay, that's good. That's one. Two. Three. Four. Five. Six. Seven. It's going to be great, I promise."

Five minutes later, Stella takes an abrupt turn off the path, straight into a cluster of trees. Another seven steps later and the trees disappear. We're standing in a grassy clearing that drops off steeply about fifty feet in front of us. There are dead trees lying across the ground, barks peeling. Now that we're not under the canopy anymore, it's actually incredibly bright under the light of the moon. It kind of reminds me of a stage—the darkness of the forest behind us, the sudden brightness, the ledge in front. The feeling that the silence is just *waiting* for you to break it. I wish I had my guitar.

"Welcome," Stella announces, "to The Ridge." She takes a seat on one of the dead trees on the ground.

"Why are we here?" Mason asks. He walks along the grass suspiciously and looks around.

"Don't you ever get tired of having all of our conversations and actions and everything else monitored all the time?" Stella says. "It's just a place where we can hang out without feeling like we're criminals. Jesus."

"Wow," Ben says. He takes a seat on another log on the ground. There's a third right behind me, and the three form a rough triangle in the middle of the clearing. Between them is a makeshift fire pit with bunches of sticks and branches in it. I wonder how long campers have been doing this, and if they've ever gotten caught. God, Sam would get a kick out of this. He used to always try to get us to sneak out in the middle of the night to go downtown and do graffiti with him. "We can't even design our own *album art*," I remember Jake saying to him once. "And you want to deface a *building*?"

Maybe it's that it's the middle of the night, when I'm used to being surrounded by Sam and Jake and Aidan and pages and pages of sheet music and song lyrics, or maybe it's just that the memory hits me out of nowhere, but all of a sudden I really miss them. My stomach clenches from the sadness, or maybe from hunger. I can never really tell when it's hunger anymore.

I take a seat on the third log. Clarisa sits down next to Ben, but I don't think he notices, because he's staring at Stella. He's actually gone from looking mildly impressed to looking like a groupie. I feel kind of embarrassed for him, to be honest.

"You okay there, Ben?" Stella asks, and Ben turns really, really red.

"Yeah," he mutters. "This is just…way cool."

He turns even redder.

"Everyone just ignore me," he says.

"You flatter me," Stella responds.

"You really do," Mason says. Apparently he has deemed The Ridge safe, because he swings his legs over Stella's log, sits down, and throws an arm around her shoulders.

"Mason," Stella says flatly.

"Hmm?"

"I will light your arm on fire, I swear to God."

"Oh, stop," he says. He's grinning now and keeps trying to make eye contact with her. "Isn't this why you dragged us here in the middle of the night?" Mason continues. "For some good old *unsupervised bonding*, you kno— Jesus, *all right*!"

Mason pulls his arm away and almost falls off the log. I don't blame him, because Stella has actually reached into her jacket pocket and pulled out a lighter.

"What's the matter?" she asks. "What's some good old *unsupervised bonding* without a campfire to bond over?"

Stella is the type of girl who would probably do graffiti with Sam.

"Do you think," Clarisa asks, "that you brought more legal or illegal things to camp?"

Stella walks to the fire pit in the center of the triangle. "Probably illegal," she says. "But only because I brought almost every contraband item on the list."

"What?" Clarisa says. "But—why would you even need, like, keys? Or mechanical pencils? Did you bring a cell phone? We don't even get service here—what's the point?"

"It's not about *using them*," Stella says. She crouches down to inspect the sticks and branches in the fire pit. "It's the *principle* of the thing."

"The principle of what thing?" Clarisa says.

"Oh, you know. Demanding our rightful liberty from dumb rules. Protesting authority. Et cetera, et cetera."

Yep. Would definitely do graffiti with Sam.

"Anyway," Stella says. She looks up at us solemnly, flicking the lighter on and off with her thumb. "It's time to get serious."

"But we were having so much fun," Mason says under his breath. It's so quiet that everyone can hear, but Stella just keeps talking. I'm starting to get the idea that Stella is only here to do the things that she wants to do at camp, and we're all just trying not to get yelled at. Or alcohol poisoned. Or set on fire.

"So, I think most traditions are stupid. And a part of me has always thought that the whole *sit around a campfire together* camp tradition is *particularly* stupid. But you know what? I actually had some good times around the campfire at The Ridge last year."

"You had a good time doing something?" Mason says. "I find that difficult to picture."

"And they even got the firewood together for you guys for the first fire," Stella continues. "So why the fuck not?"

"'Why the eff not,'" Clarisa repeats. "I forgot that was a reason to do things like sneak out in the middle of the night and possibly burn a forest down."

"Well, here goes," Stella says, smirking. She moves the flame to the edge of the firewood and the first branch catches. She lights a couple of other ones around the pit and then retreats back to her log, looking satisfied.

"I really like fire," Ben murmurs.

"Look at that," Stella says. "An emotionally troubled teenage boy who loses himself in movies and likes fire. You are really outdoing yourself with the originality here, Ben."

"I get him," I say. "It's— I mean, don't you think it's... beautiful? In, like, a haunting sort of way?"

"Look at that," Stella says again. "An emotionally troubled teenage boy who loses himself in music and really likes fire. Mason? You want in on this?"

"I'm not emotionally troub—" he starts, but Stella cuts him off.

"An emotionally troubled teenage boy who loses himself in denial," she says, "and really likes—"

"Dude," I interrupt. I'm a little concerned that one of them is going to push the other one into the fire or throw a flaming stick or something, and then we will all probably not like fire as much, ever again. I say the first thing that comes to mind. "Does anyone else know about this place?"

"I don't think so," Stella says. "Me and a couple group mates from last year found it after sneaking out one night, and we never ran into anyone else. And none of them are back this year, so... I'm Queen of The Ridge." She waves her hands around her head in a mock celebratory gesture. "Hooray."

"This is the most cinematic thing I've ever experienced in my life," Ben says. "This is it. I've peaked."

"That's quite the life you've lived, then," Mason says, and again Ben turns ridiculously red.

"I never said I thought my life was exciting," Ben mutters. "I know it's—"

"Ben?" Clarisa says, interrupting him midsentence. "Can you stop doing that thing where you write yourself off with every other sentence you say? It's kind of my thing, and you're making me uncomfortably aware of how ridiculous it sounds."

"Thanks for taking us out here, Stella," I say before Ben's face can erupt into flames. "This is amazing. Camp is actually kind of nice."

"No, it really isn't," Stella says.

"Yes, it kind of is!" I say. "I mean, the weather's good, and everyone seems pretty cool, and clearly the rules aren't that strict, and… I mean, it's a good story at least." Maybe not on the same level as doing midnight graffiti with Sam would've been, I think to myself, but not everything can be midnight graffiti.

"Wow," Ben says. He's recovered nicely—or nicely enough to speak at least. "A hopelessly optimistic depressed person."

"You have to be hopelessly optimistic when you're in a band. Otherwise, you'd just quit and go to engineering school."

Clarisa laughs. "Do you ever think about things that aren't your band?"

Well, there's calories, I think. But that's probably not the answer Clarisa is looking for.

"I guess it just takes over your life," I say. "It has to, you know? You spend years and years writing music and fighting with your band mates and changing A to Asus4 to Asus2 back to A again and releasing bad EPs and playing good shows and releasing good EPs and playing bad shows. How am I supposed to think of myself as someone outside of the band after all that?"

"By developing a 'healthy sense' of 'identity' and 'perspective,'" Ben replies, his fingers curling into air quotes every couple of words. "But you probably shouldn't ask me about that. I am as trapped by the artistic impulse as you are, Andrew, perhaps more so, considering I often feel like I am straitjacketed into a tripart dramatic narrative and I cannot get out of epitasis."

"No one ever knows what you're saying when you start talking like that, Ben," I say.

"I think I am the most normal person here," Clarisa declares.

"Please don't flatter yourself, Clarisa," Mason chimes in, and even Stella laughs.

"If you think I'm crazy, you guys should see everyone else from New York City," Clarisa says. "I'm high-strung, but at least I know I'm high-strung and I'm medicating. Or trying to medicate at least."

"New York?" I say. "Dude, I *wish* I was from New York."

Ben shoots me a skeptical look. "Andrew, you're from Washington *State*. The worst you have to deal with is hipsters."

"Don't tell me hipsters aren't that bad until you've had to deal with music hipsters. You've never been forced to listen to six minutes of white noise and then been told that it's 'artistic.' New York is... Well, New York is where the big record labels are."

"As I said. Hopeless optimist."

Clarisa laughs, and maybe I'm supposed to, too. But all of a sudden my stomach clenches, and I feel like I'm going to either throw up or cry. "I'm going to take a walk," I say.

They both look up at me. "I didn't mean it like that, Andrew," Ben says. "I'm not saying you guys aren't good enough to make it or anything. I just meant—"

"I know." I pause for a second. I don't know how to explain it. Wanting something so bad that it's all you ever think about, but thinking about it hurts because of how much you want it. "I'm not, like, offended or anything like that. I just want to think for a bit."

I get up and walk toward the edge of the clearing, where the ledge drops off. It's not that far a fall—probably fifteen or twenty feet. Part of me wants to jump. It's not anything self-destructive. More of a thrill thing. Like jumping into the crowd during a show. God, the last time I did that was, what, three months ago? At Café Racer? At 115 pounds, probably. A good show, I think; people liked it a lot. We did an acoustic version of "Still" that the crowd was really into. We should probably put it on the next EP, once this whole mess is over.

I don't think the next show we played liked that acoustic as much, though, as the one at the Jewel.

The Jewel. As soon as I've thought the words, memories from that night come flying back. December 10. A 700-calorie day, a sold-out show. When the lights came on and they were so bright that everything in the audience was blurry, impossible to see. When we started the set, how much energy in the crowd there was. When I realized that this was one of those shows that we were going to remember forever, that I could relive a thousand times and still not get tired of. And then The Incident happened, and everything fell apart.

I'm "better" now, I think as we head back to The Hull later that night. But I can't get it out of my head. I see my guitar next to my bed and think of the night at the Jewel—when we were still playing, just shattered silence and blinding lights and darkness behind us and something uncontrollable and raw in the crowd in front of us, before everything went to shit—and 700, and 2,100, and where I was then, and where I am now, and who I was then, and who I am now. *Better*, I think. I close my eyes as I take my shirt off and climb into bed.

"Crazy night, huh?" Ben says. But I don't reply, and neither does Mason. I feel bad, because we're probably fucking up whatever weird camp screenplay he's got going through his head, but at least he can just write a new one tomorrow. Once a show goes wrong, you don't get it back. I run my fingers along the sides of my chest, along the ridges of my rib cage. I miss the stage, I think. I miss who I was on it.

WEEK
ONE

BEN

EXT. HIKING TRAIL—DAY

A classic instance of MAN VERSUS NATURE as our FIVE DISSOLUTE CAMPERS struggle to overcome exhaustion, hunger, lack of motivation, the fact that this is exactly NO ONE'S idea of a fun Monday morning activity, and so on and so forth. Clarisa leans against a tree, breathing hard, eyes closed, mouth moving silently. Andrew is GULPING DOWN water from a canteen. Despite his repeated claims otherwise, Mason is clearly exhausted. Stella, of course, is the exception—she's standing with Josh in front of the rest of us with her arms crossed with the expression of someone who has been roped into babysitting particularly ill-behaved toddlers.

BEN (V.O.)

I do not feel tired.
I mean, I look tired. I can see myself breathing just as hard as Clarisa and Andrew, run-

ning the back of my hand across my forehead
to get rid of the sweat on my face. I can also
see that it doesn't work. I am still red, still
panting, and still sweaty.

But I do not feel tired. I do not feel hungry.
I have to keep reminding myself to drink water
every five minutes because I can't count on
my brain to register when my body is thirsty.
It's not a bad problem to have right now—not
being able to feel tired, that is—or at least,
it won't be a bad problem until I die of heat-
stroke or exhaustion or dehydration.

JOSH

How is EVERYONE DOING? Are you guys feeling the crisp, beautiful air flaring in your
lungs? Can you feel your heart pounding against
your chest, reminding you how powerfully, won-
derfully alive you are? Isn't it rejuvenating,
being surrounded by Earth—*real* Earth, minus the
wires and the batteries and the cords tying us
down? Everyone, breathe in with me.

Josh closes his eyes and takes a deep, long
breath. The fact that none of us join him does
not seem to bother him in the slightest.

BEN (V.O.)

I'm not really sure what to say about Josh,
other than that he is, quite literally, a hippie. A well-educated hippie apparently, since

his nametag boasts not one but two degrees, but a hippie nonetheless.

I didn't believe it at first. Up until now, I figured he was just like all the other middle-aged men who are really confused about what kids find "cool" nowadays. I mean, yeah, there were all those ridiculous jokes during introductions. And sure, he had the exact same facial hair as The Dude from *The Big Lebowski* and was wearing a Hawaiian print shirt. But, I reasoned with myself, my dad does things like that all the time! Besides, the nametag said, very clearly, Psy.D., LCSW, and a) hippies don't get that many degrees, and b) hippies don't have such good handwriting.

But then today happened.

EXT. UGUNDUZI MAIN GROUNDS—EARLIER THAT MORNING

Our campers are lined up next to the picnic tables in hiking clothes. Josh walks up and down the line.

JOSH

Before we start on this hike, let's take a second to clear our minds. Breathe deeply. And leave our regrets in the past and our worries for the future. Everyone ready? Aaaaand—breathe.

Off Stella's expression, clearly over this shit.

★ ★ ★

EXT. HIKING TRAIL—AN HOUR EARLIER—FLASHBACK
We're a mile and a half into the hike now. Andrew's energy is clearly flagging—he's a couple feet behind the rest of the group. Mason is trying to hide the fact that he's breathing hard.

STELLA

Really, Mason? After all that talk the other day, I gotta say, I really thought you were the kind of guy who could last…longer.

As Mason starts to retort—

JOSH

Stella! Let's take this opportunity to let go of our *toxic energy* and replace it with the *energy of nature*. Can you try to do that for us? You ready? Everyone else can join us, too.

Off Mason, "what the fuck" written all over his face.

EXT. HIKING TRAIL—DAY—BACK TO THE PRESENT

BEN (V.O.)

I've never watched a Woodstock documentary, but I imagine it would look a lot like this.

JOSH

All right, is everyone ready to start hiking again? We're probably half an hour from the
top, and I promise you, the view is going to
blow your minds.

STELLA

Stop being babies. This hike isn't even that
bad.

JOSH

There's that positive energy I've been looking for! All right, guys, let's start walking
again. That's the key to getting anywhere, you
know—taking the first step.

ANDREW

That is not real. You cannot be real. It is
just not possible for you to be a real person.

JOSH

Why do you say that, Andrew?

ANDREW

No one talks like that. No one. I mean, if
people did, I would know, you know? I'm from

Washington. Washington is the hippie capital of the United States!

JOSH

Hmm. No, I'm pretty sure that's Oregon.

BEN (V.O.)

Andrew doesn't say anything, and neither does anyone else, because what can we possibly say to this guy? *You are insane? Go back to the '60s? Can I have some LSD?* He would probably just laugh and say something about *channeling the energy of the woods*. This is what I get for letting my parents send me to wilderness therapy camp.

The path has gotten steep again, so we're all quiet as we hike. Eventually the only thing I'm registering is the chirping of the birds, the sound of Clarisa and Andrew breathing hard behind me, the backs of Stella's hiking boots as they go from shiny black to dulled black to brown from the dirt.

But I guess this is hiking: taking one step, and then another, and then another, and then another. Lifting the canteen to your mouth, keeping yourself alive even when you can't re-member why you're doing it. A step. A breath. A drink. Ten feet, twenty feet, a hundred feet, five hundred feet, fifteen hundred feet. A mile. Sunlight. Wind. Movement.

JOSH

And here we are.

I am so lost in my mind that I do not realize we've reached the destination until Stella
stops sharply in front of me. The trees on both
sides of the path are gone. The moss and dirt
have disappeared off the ground, leaving only a
bare outcropping of rock. Thirty feet in front
of us, the rocks drop off. In front of that is
nothing. Air. A thousand-foot drop to the forest of trees below us.

Josh spreads his arms around him and lifts
his eyes toward the sky.

JOSH

Look *around*, guys. Open your eyes.

MASON

Open *your* eyes—our eyes *are* open.

JOSH

No, Mason. That's not what I meant. I meant,
open your eyes. I meant, take it all in. I
meant, stop thinking about what to say next or
what you should have said or what anyone should
have said at any time and *look around*.

As he speaks, we fan out around him. There's
a red line of tape running across the rocks

ten feet before the cliff. I swing my backpack off my shoulders, sit down on the rocks, and try my hardest to *"look around"* as opposed to merely "looking around."

JOSH

This is the first hike. They always send me to lead the first hike. I'm sure you guys are all wondering why. You're all annoyed at how positive I am, how I seem to be living in my own world, how I can't possibly understand you. But I want you guys to think about it. When we started this hike, Stella was angry, and Mason was trying to be more angry than Stella just to prove a point, and Clarisa thought this was a waste of time. What did I do? I stayed positive. I wouldn't let negative energy affect me. I told you to breathe. To look around. To channel nature's energy. And what happened? Stella stopped complaining. Mason stopped being so negative. Everyone breathed. And looked around. And tried—I hope—to channel nature's energy. And here we are.

I think that positive energy always wins out. Perhaps you think I'm wrong. That's your right. But I hope as we keep hiking throughout the next month, and even as we share stories and hopes and fears and regrets, you remember that. That positive energy will win out. But only if you let it.

★ ★ ★

Everyone takes a second to digest Josh's speech.

ANDREW

Dude. That was pretty badass.

Stella laughs.

STELLA

Damn, Josh. You should take his word for it—Andrew here is our resident expert on "badass." I don't know if you've heard, but he's in a band.

BEN (V.O.)

I'm not really processing what anyone is saying anymore. I can hear everyone talking, but they're in the background, like a reporter on the evening news when you're not really paying attention to the television. I vaguely register Andrew replying to Stella and Stella laughing again, but there's a gust of wind and by the time the voices are carried away it feels like I'm remembering the moment instead of living it. They're sitting five feet away, but they feel incredibly insignificant when compared to everything that's stretching out in front of me: the trees, and the sky, and the jagged, bumpy line where they collide. I can see the shades of green blending into each other in the canopy; the flurry of the wings exploding out of the stillness of the sky; the clouds clustering together above us only to pull apart a few minutes later. I can hear leaves rustling below us and above us and around us and Andrew and Stella joking around behind me, somehow both a few footsteps and a universe away. The cliff drops off ten feet in front of me and then there is nothing but canopy and sunshine and wind and I can see myself sitting there, on the rocks, on a cliff, almost at the edge, almost in the air, almost floating, almost falling, and everything is so incredibly large around me and I am so incredibly small in the midst of it all and all of a sudden it breaks; the dissociation breaks and I can feel it all. Lots of people say lots of different things about euphoria, but I will describe it for you right now: I am sitting on the ground after a five-mile hike and I can feel the muscles in my legs falling in love with the sensation of rest and my soul is supernova exploding in an empty room, light bouncing off white walls and white ceiling and white floors; the breeze against my skin is a whisper from the universe that everything is going to be okay, and better, and good; it is so incredibly quiet, but the quiet sounds so, so vibrantly loud. Josh is such a hippie with his never-ending slogans of *nature* and *rest* and *energy*, but I can feel it now, I swear, running through my body and coursing through my veins and seeping into my bloodstream with every breath and I am look-

ing around, no, I am *looking around*, and it is
so beautiful, and there is so much life even
in the stillness, and in a few minutes or six
hours or one day or a couple of small eterni-
ties I will step away from the edge and walk
away. I will go back, I will return to camp, I
will say goodbye to the sky, the canopy, and
the wind and my legs will forget the sensation
of rest and the universe will start shouting
again like it always does and I will forget
this place and this quiet and this peace, but
I am here now. I am here on this mountain sitting on this air ten feet away from death and
everything else is so far away, even Stella
even Andrew even Mason even Clarisa even hippie
Josh, and I can feel the words in my head echoing and getting louder and louder with every
bounce back until they are vibrating through
my head until they are vibrating through my
body until they are everything until they are
inside me until I am light until I am stars
until I am supernova until I am nothing but
words ringing in an infinity of space.

I am trying to look at everything at once.
I am trying to hear everything at once.
I am trying to take in everything at once.
I am trying to feel everything at once.
I am trying to be everything at once.

I am everything at once.

I am everything.

I am

so

happy.

STELLA

I'VE ALWAYS MAINTAINED that this whole wilderness therapy camp stuff wouldn't actually be *that* terrible if it weren't for the, well, "therapy" part. For starters, it's obviously better than being locked up in Wethersfield all summer, where everywhere and everyone reminds me of all the shit that happened last semester. And it's nice to be away from my psychotic parents, even if they've just been replaced by equally if not more psychotic people my own age. Even the hikes are actually kind of nice, especially when they end in views like this. But the stuff that comes after all the hiking, the stuff like *this*—Josh making us sit down in a circle at the top of the hike so we can *ascend the mountain of our complex and beautiful minds*—pretty much kills it.

"Not too close to the edge," Josh warns, which is really a shame, because I was just starting to realize all the pros of hurling myself into the abyss and ending it all now. Josh gives us a minute to sit down, then closes his eyes and takes a deep breath in the way that I've been around long enough to know he's about to launch into some serious hippie-dippy shit that no one can actually understand.

"At Ugunduzi," Josh starts, "we focus on the future. We focus on the possibility of brighter days. We focus on the *ourselves of tomorrow*."

"'The ourselves of tomorrow,'" Andrew repeats. "I really dig that, dude."

"It's a grammatical abomination," I say. Because no amount of gung-ho is going to bend the rules of the English language—sorry, Josh.

"But in order to shape our presents, and in order to better our futures," Josh continues, "we must first…go back. We must go back to the past. To *our* pasts. We must not run from them. We must embrace them. Accept them. And *understand* them.

"Our families. Our childhoods. Our past lovers. These are all things that shape us in indefinable and extraordinary ways," Josh says. I feel an unpleasantly familiar twinge in my chest when he says the "lovers" part, but I grit my teeth and choke it down.

"We're, like, seventeen years old," Clarisa says. "How many past lovers could we possibly have?"

"Well…" Mason says. I keep myself from whacking him on the arm, because 1) day one seems a bit early to get kicked out of camp, and 2) Mason's the type of person who takes all physical contact short of being punched in the face as a sign of flirtation.

"I really love my parents, you guys," Ben says out of nowhere. I turn to look at him—because *what?*—and am doubly stunned to find that he actually looks like he's about to burst into tears. Now, I'm the first to admit that someone crying for no real reason during random moments at Ugunduzi is depressingly par for the course. But Ben was so ridiculously zoned out for the duration of the hike up that the whole sudden burst of emotion thing catches me completely off guard.

Just thirty minutes ago, I yelled at him to walk faster because he was holding everyone up, and he literally looked at me like I was speaking another language. And now he's on the verge of tears because of how much he loves his parents?

"Of course," Josh says. "We all love our parents. But that doesn't mean that the relationships can't be complicated, or troubled, or even unhealthy in ways that affect us to this day. Clarisa?" Josh asks. "Is there something you'd like to add?"

Clarisa has made the biggest therapy mistake there is, which is to lose control of your facial expressions and react visibly to something someone else says. Therapists are designed to sniff out that shit: any frown, grimace, half-choked sob you accidentally let out—they will sense it and put you on the spot.

"Oh, nothing," Clarisa says. Which might be the *second* biggest therapy mistake there is. Lying and saying, "Nothing," when you do get called out. It's not the *lying* so much that's the problem, really—it's the "nothing" part. I want to tell Clarisa that she's going to have to come up with some better evasive techniques than "nothing." I, for one, started a list back in freshman year of high school.

Josh stares at Clarisa solemnly. It's not long until the silence gets to her (therapy wisdom #3: get real, real comfortable with silence) and she spills.

"Of *course* I love my mom," Clarisa says. "But sometimes she's just...too much."

"Too much in what way?" Josh presses. You can tell he's really getting into this. I make a mental note to share my list with Clarisa later so she can avoid this kind of misery in the future.

"Too much in *every* way," Clarisa says. "Too much...positivity. Too much hope. Too social, too pretty, too *everything*."

"So..." Andrew says. I look over at him and immediately

feel a rush of discomfort. His arms, Jesus. They're practically toothpicks. "You feel like you're not as good as her?"

"Of course I'm not as good as her," Clarisa says. "But the thing is, I don't really care. I don't want to be, like, the prom queen, or go on lots of dates, or win a billion senior superlatives. That stuff sounds awful. But for some reason she's always thought that unless I'm doing all of those things, I'm just wasting my life. Like in the ninth grade, when our school did those ridiculous Valentine's Day roses and I didn't get any, my mother legitimately thought my life was over. Which is why I brought this entire thing up—because that was *so* long ago, and I can still hear her telling me how all she wanted was for me to be able to experience 'normal teenage things' and have 'normal teenage fun.' But I can't *do* those things," Clarisa says, "and I don't even *want* to."

There's an uncomfortable moment of silence as the rest of us wait for Josh to say something and Josh waits for Clarisa to say something and Clarisa stares directly into the ground, oblivious.

"But I still feel like I should try, I guess," Clarisa says slowly. "Because… I don't know, she's my mom. And it's just been me and her for so long."

Josh nods. He has the good sense to look grave and serious, but I've been to enough therapy sessions to know that inside he's probably doing cartwheels out of joy. Session One and Clarisa's already dishing out the good stuff. This is like a therapist's *dream*.

"Thank you so much for your bravery, Clarisa," Josh says, and I try with limited success to turn my scoff into a cough. "In the spirit of community, and of healing, and of *communal* healing, I want us all to follow in Clarisa's lead and share something from our past that we're still hanging on to today, for whatever reason. It can be a family story. It can be a story about your friends. It can be a story about yourself. It can be a story about your parents. It can be good or bad. Long or short. But it must be *honest*, guys—because we're all here to help each other and we can only do that if we're honest with each other. Do you guys want to do another breathing exercise before we begin?"

"No," I say forcefully, only to realize in horror that Mason has said the exact same thing at the exact same time.

"All right!" Josh says. "Stella, why don't you start us off?"

Josh beams at me. The other side of the edge of the cliff starts to look appealing.

"One thing about my past…" I repeat. "That I'm holding on to…"

Kevin's name springs to mind so abruptly that I almost can't believe that I'm thinking it—not after all this time, not after all the work I've done trying to lock it in a box in the back of my mind that I never, ever have to open again. But there it is, all at once, and: *Kevin, Kevin, Kevin,* and I'm so off guard and so emotionally unprepared that I squeeze my eyes shut almost instinctively. But that makes everything worse, because then I'm *seeing* him, too: Kevin at school and Kevin that night at the park and Kevin at the stupid, stupid antiprom we threw and—

"Stella?" Josh prompts.

I open my eyes. Do my best to look calm. *If you show them how much this means to you,* I think to myself, *they will never let you forget about it.*

"This past year I dated this guy," I say evenly. I have had so much practice on therapy couches and never-ending group sessions that my voice barely catches at all. "His name was Kevin. And it ended pretty poorly. What a shock, right? Dumb teenagers in high school fail to make relationship last.

"Anyway, I'm not that stupid girl who thought that we were

going to ride off into the sunset and get married. I knew it was going to end and I knew it wasn't going to end well, because these things never do. But for some reason—"

I cut off, bite my lip. Is there any way to say this that doesn't sound pathetic? Laughably melodramatic? Like I've been written into the script of a bad TV soap?

"It's harder than I expected it to be," I finish. Clarisa makes this sympathetic, sad noise that just screams how bad she feels for me, which makes me want to pull her over the edge of the mountain with me. I turn to face Andrew with the hope that he'll get the memo and start talking before Josh starts in on me, but—

"That sounds like a very difficult experience, Stella," Josh says, voice so soothing that I feel *even more* annoyed.

"It's not," I grit. "It's fine. Everything is fine."

"You don't *sound* fine," Mason says. There's a grin creeping across his face that makes me want to punch him.

"It's fine," I repeat.

"Are you *sure* it's fine?" Mason asks.

I turn away from him.

"You guys fucked, didn't you?" Mason asks, sounding positively gleeful.

"What are we, twelve?" I snap.

It's a testament to how absolutely insufferable Mason is that I actually wish Jessie were here leading this session, because there's no way she'd let him get away with saying shit like that. But instead we're stuck with Josh, so blissfully mellowed out that he just says, "Was that really necessary, Mason?"

"Guess not," Mason says. He makes his best contrite expression. I resist the urge to smack it off his face.

"Would you like to tell us a little bit more about the relationship?" Josh asks, once again turning to me.

"There's nothing to tell," I say. "It was a thing and it's over.

But for some reason my feelings are, like, two months behind my brain."

"Stella," Josh says, "the past does not simply *go away*. It stays with us. And it is just as necessary to confront and acknowledge and process the parts of our pasts that have pained us as it is those that have given us joy—in order to move on, and in order to grow."

You're literally wearing a fucking rainbow tie-dye shirt, I want to shout at Josh, because the only thing more annoying than adults speaking to you in dumb, meaningless platitudes is adults speaking to you in dumb, meaningless platitudes in a tone of voice that screams, "I AM WISER THAN YOU AND YOU KNOW IT." But I've learned that getting angry will only convince Josh that this is a Big Issue worth discussing, and that's the last thing I want.

"Thanks," I say instead. And turn, once more, to look expectantly at Andrew.

"I have a story," Andrew says hesitantly. "But it's about my band."

"That's great!" Josh says. This is easy for him to say, since he hasn't been subjected to a never-ending stream of stories about Andrew's band like the rest of us have.

"This was...*before*," Andrew starts.

"Before what?"

"Before—I don't know—before we got better. Before people started liking us more. Before whatever. The point is, we had scored a gig opening for a really big Seattle band. We were all really excited, you know? It was definitely the biggest venue we'd played, and a surprising number of people were there for the opening acts. Anyway, it went awful. The crowd really didn't like us. And then we all got psyched out, you know, 'cause people were booing and being jackasses about it. Not that that kind of stuff isn't expected when you open for a tough crowd, but it was... It was pretty shitty. And I've just never been able to forget it, I guess."

Andrew is one of those people who is painfully sensitive, and also painfully open about all of the experiences and feelings and fears triggered by how damn sensitive he is. Which is great for being a wilderness therapy camper, and not nearly as great for being a professional musician. I can see this becoming a problem, mostly because Andrew would probably rather be a successful musician than a successful wilderness therapy camper.

"Ah," Josh says. "And what did you do to deal with the situation?"

Andrew sighs. "Not anything, really. I mean, there wasn't much we could do. I just smoked, like, half a pack of cigarettes and went on a diet and swore to get better."

"Were those things really going to help you become 'better'?" Josh says.

"You guys just don't *get it*," Andrew says. "It's the only way to be successful. You have to do it. I'm not in a position to be rewriting some ancient music scene codes of conduct, you know? You have no idea how much it matters to look a certain way in order to get people to buy your music. It's *cra*—"

"That's really stupid, Andrew," Ben says.

"What?"

"You're awesome," Ben says, beaming. Then the words start spilling out of his mouth so quickly it's difficult to understand what he's saying. "Your band's music is awesome, so who gives a fuck if anyone buys it or not? You're making art. It's art it's art it's art it's beautiful."

"*That's* really stupid," Andrew says. "Yeah, it's beautiful making art, but you can't do it forever if no one buys your records. Eventually I have to, I don't know, go to college or some shit and then I'll never see my band again and— Basically we have two years to get signed or it's all over."

"That's a lot of pressure to put on yourself," Josh says. "Has anyone else experienced anything similar?"

"I used to think," Clarisa says, "that it was my fault that I had OCD. Like if I tried hard enough, I could just—I don't know—*not*. I could become a normal person and hang out with other normal people in normal places and not have to be counting things all the time, and then freaking out when the number I got wasn't safe or good."

"That's *tragic*," Ben says. He looks moved to the point of tears.

"Ben," Mason says. "What the fuck is wrong with you?"

"Nothing," Ben replies. "And nothing is wrong with you, either. Or any of us. Or anyone, for that matter. We're all... We're all *good*, I think. Good and *right*. We're all *right*." Ben keeps emphasizing certain words as he talks, as if emphasizing them could imbue them with a meaning that they don't actually have.

"Well, that's just not true," Mason says.

"Mason," I say. "You are literally a colossal asshole."

"That's not what *literally* means," Clarisa says.

"Guys!" Ben says. We all turn around to look at him. "Why are we all fighting?"

"I have a couple of explanations," Andrew says.

"No, but I mean, *why are we all fighting*?"

"Um," Andrew says. "I mean, *I have a couple of explanations*."

"I don't know how to express this," Ben says.

"Maybe you just— Maybe you just shouldn't," Andrew advises, but to no avail.

"I want you to know that I feel incredible amounts of affection for all of you even though I have only known you for a relatively short period of time and I think we're all great, and we're all going to be okay, and we should do those breathing exercises that Josh was talking about because there really is something magical and beautiful and awe-inspiring about the way we keep ourselves alive without even noticing."

No one says anything. Except for Josh, of course, who grins and spreads his arms wide, like an eagle, or like someone who is about to get stabbed in the chest by a disgruntled, emotionally volatile teenager. "Wow," Josh says. "Wow, wasn't that a great session? It was a great session. I'm so glad you guys are sharing with each other, and participating, and communicating. I think Ben's right—I think we could all use some breathing exercises."

"I think so, too," Mason says. "Don't you, Stella?"

"All right, everyone—close your eyes. Picture yourself somewhere happy, somewhere tranquil. And breathe in."

I close my eyes, take a breath, and picture myself back in Wethersfield. I'll take boredom and screaming parents and unwelcoming memories over that nightmare of a therapy session any day.

ANDREW

I'M NOT RELIGIOUS, but I pray before I step on the scale.

It is Weigh-in Wednesday. I am standing in front of the scale. I am holding my breath. And I am fucking praying.

To be honest, I don't even know who or what I'm praying to. It's not like I picture some stern, bearded guy hanging out in the sky, checking off *yes* or *no* every time I ask him for something. And I don't imagine sitting next to Buddha, waiting for him to give me wisdom or tranquility. It's more like a plea to the universe, I guess, or some grand sense of justice that obviously doesn't really exist. Like, I would obviously prefer it if God answered my pleas, and if Buddha granted me peace and self-love or whatever else. But those are obviously not going to happen, so the most I can ask is that the universe keeps the scale from reading above 125. Not out of grace or goodness or whatever else, but just out of some cosmic desire to keep me from going crazy.

It's funny, because I know that the scale *shouldn't* read above 125. I know how much I've been eating, and I know how much I weighed before, and I'm good enough at math to know how much I should weigh today. Even then—even knowing everything I've done and all the factors I've taken into account—I'm still terrified.

It's been almost five days since I last weighed myself. Who knows what's been happening with my metabolism in those five days—maybe the stress has thrown it out of sync and I've somehow gained five pounds. Maybe the God I don't believe in and the Buddha I don't pray to have teamed up in order to fuck me over. Maybe it's going to read 130, 135, 140.

It's worse because there's no preparation about it, you know? Back home, I weighed myself at the same time every day—after using the bathroom, before showering, before breakfast. I took off all my clothes except for my boxers and always stepped evenly onto the scale, right foot first, then the left. I made sure to balance my weight carefully and not touch anything else. Here, they just have you take your shoes off and step on. I don't know how much to subtract for my jeans and shirt, and also, I drank water already this morning. Everyone always told me that I shouldn't let the numbers rule my life, but it's even worse with numbers that might not even be true.

"Andrew?" Jessie says. I've been staring at the scale for a solid minute now, and she's probably getting worried. "Would you like to do the weighing blind?"

It's a tempting offer. I could step on with my back to the scale, wait for them to move the bars, hold my breath, then step off again. But then I would never know—130, 135, 140. I would never know if I could eat more, or if I should eat less, if I'm okay, or if I'm not okay, if I'm getting better, or if I'm not getting better—130, 135, 140, and I would *never know.*

"No," I say. "No, I'm fine. Thanks."

I force all of the air out of my lungs, cross my fingers, and step on, right foot, and then left foot. I close my eyes as she adjusts the scale, holding, hoping, praying, while everything I've eaten in the last five days runs through my head, the sandwiches for lunch, the soup at dinner, the pasta, the pizza, a 2,000-calorie day, a 2,500-calorie day, a bagel every morning, oh, *God*, bagels are so large and all carbs and—

"It's 124," Jessie says. "You can step off."

I step off and feel myself take a giant breath of air. "Jesus Christ," I say, "124." That's okay—124 with the shirt and the jeans and the water is probably 123.5 or even 123, and 123 is closer to 120 than 130, 135, 140.

"You were 123 when you got to camp," Jessie says, frowning.

"Yeah, I guess," I say. I need to get out of here quickly now, because I'm a terrible liar and always have been.

Jessie looks at me, concerned. "Hmm," she says. "Okay, Andrew, you're free to leave. Could you send Ben in?"

"Yes," I say. I shove my feet into my shoes and start walking before I've even tied them. I'm probably going to trip and fall, but I don't care: 124. Thank God. "Yeah, I'll send Ben in."

MASON

IT'S ALL GOING very smoothly until Andrew passes out.

Which is annoying enough on its own, if you ask me, but what makes it ten times worse is the fact that he waits until we're almost all the way up the mountain to do it. I'm looking forward to getting to the top and taking in the view and finally getting to sit down for a while after three hours of trudging along through the woods, and then all of a sudden Clarisa is saying, "Oh, my gosh, Andrew," and then I turn around to find that he's on the ground.

My first thought, of course, is that he's playing some kind of stupid prank. This is the kind of stuff that kids who think they're punk find amusing, right? Stupid kids at my high school do shit like this all the time, pretending to get sick in the middle of class or the lunchroom because they never progressed past the emotional maturity of a twelve-year-old. "Get up, Andrew, come on," I say.

"He *can't* just 'come on,' Mason, he *fainted*," Clarisa snaps, looking panicked. Clarisa panics so easily that it's hard to imagine how she's managed to remain on this planet for sixteen whole years. Then again, if Stella managed to get a boyfriend despite *that* kind of attitude—well, I guess anything must be possible.

"It's obviously some dumb prank," I say. "Andrew, this isn't funny. You're holding us all up."

"Could you stop being such a—" Stella starts, but I never get to find out what it is exactly I'm supposed to stop being, because Jessie has finally realized what's going on and breaks us all up.

"I need all of you—*all of you, Stella, that includes you*—to take five steps back. Give him *room*," she commands. Jessie crouches over Andrew and takes out her radio, but then the entire point is moot because Andrew wakes up.

"Dude…" he mumbles. He props himself up on his elbows, looking even more confused than he usually does. "What is going on?"

I know that I'm supposed to say something like, "Oh, my God, Andrew, are you okay?" in a tone of voice so concerned that it defies all reasonable expectation and offer to carry him back to The Hull or something equally ridiculous. But I just can't stop thinking about how *dumb* this all is. I could be home, doing something actually productive with my life and considerable intellect right now, and instead I'm standing in the middle of the woods with a bunch of psychos learning how to "maintain a positive" attitude or whatever else. I don't need a positive attitude. I need everyone to get their collective shit together so we can finish this stupid hike.

"Don't get up too quickly," Jessie advises. "And drink some water before you get up."

"I feel fine," Andrew says. He uncaps the water bottle and drinks all of it in one go. "I just…don't really remember what happened."

"You fainted," Jessie says. "Probably from dehydration. Don't worry, there shouldn't be any lasting symptoms other than maybe a few bruises from the fall, but still—if you were feeling faint, you should have said something and asked us to stop, Andrew, really. We wouldn't have minded."

"I'm *fine*," Andrew repeats. He stands up.

"Great," I say. "Andrew's fine, everyone else is fine—can we get a move on now?"

"Mason," Stella hisses next to me. "What is *wrong* with you?"

"What is wrong with *me*? What is wrong with *you*? I'm just trying to behave like a civilized adult here, unlike you—"

"That's your idea of uncivil?" Stella says, disgusted. "Keep talking and I'll show you uncivil, I swear to—"

"Mason and Stella," Jessie snaps. Both of us shut up. "We're going back to camp," she says firmly. "Now unless you two would like to spend the rest of the night out here with each other as company…"

Stella scoffs and starts walking.

We're all silent as we walk back, except for Andrew, who buries his face in his hands and mutters, "Oh, God," every couple of minutes.

"Andrew," Stella starts gently as Andrew continues to moan indecipherably almost forty minutes into our walk back. "Are you still feeling sick?"

"No," Andrew says. He stops walking and shuts his eyes. "I screwed up, guys," he says.

"Jesus Christ," Stella says. "You can't possibly feel like this is your fault, can you?"

"It *is* my fault," Andrew moans. He starts moving again, but now at twice the speed we were walking at before. *Good riddance*, I think as Stella and Ben break into a jog to try to keep up.

"There's no way you could've predicted that would happen!" Ben says.

"Andrew, I know you might feel disappointed or upset because we couldn't finish the hike—and there's nothing wrong with feeling that way," Jessie says, "but don't feel ashamed—"

"It's my fault because I haven't— I haven't—"

"You haven't *what?*" Stella says. She plants herself firmly in front of him so he has no choice but to stop.

"I haven't been eating," Andrew says. He's breathing hard. "I just haven't been able to do it. I can't eat this shit, guys. You have no idea what it would do to my body—I'm not used to carbs and I'm not used to meat and I'm just… I just can't."

"You haven't been eating?" Stella says.

"Oh, God," I say. This is the kind of revelation that starts a discussion that I have absolutely no desire to be a part of.

"I've just been throwing it out," Andrew says.

"You've just been throwing it out?" Stella repeats.

"Could you lower your voice, please?" I ask. Her voice is so shrill that it's hurting my ears.

"You've just been throwing it out?" Jessie echoes, so dumbstruck she's forgotten to be stern.

"There's so many people out at the tables when we eat, so no one ever really notices, and I feel bad, and I know it's wrong, and I know it's not the solution, but I just… I just didn't know what else to do," Andrew says. He brushes past Stella and starts pushing forward again. The Hull has appeared in front of us and is getting larger with every step we take. I'm just hoping I make it back inside before he starts crying.

"Every time I look at the food, I feel like I'm going to die," Andrew continues. "*I can't do it.* It was the only way."

"The only way to *what* exactly?" I say. "To wind up fainting midway through our hike?"

"Okay," Jessie says. She's evidently pulled herself back together, because she sounds, once more, like she is lecturing a roomful of kindergartners. "Everyone can head back to the common room, where Josh is going to supervise you guys until lunch. Andrew, we're going to need to speak privately."

STELLA

"WHY DON'T WE talk about what happened earlier today?" Jessie says when we're back together for group later that night.

I can think of a couple of reasons why we shouldn't talk about what happened earlier today. First of all, what is anyone supposed to say? I've been thinking about it all morning, and the only thing I've managed to come up with is "Oh, sorry you can't bring yourself to eat anything, Andrew, but at least this means that I wasn't the first one to majorly fuck up this summer."

Andrew, for his part, looks like he'd rather do anything else in the world than talk about what happened earlier today. "We don't have to," he protests, but Jessie doesn't even bother to respond.

"I just don't get it," Ben says. "Why?"

"What do you mean, 'why?'" Andrew moans. "I feel like I've told everyone a thousand times already. I just *can't do it*."

"Yes, you can," Clarisa says. "That probably sounds stupid to you. But you *can*, Andrew, you really can."

"Even if I could, I *can't*, you know what I mean?" Andrew says.

"You literally just made two contradictory statements," Clarisa says.

"No," Andrew says. "What I meant was, even if I could bring myself to do it, I *couldn't*, because it would be letting the band down."

"That's just not true," Clarisa says. "We've talked about this, right? How it's just patently false that if you gain weight you'll be 'letting your band down'?"

"We have talked about this, and you guys *still just don't get it*. You think that everything is just about me being healthy again, but it's not. It's about the band. It's about the fans. It's about being the kind of band that *has* fans. No one wants to listen to a band that doesn't look—well, you know—cool. And I don't want to be the reason why we're not cool."

"Stop," I say. Andrew sounds so sad that listening to him is making *me* feel sad. "Andrew, you're not making any sense. That literally doesn't make any sense. It's a—what's the word—my therapist uses it all the time—"

"Cognitive distortion," Clarisa supplies. "What?" Clarisa says at my surprised expression. "You're not the only one who goes to therapy, Stella. We all want to feel better."

"That's not what I meant," I start, but Clarisa has launched into an in-depth explanation of the "several different types" of cognitive distortions and how Andrew's "flawed but understandable thought process" fits into them.

"You're letting your feelings dictate your reasoning. You *feel* like you're not cool, so you assume it must be true. You *feel* like if your band fails, it must be all your fault, so you assume that that's true, too. You *feel* like bands only succeed if they look cool, so you assume that if you fail, it's because—"

"I don't really see how any of those sentences are wrong," Andrew says.

"That's the other thing about cognitive distortions," I say.

"They're basically impossible to get rid of. We might as well just accept that we're stuck with them forever."

"That's not a very positive attitude," Jessie says.

"That's funny, because I'm so well-known for my positive attitude."

"Andrew," Jessie says, "have you considered starting any medications? Josh and I have been talking about this, and we think it could be very beneficial to—"

"No," Andrew says flatly. "I'm not considering it."

"Why's that?" Jessie asks.

"I don't need it," Andrew says. He looks like he's seriously panicking now. "I can't start any drugs right now because— I just can't. I don't want to deal with the side effects now. It wouldn't go well with my lifestyle."

"Your lifestyle...of being anorexic?" Clarisa asks.

Mason snorts. "He means he gets trashed and does drugs a lot."

"That's not what I meant!" Andrew says. "Look, I just don't *need* it. I really don't. What happened today terrified me, guys. I'd forgotten what it was like before I started camp, and how I couldn't eat anything, and how tired and miserable I was all the time, and how awful that night was. And it brought it all back and I just don't ever want to be back there, okay? It's not going to happen again. I swear."

"Wait, what night?" Ben says.

"Shit," Andrew says. "Never mind."

"Please watch your language, Andrew," Jessie says.

"I don't think *never mind* are words you're allowed to say in therapy, Andrew," I say. I'm tempted to ask Jessie if this is *really* the best time to be harping on the no-language rule, but then I remember that this is Jessie we're talking to, and to Jessie, it's *always* the best time to be harping on the freaking no-language rule.

121

"All the nights," Andrew says. I catch his eye and raise my eyebrows, but he looks away hastily and starts talking to the ground instead. "I just meant all the nights. They were all bad. The point is, I don't need to go on meds."

"Of course we won't make you go on any medications that you don't want to be on, Andrew," Jessie says soothingly. "It was just a suggestion. A possibility. Because I know you do want to feel better, and the rest of us want to help you in that process. A lot of people here can attest to the fact that sometimes medication can make a world of difference."

"She's right, man," Ben says. "I was a mess before I went on meds."

"You're a mess *now*," Mason interjects.

"I was more of a mess," Ben amends.

"They helped," I admit. "I mean, they helped me get out of bed, anyway."

Andrew closes his eyes and takes a deep breath. "I'm fine, guys. I don't need it. I'll do better. I promise."

"I think you're confused about what 'better' is," Clarisa says.

"I'll eat," Andrew says. "Look, I just— I can do this, okay? I shouldn't have said I couldn't. I was being dramatic. I don't know why I said that. Look, I came to camp because I wanted to get better. I just need to try harder. Seriously, that's it. If I just make myself try harder, I can fix it."

"Cognitive distortion," I say, but no one replies.

Later, I catch Andrew in the common room before lights-out. I don't know what it is that makes me do it. Maybe it's that I'm still kind of shaken up from seeing him collapse onto the ground earlier today, and I can't get the image out of my head no matter how many times I tell myself that everything is fine, that he's fine, and that this is all par for the course at Ugunduzi, anyway, so why am I so freaked out? Maybe it's because I'm exhausted, and I always get stupidly emotional when I'm exhausted, prone to caring too much about things for no real reason just because it's late and the logical side of my brain has given up and shut down for the night. Or maybe it's just that when I walk by, Andrew just looks so... *sad*. It sounds kind of stupid—I mean, he's sad, I'm sad, we're all sad; isn't that why we're here?—but the look on Andrew's face practically qualifies as another *dimension* of sad. He looks so incredibly depressed that to leave him there all by himself seems almost criminal.

Whatever the reason is, I find myself walking over and taking a seat next to him on the couch. "Hey," I say softly.

"Hi," Andrew responds.

There's an awkward moment of silence during which Andrew looks like he can't believe that I'm sitting there, and *I* can't believe that I'm sitting there, and part of me just wants to get up and leave. *What were you thinking, Stella? That you would just waltz in and sit down and have a heart-to-heart with some random kid you met a few days ago at crazy camp?*

"How'd your conversation with Jessie go?" I ask.

"Fine."

And then again, silence.

"It's just tough," he says after a few moments. "Because it's like...I know what I need to do, and I know that I need to do it, but when it's actually time..." He trails off for a moment. He looks up at the ceiling, then closes his eyes. "I always fail."

"No one thinks you've failed, Andrew," I say quietly.

"Mason thinks I've failed," Andrew points out matter-of-factly.

"Mason's an asshole," I respond, and he laughs, and the levity is such a welcome distraction from the heaviness of this talk that I almost cry from relief.

"Yeah. I guess he is."

There's another break in the conversation. Thoughts swirl around my head, incoherent and unorganized and largely useless. There's so much that I want Andrew to hear, that I want him to know, that I want him to *believe*, but I'm so tired and I don't know how to say those things in the first place and I certainly can't make him believe them.

So instead I look up at the ceiling, too, and say, "I know."

"What?"

I bite my lip. "I know. I know what it's like to feel like something should be so easy to just…to just *do*. But it never works out when you try, and in the end you just wind up going in circles inside your head, again and again and again. I know."

Andrew looks at me. I look at him.

Neither of us is crying yet, which I suppose is a good sign.

"Well," I say. I pause, uncertain—but Andrew doesn't say anything, so I figure my time here is up. "I'm going to get to bed. Before we, you know, get in trouble for staying up past the oh-so-late hour of 9:00 p.m."

"Thanks," Andrew says.

"What?" I say.

"Just, you know, *thanks*," Andrew repeats, and the word catches me so completely off guard that I'm temporarily lost for words.

"You don't have to thank me," I manage to get out.

"I know that I don't *have* to," Andrew says. He rolls his eyes, half exasperated, half playful, and then grins in a way that makes it all too easy to see him onstage, helming some angsty teen punk band, on top of the world. "But I want to."

"You're welcome," I say. "I'm gonna just… Okay, bye."

Andrew's laughter follows me out of the room.

BEN

THE BAD NEWS is that things are tense.

On Wednesday night, we have one of those Comically Awkward Dinners—the kind you see in TV shows where no one knows what to say to anyone else and everyone just sort of looks around awkwardly waiting for an excuse to leave. Mason spends the evening pretending Andrew doesn't exist and Andrew, for his part, can't seem to say more than three words without tearing up.

The good news is that Jessie arrives Thursday morning with a distraction in the form of a lecture. "I'm disappointed in you guys," Jessie starts as soon as we're done with breakfast. "You're supposed to have a list of the materials you need in order to start working on your Camp Project by lunchtime. I know that everyone has been busy thinking about other things, but that's no excuse to ignore the Camp Project."

"Oh, shit," Andrew says. "We're supposed to be decorating this joint."

"Language, Andrew," Jessie says. "And yes. As you all seem to have forgotten, you are indeed supposed to be 'decorating this joint.'"

I get out my notebook and click my pen loudly, like people do in the movies when they are about to embark on a serious project. "Okay, guys," I say, flipping to a clean page. "Obviously we need wood stain, for the entire cabin, but beyond that, we need to figure out a color scheme."

It must work, because no one looks at me as if I've done anything particularly out of the ordinary. "Black and white," Andrew suggests. It's the first time he's looked remotely interested in anything since before the Hike That Went Wrong.

"God, no," Mason says, apparently so offended by Andrew's color choice that he can't resist replying. "This isn't one of your shitty—sorry, Jessie, I meant to say *awful*—music videos. We're not trying to blind anyone here. We should do blue and white."

"We should have some blue," Clarisa replies. "Blue is supposed to evoke peace, right?"

"Dark blue and beige," Stella says, sounding bored as ever. "Those are our colors."

"Beige?" Mason interjects. "What the hell even is beige?"

"Beige is one of those girlie colors that doesn't actually exist," Andrew explains, "like 'magenta' and 'plum.'"

"So...everyone good with dark blue and beige?" I say. Mason scoffs but doesn't protest. "Great. What about furniture?"

"Just write down *IKEA wooden living room set*," Mason says. "Like hell am I going to build a shitty desk from scratch for this."

"We should also get a futon," Andrew adds.

"Okay," I say. "What about decorations?"

Everyone, apparently, feels very strongly about decorations.

"Posters," Andrew says. "We need to get posters."

"Not if they're anything like the posters you put up in our room, Andrew. Those are embar—"

"I like posters!" I exclaim. "Plus, posters are inclusive. We can get movie posters for me, band posters for Andrew—"

"No one is going to come into the cabin and see a Nirvana poster and feel *safe*—"

"—inspirational posters for Clarisa—"

"We agreed that there wouldn't be dumb inspirational posters!" Mason practically shouts.

"What about a chandelier?"

"Are you kidding me? Ben, we are not getting a chandelier!"

"Jesus Christ, guys!" Stella says. Everyone shuts up. "This is not that complicated." She walks over to me and takes the notebook and pen out of my hands. "We're going to go around and each suggest something and then vote on it. If the majority votes it in, I'll write it down."

Stella looks up at me expectantly. "*Donnie Darko* poster," I say.

That one is voted down unanimously. "Sorry, Ben," Clarisa says. "That's just way too depressing. Christmas lights."

Stella snorts. "Clarisa, I think you spend too much time on Tumblr."

"Well, let's vote on it and see!" she says defensively. "Raise your hand if you support Christmas lights."

Clarisa and Andrew raise their hands. Mason and Stella do not. Clarisa looks at me imploringly. "Come *on*, Ben, think about how, you know, moody and ambient and atmospheric they are."

"Uh," I say, feeling Stella's glare boring into my soul.

"Pleaaaase?" Clarisa asks, eyes wide and dark and impossible to resist.

I feel myself raise my hand.

"Seriously, guys?" Mason says. He sounds disgusted.

"Let's get a guitar," Andrew says.

"You already have a guitar."

"No, I mean a guitar for the wall. Like one of those guitars you hang up above a couch or a TV or something."

"That," Stella says, "is a complete waste of a guitar. You'd never even be able to play it."

"It looks cool!" Andrew says.

"It looks stupid! What's the point of having a guitar when it's just hanging on the wall?"

"Oh, come *on*, guys—Stella got her stupid color scheme and Clarisa got her Christmas lights and all I want is a *guitar*. That's not asking for that much, is—"

"My color scheme," Stella says, "is less stupid than putting a guitar on the wall. Who does that? No one is going to walk into the cabin and be like, 'Hey, I see a guitar on the wall and now I feel super at peace.' They're going to be like, 'Hey, there's a guitar on the wall, and it looks really dumb.'"

"*Or*," Andrew argues, "they'll be like, 'Wow, there's a guitar on the wall and it's sick.'"

"First of all," Stella says, "no, they won't, because you're the only person above the age of thirteen who still says 'sick.' And second of all, no."

"It's supposed to be a vote!" Andrew says.

"I'm going to have to go with Stella on this one," Mason says. Stella and Andrew both narrow their eyes at him.

"A guitar on the wall doesn't exactly convey peace," Clarisa says. "And it could fall." Her eyes get wide at the thought. "Okay, we are not putting a guitar on the wall."

"Seriously? It's the one thing I really want in this cabin, and you're not going to let me have it?"

"Well, that's your problem for really wanting something as ridiculous as a guitar on the wall," Mason says.

"We could get a guitar *decal*," Clarisa suggests.

"That's not the same as an actual guitar," Andrew says.

"Exactly. An actual guitar could fall on you and injure you. A guitar decal could not."

"Whatever, dude," Andrew says. "Get a guitar decal instead of an actual guitar."

Over the next hour, we approve seven posters (none particularly inspirational), an air hockey table (Andrew's second proposal, mostly voted in out of guilt for vetoing the guitar), and a bookshelf. We're all feeling pretty accomplished and proud of ourselves, at least until we turn in the list to Jessie and, instead of congratulating us and telling us to take the rest of the day off, she reminds us that Art by the Fire Friday is tomorrow. "How is preparation for that going?" she asks.

"Oh, shi—shoot," Andrew says, glancing nervously at Jessie. "I've only written one verse for the song I'm supposed to be playing for that."

"Ugh," Clarisa says. "I've been trying to write a poem the entire week, and it's impossible. I don't know—can I just recite that Shakespeare sonnet they made us memorize in school last year or something?"

"How hard can it be to write a poem?" Mason says. "Give me a minute."

He grabs the notebook out of Stella's hands and scribbles furiously for thirty seconds. "Okay, here's what I got. 'All I want,'" he says, voice dropping a solid octave, "'is the serenity to accept the things I cannot change.'" Dramatic pause. "'The courage to change the things I can.'" Dramatic pause. "'And the wisdom to know the difference.'"

He looks up at us solemnly. For a minute, no one says anything.

"That's the serenity prayer, Mason," Andrew finally points out.

Mason makes a face. "So? The point is, it's not that deep

or lyrical or great, so I'm sure I wouldn't have had to try that hard to write it."

"You wouldn't have had to try that hard to write it because it's already been fucking written," Stella snaps, snatching the notebook and the pen back.

"That's *my* stuff!" I say.

"Language!" Jessie says.

This conversation must already have really stressed Stella out, because for some reason she now completely loses her shit.

"Mason," she says, spinning around to look at Jessie with a look of fury on her face that makes even me take four steps back out of sheer force of self-preservation, "has been swearing this *entire* fucking time, and you don't say *anything* about it!"

"That is not true, Stella, and I'm going to have to ask you to lower your voice," Jessie replies calmly.

Stella lowers her voice but somehow manages to sound even more furious. "Everyone swears! Everyone! But I'm the *only* one you ever call out for it. Why? What is your problem?"

"I'll admit that I haven't been able to catch each and every instance of profanity, but to suggest that I'm *targeting* you—as I believe you're suggesting, Stella—is ludicrous, not to mention incredibly disrespectful. Now, unless you have anything productive to add, I'd like to turn the focus of our conversation back to Art by the Fire Friday, which is—"

"Whatever," Stella says. She drops the notebook and pen on the floor in front of me. "It's idiotic and pointless. Art by the Fire Friday is idiotic and pointless."

"Stella!" Jessie exclaims, but Stella has already turned around and started walking away.

ANDREW

THURSDAY AND FRIDAY are bad days.

I'm not supposed to be thinking about calories, I know, but I can't help it. I'm so used to it that I don't even have to really *think* about the food before a number has already popped into my head. I'll grab a sandwich and think *300*, just out of instinct. Or I'll eat pasta for dinner and multiply fifty by the number of bites that I've had before I even realize that I have to finish the entire plate, so it doesn't even matter. Jessie has started sitting across the table from me while I eat all of my meals, which basically means that I have no way out of it.

So I sit there. And I pick at my food. And I think about how if I do this, everything I've spent the last year and a half working for might all go to shit, just because I decided that the band's success wasn't important enough to me to sacrifice everything for. And I eat, because I have to. Because Jessie is right there. I lift the fork to my mouth and take a bite of pasta. And another. And another. Make it so mechanical that I don't have time to think about what I'm doing. *Just another movement*, I tell myself. *Just like playing a guitar. Just like breathing.* So I eat and I eat and I watch the numbers flash across my eyes: 300, 500, 1,000, 2,000. And I try not to break down. Because that's the only thing I can do.

I tell myself that some things aren't worth sacrificing. I try to believe myself.

It doesn't really work, of course. By the end of every night, the numbers are lodged in my brain, and when I close my eyes and try to go to sleep, I just see the numbers floating in front of my eyes, my brain screaming at me about how that's way too high, that's way too many. The only thing that keeps my mind off all that is thinking about the show.

It's weird, because a week ago, I would've found it totally stupid. I mean, I'm in a real band, for fuck's sake. We play on real stages, in real cities, for real audiences. The idea that playing a one-song set on acoustic guitar for an audience of, like, fifty people for some weird summer camp exercise that we're all forced to do could excite me seems crazy. And yet here I am. Kind of excited.

By the time it's my turn to go on Friday night, I've been thinking about it so much that I'm incredibly nervous. The campers and the counselors are all sitting at the picnic tables. There's a fire in front of the tables, and a mic set up on the other side of the fire. On the table is an endless assortment of graham crackers and marshmallows and chocolate. I watch as everyone loads the food onto their plates, thankful that the counselors haven't made it mandatory for all of us to eat the s'mores. I'm actually last in the lineup, but I'm so nervous that I barely hear a word of what anyone else says. It's like one second, Jessie is standing in front of the mic, introducing the order and telling all of us for the millionth time about how much she loves Art by the Fire Fridays. And then the next second, she's sitting at the table next to us and calling me up. The second she says my name, it's like a jolt of electricity runs through me. Even after a hundred shows—good ones and bad ones and everything in between—the preperformance adrenaline rush never changes. And despite the nervousness and inability to speak and the fact that I'm almost shaking, I never want it to.

This is the part, I think, where autopilot kicks in. I walk up to the microphone, swing the guitar strap over my shoulder, strum a G just to make sure the thing is still tuned. The top E is off, as always, and I tune it as I talk. I can feel my heart racing, but I force myself to keep my voice steady. *Just like any other show*, I think. *Except Stella will probably throw a marshmallow at me if I fuck up.* I try not to think about that.

"Hey, guys, I'm Andrew," I say.

"And I'm in a band," Stella calls out.

"And, as my group members already know, I'm in a band," I say, smiling. "Now, obviously my band's not here tonight… but I thought I'd share this song I wrote with you guys, anyway, just me and the guitar. It's called 'Sometimes I Still.'"

I take one last look around the crowd. A quarter of the kids look bored. Some of them are even doodling away in their journals. Mason is mid-s'more, clearly more concerned about making sure the chocolate doesn't drip onto the table than listening to my song. But everyone else at my table is smiling in encouragement—even Stella—and that's what does it, I think. That's what takes away my nerves. That's what gets me to play the first note.

The thing is, I'm not really thinking when I play music. My brain is totally off at that point. There is music coming from my body, but it doesn't actually matter whose body it is, if that makes any sense. I'm just feeling my fingers move and singing the words and making sure I'm the right distance from the mic and hoping it all goes right. Even though I can hear myself, I wouldn't be able to tell you if I was doing good or not. I'm just playing, and singing, and hoping. And everything else is up to the musical gods.

The silence after a song is over is always quieter than the silence before the song started. That sounds stupid, I know, but it's true. I think it's my favorite moment. Well, maybe not the silence after the song ends itself exactly, but the moment that silence *breaks*—when the applause starts and you remember that you're supposed to be breathing and you *have been* breathing, somehow, for the past three or five or however many minutes. The moment you say, "Thank you," and just look at the audience. It's the happiest and the saddest moment of a performance, I think. The happiest because there's something so transcendent about what just happened. The saddest because it's over, and you're yourself again. At least until the next song starts.

"Andrew," Ben says when I've walked back to the table. I swing my guitar off my shoulder and lay it on the grass next to us. "That was awesome."

"Yeah, that was amazing," Clarisa says.

"That part in the middle, with the, you know, *noo-noo-na-na-nah*—" Ben does an impression of the bridge of the song that would offend me if I weren't so relieved "—was awesome."

"Thanks," I say. I wish there was a nice way to tell him how terrible his air-guitaring is.

It's funny, because once you get off the stage, all you want to think about is the performance. Every note, every beat, every lyric. The quiet moments, the build, and the explosions of sound. You want to remember it all, even though you were barely conscious when you were actually performing.

The 2R counselor is at the microphone now, thanking us for coming as if it wasn't a mandatory event. She tells us she's proud of us all, and amazed by the quality of our work, and can't wait to see the performances we have in store next week. I can't, either, to be honest. It's kind of addicting, being someone else.

CLARISA

MAKING SURE THAT my mother thinks that I'm having a good time at camp is probably more important than actually having a good time at camp. I'm used to not having a good time at things that involve interacting with other people at least. I've long resigned myself to a lifetime of avoiding unnecessary social situations at all costs and, if forced to go, standing in the corner awkwardly while more exciting people talk around me. My mother, on the other hand, has *hopes* for me. She wants me to put myself out there and have some normal teenage experiences with "kids my age." I mean, that's why everyone goes to camp, right? I'm not sure how to explain to her that "normal experiences with kids my own age" at wilderness therapy camp means living with a roommate who has brought an arsenal of banned items, across the hall from someone who is probably a sociopath. //

"Yo," Mason says as we're all hanging out on Friday night. "Let's play a game." "We are *not* playing Spin the Bottle, Mason," Stella starts. "I don't care what sort of argument you make." "I wasn't going to say Spin the Bottle!" Mason says. "For me to suggest that would require some baseline level of interest in kissing any of you, which is notably absent. No, we should play Never Have I Ever." //

"I don't know what that is," I say. "Okay," Mason says. He holds out his hands in front of his chest, palms down and open. "So everyone starts with ten fingers, like this. We go around in a circle, and everyone says something about themselves that starts with 'Never have I ever...' *something*. Then anyone who has done that thing has to say, 'Oy,' put down a finger, and take a shot. The first person who runs out of fingers loses—or wins, I guess, depending on your 'values' and 'morals' or whatever." //

Mason says "values" and "morals" as if they're not actually real things, which makes me extremely concerned about playing any kind of drinking game that he endorses. "Wait, hang on a second," I say. "The person who loses—wins—whatever— would end up taking *ten shots*. That's ridiculous, Mason. No one here could take ten shots and survive." Knowing my life, it's highly unlikely that I'll be putting down more than two fingers over the course of the night, but I'd still prefer everyone to stay alive. I'd have a pretty difficult time explaining to my mother what happened if someone died of alcohol poisoning tonight and the camp got shut down. //

"Half a shot, then," Ben says. "For every finger you put down, you have to take half a shot. You in, Clarisa?" Everyone looks at me while the internal struggle plays out. On one hand, the shot glasses are disgusting and the very prospect of drinking something out of them gives me anxiety. Plus, I'm terrified that I'll get drunk and then lose control and do something really stupid, like forget to brush my teeth or put my pajamas on over my clothes. But on the other hand, part of me really wants to do it—maybe because I'm tired of being the only teenager in America who sits stuff like this out, every single time, maybe because this is a defining element of the camp experience that I've created in my head, maybe just because I want to prove that I can. //

"I'm in," I say. And then, realizing what I've just said: "Oh, wait, God, no. I can't do this. No—I have to. I'm going to." I can hear my voice rising to panic level. "I'm going to do this, guys!" //

"Dude," Andrew says, "okay, we believe you." I squeeze my eyes closed. "Just pour the shots before I change my mind," I say. "Ooookay," Stella says. She fills each glass halfway. "I guess I'll start. Never have I ever been to Europe." //

Ben, Andrew, and Mason all say, "Oy," and put a finger down. Ben stares at Stella and me, shocked. "You two are missing out," he says. He looks toward the ceiling, as if the whole of Europe is actually just above our cabin and accessible if he just stares hungrily enough. "Europe is beautiful. And filled with the *romances and stories and scars that history has overlain on its land*, you know?" "Beauty and romance," Stella says, imitating Ben's dazed, dreamy tone, "my two *absolute* favorite things." //

Then there's Mason, who has jumped into this game with an alarming level of enthusiasm. "Never have I ever," Mason says, "been blackout." "Well, that's surprising," Stella says. She refills her glass and drinks it. "Considering how badass and edgy you pretend to be." "I don't pretend to be edgy!" Mason says. "That's Andrew." //

I'm starting to see the appeal of Never Have I Ever. You learn a lot of fun things about each other—things that could always turn into blackmail material later, which I guess is a plus. But at the same time, I'm not so sure I needed or even wanted to know that Mason and Stella are the nonvirgins among the five of us. And I definitely didn't need to know that Mason had sex for the first time when he was fifteen, or that Stella lost her virginity earlier this year to the guy she brought up in therapy and then refused to talk about. "I just felt like it was something I should do. So I did it," Stella says. "It was pretty whatever," she adds. //

"Pretty whatever?" Ben says disgustedly. "Never mind, Europe would be wasted on you." "Just go, Ben," Stella says. He stares into his shot glass for a couple of seconds. "Okay," he says. "I have one. Never have I ever tried to commit suicide." //

"Dude," Andrew says. "Who brings that up during a game of Never Have I Ever?" "Oy," Stella says. We all stare at her as she raises the glass to her lips and drinks it. She looks remarkably calm for someone who's just admitted that she's tried to kill herself. From sex to suicide in half a minute, I think to myself. No wonder this is the game of choice for bored suburban teenagers. //

And then it's my turn. "Never have I ever," I say, "been in love." Because that's the type of thing you're supposed to bring up during games like this, things that are kind of corny and personal so people get a kick out of hearing it but also not that specific so as to make people uncomfortable, right? "I'm in love with life," Ben says. "Does that count?" "Mason is in love with himself," Stella says. "Does that count?" //

"Never have I ever been sent to the principal's office," Ben says. I think guiltily of the time I refused to come back from recess in the fifth grade because we had been outside for an "unsafe" number of minutes. "Well, guys," I say, more to myself than anyone around me, "this is it." I take a look at the glass in my hand and suddenly regret my decision to stay up with everyone instead of just going to bed. This is what happens, I think, when I try to *be social* and *integrate myself into the community* and *put myself out there*. I end up drinking for the first time at an illegally held 1:00 a.m. meeting while at a summer camp for crazy people. "Anyone have any advice?" I say. //

"Hold your breath," Stella says. "And drink it really quickly, and then chug some water, and then suck it up and get over it." "Glad I have you here to support me in my moment of need, Stella," I say. And then, before I can think too hard about it and totally lose my composure, I take the shot. I chug some water. And I almost throw up. "That was *terrible*," I gasp. //

The taste feels like it's all over my mouth, and the alcohol immediately starts burning in my stomach. It's not just uncomfortable. It actually kind of *hurts*. "Why do people do this?" I say. "There seem like such more fun ways to kill your brain cells slowly. Like playing contact sports or something." "It'll get better," Ben says. //

"Speaking of ways to kill your brain cells," Mason says. "Never have I ever smoked marijuana." "Huh," Andrew says, "I kinda figured *everyone* had smoked weed by now." "Marijuana," Mason announces, "is fucking stupid. It literally makes you fucking stupid." "You're already fucking stupid, Mason," Stella says. "It's not like you have that much to lose." //

Her attention is somewhat diverted as I take my second shot of the night. "There's no way," Mason says. He stares at me as if I've suddenly sprouted tentacles or become a talking potted plant or something. Everyone else has similar incredulous expressions on their faces, which I find pretty insulting. I mean, am I really so unexciting a person that the idea of me trying the most commonly abused drug in America is utterly unfathomable? Marijuana practically doesn't even count as a drug. It's more like, I don't know, speeding on the highway, or not coming to a full stop at every stop sign you hit. //

"*You've* smoked weed?" Andrew says. "Dude, mad respect." Now I can't tell what's worse—being judged for doing something illegal that everyone else does, or being "mad respected" for doing something illegal that everyone else does. "It was an attempt to make me less crazy and anxious," I explain. "But it didn't really work. In the end, it just made me more crazy and anxious." "Is that even possible?" Stella asks. //

It takes five more rounds for someone to lose all ten fingers, and that person ends up being *Andrew*. Turns out, Andrew has not only been to Europe and smoked weed, but has also gone skinny-dipping, run away from home, and gotten in a fistfight, because *of course* the 110-pound anorexic kid from the suburbs of Washington would win the game of Never Have I Ever. I think about putting that in my next letter to my mother and have to stifle a laugh. "This is fucking ridiculous," Mason says flatly. "I can't believe you've done more shit than I have." "It's not my fault!" Andrew says. "I don't know, dude, things just *happen* to me!" //

"Never have I ever abused any word as much as Andrew abuses the word *dude*," I say, even though the game is technically over. I look down at my hands. I have four fingers still up, which means I've put six fingers down over the course of the game, which means I've taken three full shots of alcohol, which means— "Oh, God," I say out loud, "I totally forgot to keep track of how much I was drinking." "Yeah," Stella says, "that would kind of be the point of playing the game." She looks at me, amused. "Welcome to the life of an ordinary teenager, Clarisa." //

"Guys, what if I'm drunk?" I say. My words sound somehow amplified as they come out of my mouth, and also slower. The room feels really bright. Really, really bright. Really, really, really, *really* and, oh, *God*, all of a sudden I am having a lot of difficulty counting and a lot of difficulty parsing through my thoughts and a lot of difficulty trying to remember whether that's the correct usage of the word *parsing* or not and a lot of difficulty trying to slow my thoughts down and a lot of difficulty trying to motivate myself to *care* about whether or not I can slow my thoughts down.

"I am utterly incompetent right now," I announce to the group, for reasons I'm not entirely sure of. I take inventory of the faces around me. Stella and Andrew look concerned. Ben and Mason just look amused.

"I think you're drunk, Clarisa," Ben says.

"I think *you're* drunk," I say, and laugh, because I am hilarious.

"Hmm," Ben says. "I think those may both be accurate statements."

Okay, Clarisa, I think to myself. My inner voice is a lot less bitchy and annoying and a lot more nice when I'm drunk, I think. It's quite liberating. *You have read about this. You have watched movies about this. You have talked to your friends about this. You can do this!*

"I can do this!" I say, perhaps more loudly than necessary.

"Oh, God, Clarisa," Stella says. "You're one of *those* drunks."

"What's that supposed to mean?" I say. I really like Stella, despite the fact that she's not a very nice person. She's kind of like a cat who you love despite the fact that it constantly scratches you and never, ever wants to spend time with you and is generally a jerk except for when it needs you to feed it. I think the metaphor in my head right now is that Stella is a cat. I'm going to need to return to this line of reasoning when I'm sober.

"I want to go to The Ridge," I say, because all of a sudden that seems like the best idea anyone has ever come up with, ever. We can light a fire. We can talk as loudly as we want without the counselors hearing. At The Ridge, the possibilities are endless.

"We are not going to The Ridge," Stella says. "It's 1:35 in the morning. They're going to do bed checks in, like, twenty minutes."

"We can go after the bed checks!" I say.

142

"We can*not* go after the bed checks," Stella says, "because then it'll be after 2:00 a.m. and I want to go to bed."

"Oh, *whatever*," I say. I don't think I've ever said the word *whatever* in my life. I add that to the list of things that are liberating, which now consists of two items: being drunk and the word *whatever*. I like lists. I add lists to the list of things that I like, which now consists of three items: being drunk, the word *whatever*, and lists. "Tomorrow's just like any other Monday—we'll be tired in the morning, but we'll be fine. Didn't you guys go to high school?"

"Tomorrow's Sunday," Andrew points out.

"Oh, *whatever*," I say.

"I'll go to The Ridge with you, Clarisa," Ben says.

"Oh, *whatever*," I say. "Wait."

"Yeah, absolutely not," Mason says. "If I go, I'm going to end up as the de facto chaperone, and when someone does something stupid, which *someone will*, it'll be my fault again. I am not interested."

"Stella," I say. I feel like saying her name over and over again will convince her to come to The Ridge with me, so I do it. "Stella, Stella, Stella, Stella!"

She gives me a look—no, *the* look, the Stella look, where you kind of want to melt into the ground but you also kind of want to give her a hug because how terrible must it be to go around giving people that look all the time!

"No," Stella says flatly. Stella is almost as terrifying as my inner voice.

"*Andrew*," I say. "Andrew, come to The Ridge with me."

"I'm really tired..." he says. He shifts and runs a hand through his hair, which is way better than my hair. I feel a wild, narrowly suppressed urge to reach out and touch it. "Can't we go tomorrow?"

"Well, we could, but then it would be tomorrow, and not today," I say.

"Goddamn it," Mason says. "Just go with Ben."

I turn to Ben. "Ben, come to The Ridge with me," I say.

"I already agreed to do that, Clarisa," he says. "Like, five seconds ago."

"Oh, right. I forgot."

"If one of you guys dies," Stella says, "I'm going to be pretty pissed."

"That's the nicest thing you've ever said to me," I say. I feel like I might start crying.

"That's the nicest thing I've ever said to anyone," Stella says.

"Really?"

"No."

"It's quarter of," Mason says. "We need to get back into our room."

"Oh, *whatever*," I say. This phrase is the best discovery I have ever made. "Okay, Ben, you're going to come back after the bed check, right?"

"Yeah," he says. "Although," Ben adds, putting on his shoes, "there's, like, a ninety-five percent chance that you're going to have fallen asleep by the time they do bed checks."

"I'm not going to fall asleep," I say.

The boys leave the room, and I turn around to face Stella. "I'm not going to fall asleep," I tell her, just for good measure.

She rolls her eyes. "Well, you have to at least pretend to."

"Okay," I say. "I can do that." I get into bed and squeeze my eyes shut. My thoughts are racing. I'm thinking about camp, and The Ridge, and how great it's going to be to experience it like a normal person for once, and about my mom, and whether or not she would be proud of me right now, and the numbers, and how nice it is to have gotten away from them for once in my life. I'm thinking about alcohol and the feel of it burning in my stomach and in my veins and all through my body and how it should bother me, it really should, because it's so dirty, and it's so dangerous, but how it doesn't, really, right now. Time is moving really quickly but really slowly at the same time. *Quickslow*, I think, *quickslow*. One of the counselors opens the door and I can feel the light from outside hitting my eyelids and then fading away as the door closes. *Quickslow.* The lights are back on in the room and I am putting on my shoes and getting a hairpin from Stella so I can unlock the back door. *Quickslow.* Ben is standing in our room.

"You good?" he says.

"Yes," I say, and I mean it in so many ways.

A wall of humidity hits my skin the second I step outside. It feels like walking into another universe. It's dark and muggy and the trees are shadowy and imposing in the distance, silhouetted against the mountaintops, and even though I've walked out of this cabin twenty-eight times in the past week, it feels different this time. I'm not trying desperately to count all of the trees before they turn into monsters and the forest swallows me whole, and I'm not staring furiously at my feet trying to count the monster into nonexistence. I can look at the sky. I can look at the stars. I can look at Ben.

"Hi," I say.

Ben looks at me, eyebrows raised. His hair is disheveled from the wind. "Hi," he says.

"Sorry," I say, but I'm not quite sure what I'm apologizing for. Perhaps just for breaking the silence, which feels safe and comfortable and somehow sacred. We step into the forest together, side by side, and the wave of nausea that's supposed to hit never does. The canopy eclipses the moon and the cabins disappear behind us and it's dark all of a sudden—really dark. "It kind of feels like I'm seeing things for the very first time, you know?" I say.

Ben laughs and shakes his head. "You know, Clarisa, if I ever said anything that dramatic..."

"You say things that are that dramatic all the time, Ben," I say. "You barely say anything that *isn't* that dramatic, which is why no one takes your dramatic statements seriously."

"Ouch," he says. He looks at me with a terribly hurt expression on his face.

"Oh, God," I say. "Was that rude? I didn't mean it to be rude. It just kind of came out of my mouth. I don't even know what came over me. Please don't be offended, I just—"

"Clarisa," Ben says. I'm so panicky that I've stopped walking and started waving my arms around, yelling at nothing in particular.

"Yeah?" I say.

"I was kidding."

"Oh. Right."

He smiles reassuringly at me. I wonder if being drunk is supposed to make me better at picking up social cues. Maybe that doesn't kick in until the fourth or fifth shot. I make a note to go for that next time we drink.

A couple of minutes later, we reach The Ridge. The brightness hits me full in the face and everything ahead of me suddenly comes into sharp focus. It feels like I'm in a different forest now, standing at a different campsite, and Ben and I are different people who could be living different lives.

"It's...different," I say.

"What do you mean?"

"It just looks different, now that I'm actually looking at things. You know?"

"Yeah," Ben says. "I mean, no, not really. I mean, sort of. Look, let's go sit over there."

We make our way to the actual ledge, where the grass thins out and the ground gets rockier and rockier. I follow his lead as he takes a seat at the edge, leans back on his hands, and swings his legs back and forth in the air, ever so slightly. I watch his legs move, almost in slow motion, almost as if a stop-motion film is playing inside my head. *Quickslow.* "Don't jump," I murmur.

"Wasn't planning on it," he says. He looks at me. "How are you feeling?"

"I feel…good," I say. And it's true. It's calm and quiet and the voices inside my head aren't screaming and I wasn't lying when I said that it feels like I'm looking at everything for the very first time. It's hard to notice things like the moon when you're staring at your feet or straight ahead or at the inside of your eyelids. It's hard to notice things like the shape of the trees, the texture of rocks, the way space expands in front of your feet.

"That's good," Ben says. He looks at me, and then back at his legs, and then back at me. A piece of hair falls in front of his eyes and he brushes it out of the way.

It's hard to notice things like the green in people's eyes, or the way it feels to really look at someone, or the way it feels to really be looked at.

Ben puts his hands out in front of him. "Wanna play another round?"

It takes me a minute to figure out what he's talking about. It's so quiet at The Ridge, and so well-lit even in the middle of the night, and life is still moving so *quickslow*ly, and I forget that everything that happened fifteen minutes ago wasn't entire years removed.

"We don't have any drinks!" I say.

"A bit soon to become an alcoholic, don't you think?" Ben says. "We don't have to drink. Just play for shits and giggles, you know? Here, I'll start. Never have I ever been to Canada."

I put a finger down. "My dad lives there," I murmur.

"Ah," Ben says. He lies back on the ground and folds his arms over his chest, so that I have to turn to look at him when he talks. "Your parents are divorced?"

"Yeah," I say. I've explained the situation to so many therapists that I hear the words coming out of my mouth before I've even thought about them. "They have been for as long as I can remember. I honestly haven't even gone in, like, ten years."

"I'm sorry," Ben says.

"For what?"

"You know, for…for them being divorced, and whatnot."

I can't help but laugh at how uncomfortable he looks. He props himself up on his elbows and then seems to change his mind again and lies back down. "It's really not a big deal," I say. "I mean, over half of marriages nowadays end in divorce. So if yours aren't…tell them congratulations, I guess."

"My parents are together," Ben says slowly. "But that's not really the kind of stuff we talk about. Actually…" He trails off, seems to struggle with his words for a moment. "Actually, we don't really talk about much of anything. They're kind of…aloof, I guess."

"Aren't you *thankful*?" I say before I can stop myself. I know my first reaction should probably be sympathy—because Ben looks sad about it, even if I can't possibly understand why—but aloof parents sounds like a godsend.

"Thankful?" Ben asks. He looks genuinely puzzled. "Thankful for what?"

"Like, my mom is superinvolved, and she wants to know pretty much everything about my life, but all that really does is make me feel like…"

I trail off. Try to figure out a way to say this that doesn't make me feel terribly pathetic.

"Loved?" Ben says.

"Of course it makes me feel loved," I say. "But it also makes me feel terribly inadequate sometimes. Because I'm never going to be the prom slash homecoming slash everything else queen that she was, you know what I mean?"

"Yeah," Ben says.

"Not that I would even be a good homecoming queen. I don't think I even know the names of most of the people I go to school with."

He laughs, and I wonder how it is that even though I've known him for a week, something about his laugh sounds completely new to me.

"How's the view from the ground?" I ask.

"Starry," he says. "Inspiring. Wondrous."

"Well, with reviews like that…" I put my hands behind my head and lie back. I'm surprised by how comfortable the ground is. I could sleep here, I think. Of course, I would get kicked out of camp tomorrow morning, but maybe it would be worth it. I'm comfortable. I'm happy. The ground underneath me is flat and smooth and cool and the sky above me is clear and infinite. "You know," I start, and then trail off.

"Yeah?"

I feel myself hesitate before I start to talk. "When I was younger, I used to love the night sky. I think that's what happens when you grow up in New York—every time you see two stars it feels like there's magic in the world. Anyway, I would look at star charts and read astronomy books and drag my mom out camping at least twice a year just so I could actually see the actual stars in the actual sky for once. There was something so amazing about it all to me, you know? The fact that there were all of these stories, just written across the sky. Because each one of them is a story, you know. Scorpius, the slayer of Orion. Sagittarius, the centaur, drawing a bow in preparation for battle. Lyra, an eagle carrying a lyre to its place in the sky. I don't know, Ben, I just loved it. And there was also something so peaceful about it. About the fact that there were so, so many stars and they were so, so far away but also—I don't know—they were always there. And they were always beautiful."

I try for a second to find some of the constellations. Scorpius. Moving left, Sagittarius. Moving north, Lyra. I used to know each star by heart.

"And then what?" Ben says.

I tilt my head to the side so I can look at him. There are freckles dusted across the bridge of his nose, the tops of his cheeks. "And then I stopped. The OCD kicked in. I couldn't look at the sky anymore for longer than five seconds without being overwhelmed by the stars and how many there were and how uncountable it was and how unsafe it would make me feel."

"But tonight...?" he says. He tilts his head, too, so we're looking right at each other.

"It feels like there's a part of me that's just—I don't know— switched off."

We lie in silence for a moment.

"Never have I ever," Ben says, "seen a sky like this."

"You've never been camping?" I say.

"No, not really," Ben says. "My parents aren't really into it. And neither am I. I don't really leave the house much actually. This—" he waves his hand around him "—isn't really my thing."

"Yes, I suppose being stuck in upstate New York with no electronics would make it rather difficult to watch movies..."

"Exactly," Ben says. "And who needs fresh air and exercise when you have movies? I mean, who needs human contact when you have movies? Who needs anything else, really, when you have movies?"

"I'm with you there," I say. "As little human contact and

reality as possible, thank you very much. My career plan is currently to become a hermit."

Ben laughs. "Okay, I have another one. Never have I ever broken curfew."

"Nope."

"What? Huh. Never have I ever snuck out of the house."

"Nope."

"Never have I ever shoplifted."

"Still no, Ben."

"Never have I ever smoked a cigarette."

I laugh. "Ben, I think you're confused. I'm not a very exciting person."

"*I'm* not an exciting person!" Ben says, as if we're fighting over a medal or something.

"Never have I ever been in a relationship," I say.

"Nope."

"Never have I ever skipped school."

"Nope."

"Never have I ever abused prescription drugs."

"Ha. No. I mean, I already said that I'm not interested in killing myself."

I fall silent, momentarily out of ideas.

"I guess we're both boring," he says. His voice is so quiet that I have to strain toward him to even hear what he's saying.

"I guess we are," I say.

We're silent again.

"Why'd you want to come out here?" Ben says.

I look at him. "Honestly?"

"I wouldn't ask if I wanted you to lie to me, would I?"

"I was drunk."

"You *are* drunk."

"I am drunk."

"Mmm."

Now Ben is staring into the sky. I wonder if he knows the stories behind Pegasus or Pisces or Cygnus. They would make great movies, I think. But these things are hard to see when you're lost in the numbers, or your surroundings, or your own head.

He turns back to look at me.

"Do you want to go back?" I say.

"We can go back," he replies softly. "Or we can stay. It's really up to you."

"Okay," I say.

We lie there for a couple more minutes, silent. *Quickslow* moments play back in my head—me, taking the first shot; the alcohol, settling in my stomach; the drunkenness, clobbering me over the head. Sneaking out, walking, sitting. Ben.

"We probably should," I say. I don't know if it's the alcohol wearing off or just the fact that we've been out for over an hour now or the silence pressing at me from all around, but I suddenly feel like there are thoughts bubbling up inside my stomach that I can't figure out, much less describe. I want to ask Ben if he's ever felt this way—like there's so much inside him clamoring to get out at once that he can't let anything out at all for fear of exploding. I feel like that with words sometimes. But now it's not just words—it's words and something else, something unfamiliar and muted and desperate.

"All right," he says. He's still staring upward.

Ben has a very gentle voice, I think.

He pulls his knees up to his chest and then stands up. Extends a hand to me. "I would never take that if I were sober," I tell him.

"The offer stands," he replies.

"I'm not so drunk that I need help standing up," I say.

"The offer stands," he repeats.

I take his hand and pull myself up. "Thanks," I say.

I wonder if he's ever going to stop looking at me like that, with the smile, with his head tilted slightly to the side. It would be nice, I think, because then I could stop trying to figure out why he's doing it. But it also wouldn't be nice, I think, because of the things that are hard to notice sometimes, like the windswept hair, or the green in people's eyes, or the freckles dusted across their cheekbones.

"What are you thinking about?" I ask him as we walk.

"Oh, you know," he says. "Movies. Things. People."

"What kinds of people?" I ask.

It's too dark to see clearly, but I hear him laugh.

"What?" I say.

"Nothing, Clarisa," he says. "But shh, we're almost there and I don't want someone to hear us."

Neither of us says anything again until we're back inside The Hull. The moisture in the air disappears. I feel a blast of cold air at my skin, and the perpetual thrum of the AC beats insistently against the silence. The fluorescent lighting is somehow both brighter and less illuminating than the moon outside. I feel slightly dizzy.

"Clarisa," Ben says.

"Yeah?"

He hesitates for a second. "All kinds of people," he says. "Boring people. I'll see you tomorrow." He turns and starts walking back to his room.

"I—" I start, but I realize I have no idea what to say to that. "Okay," I say. "See you tomorrow."

The clock in my room reads 3:34 a.m., which means it's a really good thing we didn't stay out there longer. I try to get ready for bed with the lights off, so I don't wake Stella, but it doesn't go very well: I step on a shot glass and trip over her books as I make my way to the bathroom, and the noise wakes her up, anyway.

"Jesus Christ," Stella says. Her voice is muffled by her pillow. "Are you just getting back now?"

"Sorry," I say. "Sorry, I didn't mean to wake you."

"It's fine," Stella says. She sits up in bed. "Drink some water."

"I'm *fine*," I say.

"I know you're fine," she replies. "But you should still drink water. Come on, don't make me get up and force it into your hand."

I roll my eyes but pour myself a glass of water from the sink.

"Clarisa," Stella says.

"Yeah?"

"Don't do it."

"Don't do what?"

"Just...don't...you know, with Ben. Just don't do it. You didn't already, did you?"

"What are you *talking* about?" I say, climbing into bed.

Stella sighs and pulls the covers over her face. "You know what I'm talking about. He's pretty cute and you're pretty desperate and it seems like a pretty good idea, but it's not. Trust me, okay?"

Maybe the alcohol isn't leaving my system as quickly as I thought it was, because I'm suddenly more frustrated than I have any right to be. "Oh, for God's sake, Stella," I say. "We didn't even *do* anything. We literally just sat around at The Ridge and hung out. You could've come if you didn't want to go to sleep so badly."

I stare at the ceiling as if it's the sky, trying to remember the constellations. I wish I could imprint them onto the roof with my mind before I forget them. Things like this are hard to see sometimes, and I don't know when I'm going to be able to look again.

"You really didn't do anything?" Stella says.

"We really didn't," I say. I imagine Scorpius, Sagittarius, Lyra etched into the wood above me. The scorpion, the archer, the lyre. And then, moving northward, Hercules. The hero. Fighting a battle in the sky that never ends.

WEEK TWO

STELLA

A LIST OF meaningless expressions that make me want to hurl myself off the nearest cliff:

"I really think you could benefit from a positive attitude."

"Perhaps you should think of this experience as an opportunity, instead of as a punishment."

"I'm on your side, Stella, even if you don't realize it right now."

"In order for us to help you, you have to *want* to be helped."

"Have you taken a moment to reflect on how much you have to *appreciate*?"

Jessie manages to hit every single one of these in the individual session we have after my charming little blowup the other day, and I swear to God that I have never, *ever* been less moved by a lecture from a disappointed adult. And trust me—when you've pretty much made a life out of disappointing adults in the way that I have, that's really saying something.

There is one moment shortly after Jessie's *"you have to want to be helped"* diatribe when I feel a twinge of emotion—just the slightest bit, just the faintest hint of guilt creeping up to the front of my mind before I can stop it. But then I remember that I never asked to be helped like this, that I didn't even want to come here the first time, much less a-fucking-gain this summer, that this is all Jessie's fault—and the guilt evaporates before I can process that it existed in the first place.

On Sunday afternoon, we all sit down for our second weekly Mystery Movie Screening, an event that qualifies neither as a mystery (because the camp did the exact same film rotation last year, in the exact same order) nor as a screening (because we are people of exactly zero importance crowded into a cabin in the middle of nowhere).

"Today's movie is *Girl, Interrupted*," Jessie says. "We like to show this movie every year because we find that it fits in very nicely with our second Camp Ugunduzi principle, which is 'forming authentic relationships.' When we watch this movie, we can see that there are so many ways in which people form relationships, and trying to divide those into categories as black-and-white as 'healthy' and 'unhealthy' can oftentimes be an impossible task. Before I start the movie, I want to pose a few questions to think about. How do we make sure that the relationships we form are healthy and authentic? And how can we maintain them?"

"Something about self-respect," Ben says.

"Something about not being codependent," Clarisa says.

"Something about not forming relationships with people at wilderness therapy camp," Mason says.

"Ugh," I say.

"What was that, Stella?" Jessie asks.

"Sorry," I say, "but seeing as my knowledge of healthy relationships is exactly zero, I think I better save everyone involved and stay out of this conversation."

"What about with *Kevin*?" Mason asks in an insufferable singsong voice. *This proves it*, I think. Never mention anything you don't want to talk about in therapy even once, because

Lord knows that's the one thing everyone will take it upon themselves to remember until the end of time.

"This isn't about Kevin," I say.

"Who is Kevin?" Jessie asks.

"Her boyfriend," Mason volunteers, and I feel myself clench my teeth almost reflexively.

"*Ex*-boyfriend, I think," Andrew amends. Fucking Andrew, always trying to make everything better.

"Ah," Jessie says. "And that was…an unhealthy relationship?"

"What does it matter? It's over," I say. I sound whiny, even to myself, but I can't help it. I don't want to talk about this. I don't even want to *think* about this.

"Well, reflection and hindsight and understanding are always important," Jessie says. "In all areas in life, but perhaps especially in our romantic relationships, which can have a huge impact on our—"

"Jesus," I say, because the last thing I want is to listen to Jessie prattle on about how *impactful* romantic *relationships* can be in our *formative* years and all that psychobabble. "Yes. It was unhealthy, okay? Are we all happy now? It was an unhealthy relationship and it went down in flames. But who cares? That's just how relationships *are*."

"Oh, I don't know," Andrew says. "I think… Well, I think the relationships I've formed here are some of the most healthy and authentic ones I've ever made, to be honest. I mean, other than with the guys, of course," he adds.

There's a moment of silence during which everyone looks touched and doesn't know what to say. I don't know what to say, either, because Andrew never means any harm and everything he says is genuine and something about insulting him just feels like kicking a puppy. Andrew is always looking at people like they can actually tell him something or help him somehow, and I don't know how to react short of reassuring him that his trust in the human race will disintegrate soon enough, and then he'll spend a significantly smaller portion of his life feeling disappointed.

"I feel the same way, Andrew," Clarisa says softly.

"You do?" Ben says. He turns to look at her.

"Yeah," she replies. She smiles.

"Well—me, too," Ben says.

Mason groans and rolls his eyes. "Don't expect me to say anything positive here," he says. "I'm not going to enable this feel-good nonsense."

But Andrew isn't even looking at Mason. Andrew is looking at me.

I shouldn't encourage this, I know. I should be like Mason and remain staunchly realistic in the face of overwhelming pressure to enable a sappy moment that will only lead to disappointment. I'm above this, I don't need this; the movie hasn't even started yet and I can only imagine how bad the discussion afterward will be. But then I look at Andrew, and the way he's looking at me, and then, somehow, I hear myself start talking. "Yeah," I say. "Yeah, this is— It's nice, with you guys."

MASON

WHEN MY PARENTS told me that they were sending me to this godforsaken camp to spend one whole perfectly good month of summer, they said that they were doing it because they thought it would allow me to—ahem—"learn." My mother's exact words:

"We think this camp might be good for you, Mason. That you'll learn so, so much. From the program, and also from the people around you."

She said it in the tone of voice that's impossible for anyone to say no to, really; that reminds my dad of what a great, loving, caring person he married and guilts him into doing whatever she asks for, no matter how unreasonable. That tone of voice is how my mother got herself elected president of the PTA even though her son is a well-known troublemaker; it's why the neighbors always invite her to our annual Labor Day block party even when they "forget" to ask the rest of the family; it's why, after all these years and all these incidents, everyone we know always concludes that "the problem can't be the parenting—I mean, have you *met* the boy's mother?"

So my dad agreed to give camp a try ("oh, *honey*," my

mom said, teary as usual), and it wasn't long until I packed my bags and my books and my sanity and boarded a flight to Nowheresville, New York, home of the one and only Camp Ugunduzi.

Well, it's been one week, Mom. And I've learned exactly two things:

The program is stupid (I mean, we're spending our weekends doing interior decorating for a six-hundred-square-foot *cabin*, for God's sake) and the people have absolutely nothing to teach me.

Which brings me to my two conclusions of the week:

#1. This camp cannot fulfill the mission my mother initially hoped it would.

Ergo:

#2. I might as well go home.

Josh doesn't understand the logic when I try to explain it to him in our therapy session at the beginning of the week. "But how can you know that? How can you know that you have nothing to learn when camp isn't even half-over?" he asks, touching his beard. With every stroke, a solid quarter of his hand disappears into the mass of hair erupting from his chin. It's really quite distracting.

"Um," I say. "Have you met the people at this camp?"

"I believe I have, yes," Josh says.

"So…"

Josh just blinks at me. Everyone thinks Josh is so cool just because he has a deep voice and a toothy smile and a long beard. What everyone has managed to miss is that nothing he says makes any sense at all. Is it ethical to put five at-risk teenagers in the hands of someone whose wardrobe is ninety percent tie-dye shirts? Because I'm pretty sure the answer is no.

"Look," I explain. "Clarisa spends, like, five minutes scraping the food off her plate every meal before throwing it away even if she's eaten it all. Have you noticed that? It's weird. Ben thinks his life is a movie. Andrew weighs less than my dog at home. And Stella hates me for *no* reason. Like, no wonder no one gets me here. Everyone else is crazy."

"Hmmmmm," Josh says.

"Exactly."

"Have you considered that perhaps…your own, personal attitude toward camp is affecting the way your peers treat you?"

"You're saying that *I'm* the problem?" I ask, incredulous. "Clarisa's cleaning phantom spaghetti off a plate she's about to throw into a trash can and *I'm* the problem?"

"We all exude energy," Josh says. He's got that glimmer in his eye that he gets when he starts talking about things that he may as well have read in an astrology guidebook. I watch as his fingers continue to slide in and out of his beard, almost rhythmically, as he talks. "This energy is invisible, of course. You cannot see it. You cannot smell it. You cannot touch it. But it is evident in the way we speak. The way we look at other people. The way we interact with the world around us.

"Have you considered that perhaps the energy you are receiving from your peers is simply a reflection—a deflection, even—of the one you exude toward them?"

"Argh," I say. "This is way worse than when my parents made me go to the school guidance counselor for a year."

"Understanding breeds understanding, Mason," Josh says. "If you give it, you will receive it."

"What, did you get that from *Star Wars* or something? What is it, like, a Yoda quote?"

"A Yoda quote it is not," Josh says, a smile sliding over his face.

"Look," I say. "I don't *need* understanding. I don't *need* to understand why Ben is way too in-his-head for his own good or why Andrew is way too obsessed with his band. I just need to *know* that those are objective facts, and get the hell away from the crazy people. But, thanks to my parents, I'm stuck here for three more weeks, so the least I can do is try to make everyone understand that they're being completely ridiculous. That's why it's *really* upsetting that Stella is yelling at me all the time. She obviously doesn't get that I'm right."

"Scorn breeds scorn," Josh replies. "Disdain breeds disdain. The energy...always...reflects." He leans back in his seat and smiles in satisfaction.

"What about nonsense?" I ask. "Does nonsense breed nonsense?"

"Very clever, Mason," Josh says. "You know, our time is up for today. But we'll continue this discussion tomorrow. When, hopefully, receptiveness will—"

"Yeah, yeah," I say, scrambling up and out of the chair. "Receptiveness breeds receptiveness. Trust me, I get it."

BEN

IF LIFE WERE PERFECT, everyone I ever encountered would be a stock character.

If everyone were a stock character, I wouldn't have to worry about deciphering people's actions or words, because their intentions and fears and desires would always be clear. Life would be a lot simpler, because we would all know the roles we play and how we're supposed to play them. We wouldn't even have to worry about what unoriginal and boring people we were, because stock characters don't think about breaking out of the molds screenwriters build for them. And we'd be okay in the end, because stock characters exist for the purpose of making simple, easy narratives, and simple, easy relationships, and simple, easy happy endings.

I've been building dramatic, narrated scenes out of hikes and group therapy sessions and exciting late-night activities for a week now. It's easy to see how the five of us could be characters in some poorly plotted, heavy-handed camp movie. Andrew, with his six pairs of black skinny jeans and beautiful, haunting songs, is the tortured artist. Stella is the Hawksian woman, never afraid to speak her mind, and Clarisa is her foil, a classic introvert with a great deal of wisdom buried underneath her shy, quiet exterior. Mason is the quintessential asshole who eventually reforms, probably after falling in love with Stella, or with Clarisa, or with Andrew, if it's the type of movie that's trying really hard to win an Oscar. The point is, Mason falls in love, and the power of love is enough to turn him from his selfish, manipulative ways.

And me? I can't help but cast myself as the Byronic hero: withdrawn, prone to emotional outbursts, yet endlessly charismatic. I constantly defend Clarisa against Mason's cruel words whenever he's fallen into one of his moods, which is always, because quintessential assholes are like that. I inspire Andrew's music by being so captivatingly miserable, and I capture Clarisa's heart by being so aristocratic and refined, and even Stella respects me because I'm so worldly, and the counselors are all impressed by how willing I am to grapple with truths—hard truths, even terrible, *shattering* truths—and my legacy at the camp lingers even after I leave, for generations and generations to come. Tales of my character—and my dramatic escapades, of course, for what is a Byronic hero without dramatic escapades—are passed down from year to year, and there is one day even a cabin named—

"Ben!" Clarisa says.

"Oh," I say. "Sorry. Hi." The crown jewel of the future Camp Ugunduzi grounds, a giant cabin with the letters *BEN-JAMIN HARPER* across the top in imposing, stone lettering, fades before my eyes. It's replaced by the small cabins and picnic tables of the current Camp Ugunduzi grounds, where Jessie and everyone else are talking and listening to Andrew play guitar. From the volleyball court where Clarisa and I are sitting, their voices are indiscriminate, the notes faint.

"You're doing that thing again," Clarisa says. "Where you

disappear into your own head for, like, minutes at a time, and you start muttering phrases that don't make any sense."

"Sorry," I say. I put my arms against the ground and lean back, but the surface of the court is blisteringly hot, and I pull away, wincing. "Ow, that hurt. Anyway. I was just thinking."

"What about?" Clarisa asks. There's a gust of wind that lifts her hair off her shoulders, and I can't help but lose my train of thought as I watch her pull it into a ponytail.

"Um," I say. "Well, this is going to sound weird, but...I was thinking about Byronic heroes. More specifically," I add, "being one."

Clarisa raises her eyebrows at me. "Being a Byronic hero?"

"Yeah," I reply. I grin sheepishly at her.

"Well," Clarisa says uncertainly, "how goes being a Byronic hero?"

I can't help but laugh. If I were talking to anyone back home right now, they'd tell me to shut up and stop being ridiculous. And here I am now, with Clarisa looking inquisitively at me because she wants to know how being a Byronic hero goes. *This is it,* I think. *The Moment When Everything Changes.*

"Fantastic," I say. "I've never found a film trope that represents my personality more."

Clarisa snorts. "You do know that Lord Byron scandalized the British public with his ill-advised and reckless love affairs, right? If you're trying to have any ill-advised and reckless love affairs, you're either going to have to start sucking up to Stella a lot more or stop zoning out every time we hang out. Oh, my God, I can't believe I just said that."

Before I can respond, Jessie yells our names from over by the picnic tables. "It's time for dinner!" she shouts. I'm privately grateful for the interruption, because not even a thorough analysis of the relationship between the Byronic hero and the classic introvert prepared me with a response to what Clarisa just said.

"We're coming!" I call back at Jessie. But neither of us moves.

"I probably just should've lied," Clarisa says, smiling ruefully, "and told you that you're the most Byronic of the Byronic heroes, or something like that."

"No," I say. "I'm glad you didn't lie. You're right. Hey, maybe Andrew can be the Byronic hero."

Clarisa rolls her eyes and stands up. "Ben," she says.

"Yeah?"

We start walking toward the picnic tables, where everyone is eating dinner. Stella looks like she's already started yelling at Mason, and Andrew is well into his nightly routine of moving his food from one side of the plate to the other for ten minutes before bringing himself to eat any of it. I wonder if Clarisa can tell that I'm walking slowly on purpose, trying to stretch out the amount of time before we get there.

"The Byronic hero is great and all," she says. "But I think I'd rather have a real person. Now hurry up, I'm hungry."

CLARISA

I'VE NEVER CONSIDERED myself "bad with guys." This is not to say that I consider myself "good with guys," mind you. I have a lot of characteristics everyone seems to think automatically doom me to a fate of dying alone with ninety cats: shyness, inability to make eye contact, inability to start a conversation, inability to *hold* a conversation, bra size that's too small, dress size that's too large, the list goes on. But I don't think I am, mostly because I don't consider myself *anything* with guys. I was never really interested in them when I was younger, and I was too busy thinking about other things after the OCD kicked in. I never learned what it is girls are "supposed" to do or "not supposed" to do around guys, so I've never been able to plan my life around only doing things that guys like. When I told this to my ninth-grade best friend, Carmen, she gave me this sort of pitying look, as if the worst thing for a girl to not know these days is what guys like. //

Anyway, I didn't read nearly enough *Cosmo* or *Seventeen* to know what I'm supposed to do around guys in general, much less guys I have present-but-as-of-yet-undefined-and-quite-confusing feelings for. This means that I have no idea what

I'm supposed to do around Ben. And *that* means that I've just been winging it and hoping I don't say anything too stupid. I almost did the other day, I think, when I basically told him I wanted to have an "ill-advised and reckless" love affair, but I rescued myself by quickly changing the subject and Ben never brought it up again. As far as I'm concerned, the best strategy concerning all things guys is actually total and unabashed ignorance. Which is a good thing, too, because that's the only strategy I know. Besides, I have something more important to worry about right now, and that's Stella. //

Ever since watching *Girl, Interrupted* on Sunday night, Stella's been really quiet. I felt relieved about this at first, and I think everyone else probably did, too. It was nice just to be able to say things without being afraid that Stella would jump on it and say something snide and sarcastic for no apparent reason. But then Monday came and went, and she still wasn't talking very much, and then Tuesday morning came and went, and she *still* wasn't talking very much, and then Tuesday at dinner Mason was being absolutely insufferable, and she *still* didn't say anything. "Dude, are you okay?" Andrew asked her at group that evening, and she just said, "I'm fine," totally seriously. Not in a snappy way, like she usually talks, and she didn't even get on Andrew's case for using the word *dude*, which has kind of become the go-to camp joke. Just "I'm fine," and then nothing. //

So on Tuesday night, I take it upon myself to make her feel better, or at least to figure out what's wrong. It's a daunting challenge. But if my ignorance about Stella's personal life is anything like my ignorance about what to do around guys, I think I have a pretty good shot. And everything does go really well, at first. We all go to bed early that night, because we have a big hike the next day, and there's no talk of anyone sneaking into anyone's room or out to The Ridge or anything.

Stella and I are both back in our room by 10:30, which gives me a whole hour and a half before the first bed check. It's all great up until I actually try to talk to her, at which point the fact that the person I'm trying to have a deep and meaningful conversation with is Stella becomes a problem. //

"So," I start, "how've you been?" Now, personally, I think this is quite a reasonable way to start a conversation. But maybe this is another one of those things that they tell you not to do in *Seventeen*, because Stella just looks up from the notebook she's writing in and narrows her eyes at me. She doesn't even respond. She just looks at me for a solid ten seconds and then goes back to writing. I wait a little, thinking that maybe she's just formulating an insightful response, but that turns out to be a bit optimistic. "What are you writing about?" I say after a minute of silence. //

Stella puts the pen down on the desk, runs a hand through her hair, and sighs. Like, *really* sighs. I know that sigh, and it's never a good sign. It's the kind of sigh that people sigh when they are undergoing a premature midlife crisis, or have lost all hope in humanity, or have just been told by their mother that they're spending a month of summer this year at wilderness therapy camp. "I'm writing about..." She trails off and sighs again. "Nothing." //

"Nothing? You're writing about nothing?" "Ugh, Clarisa," she replies. "Why does it even matter what I'm writing about? Why do you care what I'm writing about?" I phrase my next words carefully. "Well, you've seemed a little...you know, different, for the past few days." //

Stella looks at me levelly. "I wasn't aware that I was supposed to be the exact same person every single day," she says. "And I wasn't aware that that concerned you. But by all means, if it makes you feel better, I will abandon my attempts at self-improvement and resign myself to a life of stagnation." "I don't know," I say, "I just kind of wanted to talk. Can we talk?" "You want…to…*talk*," Stella says. //

"All right, Clarisa, what do you want to talk about?" "Well, like, how are you? You've been really quiet recently," I say. She rolls her eyes. "I also wasn't aware that being *quiet* wasn't allowed here," she says, and I finally understand how parents feel when they complain about unresponsive kids at the dinner table. "Well, it's…it's unlike you," I reply. "Right," she says, "because you would know what is *like me* and *unlike me* given that we've known each other for a whole—hmm, let me think about this—*week*." //

"Look," I say. I know that I'm the one who started this conversation, and that maybe it's my fault for doing that, but I'm honestly getting a little annoyed now. *I just want to know if you're all right!* I want to shout, but I can't think of a better way to make Stella give up on the conversation and go to bed. "All I'm saying, Stella, is that people care about you, and care about how you feel, and care about whether or not you talk at dinner, even if you don't think so, and I just wanted to see if everything was all right and I'm sorry if you feel like—" "You literally. Don't. Know me," Stella interrupts. //

"I don't *know* you? What is this, middle school? I know that you're smart, just from having conversations with you, and I know that sometimes you can actually be a nice person, because I've seen it before, and I know that every time anyone brings up Kevin, you flip out, so you must have had feelings about something at some point in ti—" "Look, Kevin is *no one*, okay?" Stella interrupts. "I don't even know how this became such a big deal. Kevin and I met last semester at school and maybe made out a few times, but hey, it's the twenty-first century and everyone is making out with everyone else these days and it's *no big deal*. Everyone just needs to fuck off and leave me alone because *I'm fine*, and Kevin *doesn't matter*, and it's *none of your business, anyway*." //

I'm suddenly exhausted. I don't want to fight with Stella. I don't even really want to talk to Stella anymore. I just want to go to bed and wake up with a different roommate, one that I can have an ordinary two-minute conversation with a few times a week, just so I feel a little bit better before getting in bed. "Look, people want you to be okay, okay?" I say. "I thought I'd tell you, in case you didn't know. You can take it or leave it." //

I watch Stella stare into her notebook, expressionless. Fifteen seconds pass, and then thirty, and then a minute goes by, and I resign myself to the fact that she's not going to reply. I close my eyes, give myself seven deep breaths. *You tried*, I think, *and there's nothing else you can do about it now*. I open my eyes again, ready to go to bed, but Stella's staring at me with an expression that freezes me in my chair. I've seen this look before—on movie screens and in mirrors, but never on Stella. She looks desperate, like she's on the verge of tears, like there's something she wants to say but can't. //

But then she closes her notebook and stands up. She turns away, walks to her bed, and starts changing into pajamas. I can't see her face anymore, and I'm not sure that I want to. Part of me wants to seize this moment—*look*, I want to say, *look, you're obviously feeling something right now, so just talk to me about it, come on*—but I can't bring myself to do it. Stella changes and I look away and by the time she turns back to face me and speaks again, she looks fine. "Thanks for the offer," she says. "But I'll leave it." //

I've had this conversation before. Multiple times—with my friends, with my mother, with my first therapist, with my second therapist. I've had this conversation more times than I can count, in fact; but the funny thing is, I'm always on the other end. Shutting people out, turning away, making it to the verge of a much-needed emotional breakdown and somehow catching myself at the last minute. I figure that that should give me some sort of advantage in this situation—I mean, I've lived it, right?—but here I am, sitting in our room, unmoving, as Stella walks to the bathroom, brushes her teeth, climbs into bed. I'm full of memories, and things that I want to do, and things that I *should* do, but I'm just as helpless as Carmen, or my mother, or Dr. Manning. "Good night," I hear myself say. //

I'm not sure why. It's such an anticlimactic end to the conversation, and it's probably stupid that I'm even trying to salvage it, and I figure Stella's either going to say something sardonic and insulting or just ice me out, so what's the point? But Stella surprises me, this time. "Good night, Clarisa," she replies, and even though I can't see her face, I can't imagine her saying it with an angry expression. There's a part of me that feels like I should be really touched at her response and give her a hug and start crying or something—because this feels like one of those moments that people talk about in therapy for years and years afterward, trying to figure out what it really meant and how it changed everything, and because I can already picture Ben telling me tomorrow that when I said, "Good night," I really meant something so much more than "good night," and when Stella said, "Good night," *she* really meant something so much more than "good night," and because maybe, after years and years of therapy, I'll come to the conclusion that Ben was right. But in the moment, I can't feel anything other than relief that my failed attempt at a deep conversation with Stella is officially over. If the last few days have been any indication, I am way better with guys than I am with Stella. //

ANDREW

WEDNESDAY MORNING IS when it all starts to fall apart.

I don't know how I managed to convince myself of this, but when I stepped into the nurse's office, I actually thought it wouldn't be that bad. Maybe because it's what I've been telling myself the entire week to get myself to eat:

"Don't worry, Andrew, it's not that bad!

"It's just a full dinner after the full lunch and the full breakfast you already ate—no worries, dude!

"Two thousand calories isn't that bad, man, just go play some guitar!"

I spent the entire week shoving food down my throat through sheer force of denial. And now here I am, and there the scale is, and there the numbers are: one, and then a two, and then a nine. Red block letters: 129.

Josh must notice that I'm staring at the numbers, frozen, because he pulls his chair up so that he's sitting right next to me. "Your body," Josh says, all patient and mellow, "is recovering."

"Dude," I reply, not patient and definitely not mellow. I feel myself fall into the chair next to the scale. "I don't give a *fuck* if my body is recovering."

We're not supposed to swear around the counselors, and Josh raises his eyebrows at me, but I don't care. I'm breathing hard and I can't think straight. It's almost like I've just finished a show, except there's no excitement or happiness or relief. The feelings are all wrong. "Oh, God."

"Andrew," Josh says. "Relatively rapid weight gain is normal in the first few weeks of anorexia recovery. Most of the weight you gain during this time is just your body stabilizing after months of malnutrition. Five pounds is actually—"

"Five pounds is actually what?" I demand. "Five pounds is actually *what*? Five pounds is a fucking shit ton! Five pounds is— Oh, God. Five pounds. I haven't weighed this much since last year."

"Andrew, the fact that you haven't weighed this much since last year is a reason to be happy. It is terrible that you haven't weighed this much since last year. Your body—"

"It's terrible that I gained five pounds in a week! You're going to tell me that that's healthy? Fuck, Josh. That's, like, almost a pound a day!"

"Yes, Andrew. I'm going to tell you that it's healthy."

I've never lost my temper easily. You can't, when you're in a band. Or, at least, you can't and expect to stay together for long, anyway. I've just never had the energy to get really mad at people and yell at them for longer than a few minutes. Now, though, for the first time in, like, a year, I'm furious. I don't even know why. It can't be at Josh, because he hasn't really done anything other than try to convince me that this is okay when it's obviously not. But that's not his fault. He doesn't get it like I do. I guess it's just everything over the past week building up inside me. Being forced to eat, trying not to think about it, thinking about it, anyway, not being able to record music, not being able to talk to Jake or Sam, not being able to do *anything*. It's like the anger is exploding out of me. And honestly, it kind of feels good.

"I don't give a fuck!" I shout. If I had my guitar right now, I would throw it against the wall, the way people do in the angry rock music videos I've never liked watching because they have no plot or substance. I get it now. Plot and substance are overrated when your vision is blurring from anger. "I don't give a fuck if it's normal and I don't give a fuck if it's what my body needs and I really, *really* don't give a *flying fuck* if it's *healthy*, I really don't, and how would you know, anyway? How would any of you guys know? I was *fine* before this. I was *fine* and I was healthy enough after I stopped smoking and the band was doing fucking rad and *I was fine*."

"I understand that you feel this way, Andrew, but try to recognize that—"

"*Try to recognize what?* That I gained five pounds in one week of camp because you all told me that I need to eat way more than I need to eat? I've never eaten that much in my *life*, even before I started losing weight. Try to recognize what, Josh, tell me what the fuck I'm supposed to be recognizing right now, because *I think I fucking recognize it and you fucking don't*. That all the work I've done over the past few months to get to where I was—"

"Where were you, Andrew?"

"We were going to get signed! We were going to release another EP and then do our first tour of the Northeast and we were going to get big. We were going—"

"You can still do all of those things," Josh says calmly. "But I didn't ask where your band was. I asked where *you* were."

"I was fine," I say. I know what he's trying to get at and I'm not going to let him get there, because it doesn't matter, because I don't want to think about it, because that's not the point, because none of that is the point, because *I don't want to think about where I was six months ago.* "I know what you're talking about, and I was *fine*—it wasn't a big deal. These things happen when you tour and—"

"Andrew, you had—"

"I don't want to talk about it!"

Josh stares at me for a few seconds in silence. *Come on*, I think. *Lecture me about swearing, lecture me about yelling, lecture me about something. See if I care.* But he doesn't. He just looks at me. And then he sighs. Some part of me feels bad about this, but I push it away. "This is the wrong time and place for this argument," Josh says. "But maybe you want to bring it up in group."

"I don't want to bring it up in group," I say.

"I think it could be very helpful, Andrew. I think other people might be able to—"

"I don't want to bring it up in group."

"You don't want to bring it up in group," Josh repeats. "Okay. That's fine. You don't have to."

"Great," I say.

"But I hope you'll bring up your feelings during therapy today, Andrew. Don't let them fester inside you."

It's so cute, how Josh thinks that if I just bring up my feelings during therapy, it'll change the fact that I've gained five pounds in a week without even knowing it. At this rate, I'll be 160 before camp is over. The thought makes me want to start shouting again.

"Fine," I say.

"Okay," Josh says. "You can send the next person in."

"Fine," I say again.

Josh looks worried as I leave, but it's hard to feel bad for him when I can barely keep my voice down and I feel like I'm about to explode.

When I get back to the eating area, everyone at our table

is staring at me. "You were in there for twenty minutes," Ben says. "Are you okay?"

"I'm fine," I say. "Someone else can go in."

I slide into my seat at the table. There's a bowl of oatmeal sitting in front of me. "I can't do this," I mutter.

"You can't do what?" Ben says.

"Fucking hell," I say. "Nothing. *Nothing*. I'm fine. Go get yourself weighed, dude, goddamn."

"Um," Ben says. "Clarisa just went in, but I'll go next, if it makes you feel better. Are you sure you're fine?"

"I'm all right," I say.

"Okayyyy," Ben says. He takes a breath like he's going to keep talking, but then Clarisa comes back out. "You're up," she says to him.

I'm pretty zoned out for most of the hike. Josh is leading it, which I guess should make it one of the less boring ones. But he keeps saying things about how amazing it is that we can even hike at all, and how we should be grateful for our legs, and our arms, and our breath. "Our bodies," he tells us, "are all small miracles. They allow us to hike. They allow us to see. They allow us to hear music, and to make it."

Josh looks at me when he says that last line. *Small miracles*, I think. The only small miracle I'm interested in right now is getting out of camp and back to the band without gaining any more weight.

MASON

IF I WERE at home, I would have just finished my morning cup of coffee.

I would be sitting on the deck, enjoying the fresh air. Summer in Bethesda is muggy, humid, and generally miserable, but our backyard is woodsy and shaded, so it's bearable, and there's always the pool for days when the heat gets really bad. By lunchtime today, I would be three or four hundred pages into Mann instead of the one hundred and twelve I've currently read, because I would actually have time to read every day as opposed to getting dragged on hikes I don't want to go to and to therapy sessions I don't need with people I don't want to be around. I would spend the afternoon working on college applications, and I would go for a run in the evening, after sunset but before the crickets get going. I would certainly not be sitting on the floor of the ridiculously named "Safe Space Cabin," trying not to suffocate from the fumes of five open paint containers on the ground and listening to Ben shout at us from the front of the room.

"We are in a state of emergency!" Ben declares, waving a pen. He looks ludicrous.

"I thought we were in the state of New York," I reply.

"Camp is almost half-over!" Ben continues. "And we have made almost *no* progress with the safe space. We haven't arranged the furniture. We haven't put up the guitar decal Andrew wanted so badly. We haven't even painted the damn walls."

"Uh, slight correction, dude," Andrew says. "I didn't want a guitar decal. I wanted an actual guitar."

"We've done nothing!" Ben screeches.

He's not wrong. The materials we asked them to order arrived on Monday, and theoretically we're supposed to have done *something* between then and now. But on the other hand, this entire project is stupid and of exactly zero therapeutic benefit, so I feel fairly justified in blowing it off.

"Are you guys listening?" Ben demands.

"It's kind of hard not to," I say. I wish Jessie, who's sitting at the back of the cabin watching this unfold with an amused expression on her face, would tell Ben to lower his voice or something, but the counselors have apparently decided to take a hands-off approach to this project and left us to flounder through it alone. Well, not alone—together, with each other, which is even worse.

"We have to *do something!*"

Ben full out bellows this last line.

"Well, what do you want us to do?" Clarisa asks.

Ben, in true Ben fashion, looks confused now that someone has decided to take him seriously. "Um," he says. "Well, I guess we should start with painting. Everyone should take a wall and a container of wood stain and just, you know, paint it."

Stella groans from the floor. "How is this even legal?" she says. But she stands up and grabs a gallon of paint, anyway. "Dibs on the back wall."

"All right," Ben says. "Everyone else, mobilize!"

"What are we, the Power Rangers?" Andrew grumbles. But he, too, grabs a can of paint and starts in on one of the side walls.

Ben looks at me, clearly expecting me to get up and follow everyone else. I turn to the next page of my Mann novel.

"Mason," Ben says.

I look up at him. "Yeah?"

"Aren't you going to, like, help?" he says.

"Ah," I say. "Hmm. Well. No, I don't think I am."

It may seem like a stupid thing to pick a fight about, but it is actually imperative that Ben doesn't think he can put himself in charge of a situation just by yelling at the rest of us. If he does, he'll never stop doing it, and then I will not make it through my Mann novel, and probably not even make it through camp with sanity intact.

"What?" Ben says.

"Look, you don't need me!" I explain. "There's four walls, and four of you guys, not including me, and you've all claimed cans of paint. Well, everyone except you, Ben, but this entire thing is your party, as they say. So I'll do everyone a favor and just sit this one out."

Ben's face is all too easy to read—he goes from confused to startled to angry and then back to flustered. "That's ridiculous," he says. I start counting down the seconds until he flushes red. "You have to help."

"I have to help," I repeat, smiling. "There are four walls, and four people other than me. Why do I have to help, Ben?"

"You have to help because…because—"

"Because Ben and I are going to paint the front wall together," Clarisa says, standing up from the floor. "And it's totally fair," she adds, "because that wall is basically twice the size of Stella's." She pushes the last can of paint toward me with her foot.

It takes me a second to register what just happened.

"Holy shit," I say. "You are such a—"

"Really intelligent person who happens to be completely correct in this situation," Clarisa says. "I know. Means a lot coming from you, though, Mason."

"Jesus," Ben says, staring at Clarisa. I'm ninety-five percent sure he just came in his pants.

"All right," I say, because the only thing that makes defeat worse is refusing to admit it. I close *Doctor Faustus*, grab the can of paint and walk backward to the wall, smiling at the two of them to indicate just how unfazed I am. I'm not even mad, to be honest. It was an impressive maneuver, and I'll get her back later. Clarisa doesn't have the experience or the stamina to last against people like me. "That was well-played, Clarisa."

"It's not a game," Stella says from across the room. *Oh, God*, I think. *Not her, too.*

"Everything is a game," I say coolly. "The only people who don't know that are the ones who have already lost."

Stella makes a face that makes her look constipated. "Are you serious, Mason? Just give it up already."

But "give it up" isn't the sort of thing that's in my vocabulary, and nothing pisses me off more than annoying girls like Stella talking to me like they're more intelligent than me when everyone knows that they're not. "Excuse me," I say. "I must have missed the part where someone asked for your input."

"Excuse me," Stella echoes. *"You* must have missed the part where *no one has* ever *asked for your input, Mason.* You think you're better than everyone else because you sit there in the corner all day reading boring old novels and thinking you're hot shit? Well, guess what, Mason? You are literally *the only person here* who thinks so. NO ONE THINKS YOU ARE

COOL. NO ONE THINKS YOU ARE SMARTER THAN HER. AND NO ONE THINKS YOU ARE ANYWHERE NEAR ATTRACTIVE ENOUGH TO JUSTIFY YOUR BLATANT NARCISSISM."

It takes me a minute to realize that my mouth has fallen open in shock. It's not that I'm a stranger to unbalanced teenage girls yelling at me for no reason, because I'm not. But what I can't believe is that no one reacts at all. No one even looks *surprised* that Stella has completely lost her shit. *Am I literally the only rational person in this room?* I think as I catch Andrew's eye and watch him shrug and look away. Even Jessie appears to be too exceptionally absorbed in a book that she's reading to call Stella out for swearing, which she does *every fucking day.*

"Okay," Stella says. "I'm going to go paint now."

"She's not wrong," Clarisa says gravely.

I turn to Ben, but Ben is still staring at Clarisa with a sort of shell-shocked awe. If he has so much as *heard* a word of what Stella just said, it's impossible to tell.

I'm not the kind of guy who cares about what other people think of me, because the truth of the matter is that most people are wrong about most things, most of the time. But I'm also not the kind of guy who allows himself to become the brunt of a joke, even when the jokers would appear to the rest of the world to be nothing more than a constituent of laughingstocks.

"You're right," I call out to Stella.

"What?" Stella says. She spins around so rapidly that a trail of paint goes flying off her brush and splatters across the floor.

"You're right. I've been butting in where I'm not needed."

This, of course, is a complete lie on my part. I've been butting in where I'm absolutely needed, but what I've failed to appreciate is the extent to which my help just simply can't be appreciated by these people. Out of nowhere, Josh's words from that pointless therapy session earlier this week spring to mind. They echo in my head: a bright, shiny solution that somehow I haven't seen yet.

Understanding breeds understanding, Mason. If you give it, you will receive it.

I said it was stupid at the time, and of course I was right. It was a stupid idea, and it still is. Understanding? How am I supposed to be understanding of behavior that is, quite frankly, completely illogical?

But what Josh *should* have said is this:

The facade *of understanding breeds the* facade *of understanding.* Weak people like Stella and Clarisa and Andrew and Ben need to feel like other people understand them even when they're being unreasonable—perhaps *especially* when they're being unreasonable. When they don't, they lash out to protect their own egos, choosing *not* to understand more rational points of view as a defense mechanism. The only way to receive the understanding that I deserve—that I would get from any actual functioning human being—is to make them think that I'm giving it.

Is it dishonest? Sure. Is it an insult to my own intelligence, selling out to the crowd and selling myself short? I'm not delusional enough to deny it. But if what it takes to make it through camp without the Merry Brigade of Psychos breaking down into hysterics and calling for my head every few days is to let them think they have the upper hand, then so be it. The only thing that really matters, after all, is that *I* know the truth.

"It's fine," Stella says. She goes back to painting her wall, and I grit my teeth and start counting down the days until I get back home.

STELLA

WE'VE REACHED THE point in camp when everyone has started losing their goddamn minds.

I mean, who can blame them, really? We've been trapped in the middle of the wilderness for almost two weeks. The days have blended into one long sequence of a) talking to each other, only to regret attempting to be social, and b) not talking to each other, only to regret attempting to be solitary. The only thing that could make us insane faster, I think, is if we were all huffing paint. Oh, wait—we're doing that, too.

After lunch, Andrew grabs his guitar and a notebook from the cabin and heads off to sit by himself under a cluster of trees at the edge of the main grounds. He starts writing some weepy song about feeling angsty and misunderstood, and my seventh-grade Fall Out Boy phase left me with enough angsty and misunderstood to last a lifetime, so I'm not exactly sure why I walk over and sit with him. It's probably the acoustic guitar, which I've always maintained is the one instrument worth learning. So worth learning, in fact, that I've never allowed myself to ruin it by actually trying to learn it and finding out that I suck.

Andrew doesn't say anything when I sit down next to him. This is fine by me, because I'm not quite ready to tell him that "And when we meet again / I'll be thinking of all the things I should have said" is an awful lyric. He writes his weepy song, stopping every few minutes to scribble something in his notebook, and I work on the short story I've been writing for the past few days. I'm halfway through the fourth scene when Andrew stops playing and looks up at me.

"Do you like it?" he says.

"Uh," I say. I was not prepared for this. I was counting on Andrew to be one of those artists who never asks other people what they think of his or her work due to the line of reasoning that "it sucks, anyway, and why subject myself to that sort of undue embarrassment"; that is to say, I was counting on Andrew to be kind of like me. "It was...cool," I say.

"Well, what'd you think of the lyrics?" Andrew asks.

I wince. "Well," I say. "Well, I wasn't really listening, because I was, you know—doing my own thing. But they seemed...you know. Lyrical."

Andrew raises an eyebrow at me.

"Okay, honestly, parts of it were kind of cliché. But I really liked the melody, so you should definitely still do something with it."

"Ugh," Andrew says. "I'm too depressed to write good music." He takes the strap of the guitar off his shoulder and puts it next to him and then sprawls out on the ground on his back. He throws an arm over his face to shield himself from the sun, while I lament the fact that there isn't anything you can do to shield yourself from other people's feelings, which are just as deleterious as UV rays despite the fact that they probably won't give you skin cancer or make you blind.

"Don't be depressed," I say. "There's no point. And if you're going to be depressed, anyway, don't expect other people to be able to help you, because on that front there's *really* no point."

Andrew sits back up and looks at me, eyes narrowed. "Do you say shit like that to your friends?" he asks.

"Friends," I scoff. "What's the point of having *friends*?"

Andrew groans and falls back to the ground.

"I was being sarcastic," I say.

Andrew doesn't say anything. It's possible that he twitches a little, but that could just be the sun and its damn UV rays making me see things. *Holy shit,* I think. *I just may have killed him.*

"Look," I say somewhat desperately. "Why are you depressed?"

Andrew moans a little, into his arm. I breathe a sigh of relief, because the fact that he's responded means that he's still alive, and then a sigh of disappointment, because the fact that he's responded also means that he probably wants to talk about his problems. "I'm too fat."

"What?" I say. "Jesus, this again."

"It's always this," he says miserably.

"I know," I say. "But—I mean, you seemed to be doing really well with it! You were eating and talking about your problems in group and joking around. I mean, joking around about a problem is the number-one way to indicate to everyone that you're doing just fine, thank you very much, and no one needs to spend any time worrying about you or trying to fix you or— Oh. You were doing that thing where you pretend to treat an issue like it's no big deal to get everyone to leave you alone, weren't you?"

Andrew raises his head and shoots me a look. "No," he says. "Who *does* that? That sounds like the number-one way to make your problems worse."

He picks up the guitar and starts playing the song from before. Now that I'm paying attention, it's actually surprisingly beautiful. I listen as he plays six short notes followed by one long one, and then another seven notes in the same rhythm, but higher in pitch. He cycles between the two lines, and somehow it feels like the entire thing is building and building, even though it's all so quiet. There's a gliss at the end of every long note that makes them sound brutally sad, and I feel myself holding my breath every time he plays one of them, thinking that that's it, that's how the song ends, and now I'm going to have to say something ridiculous and cliché like, "That was really beautiful, Andrew," something that doesn't even begin to express what I'm really feeling, or what the song really is, and then he'll just look at me and I'll just look at him and it'll be like we're in some stupid music video waiting for the sappy violin to kick in with a children's choir to really drive the angsty and misunderstood point home. But the song doesn't end. Andrew holds the note just long enough to make me afraid for the silence that follows, and then jumps back into the next line. For a few minutes, I'm so distracted listening to the notes and watching his hands move up and down the neck of the guitar that I forget that I'm supposed to be arguing with him.

"The point is," Andrew finally says, "now that it's actually happening—now that I've actually gained a ton of weight—I feel like I've *really* messed up, you know? Like before, it wasn't real. It was something I could choose to do or not to do, even though I knew I was supposed to do it. But now it's too late." He squeezes his eyes shut but keeps playing. The way he's talking over the melody—slowly, carefully, breathing between every few words so that the notes fill the air again—sounds almost like he's onstage, introducing one of his songs.

"Now it's like…I've ruined it. I've actually gone and ruined it. I've ruined our chances of becoming one of those bands that everyone is super, crazily into, you know, playing sold-out shows in huge arenas all over the world full of screaming fans who live and die by our music. And would live and die by *us*," he whispers.

"But what if you don't really want to be one of those bands, anyway?" I say. I keep my voice low, because something about drowning out the music feels wrong. Six notes, and then a seventh. My breath catches in my throat. "What if you don't want to be one of those bands that people only like because the lead singer is hot for a few years, and then gets really washed-out really fast when they hit middle age? What if you don't want to have fans who actually give a shit—no, who actually like you less—because you gained a few pounds? Not because you got fat, but because you recovered from fucking anorexia, Andrew, from being so sick that you could actually, you know, die? What if you want to be one of those bands that people like—that people like *me* like—because the lead singer is a cool person and the music—" two notes "—is actually—" two notes "—fucking—" two notes *"—beautiful?"*—and the last, held, ringing in the air.

Andrew holds his hand over the strings like he's going to keep playing, but doesn't pluck any of the strings. His eyes are still closed. "Do you remember that thing you said a few weeks ago about that thing? When you think something but it's just wrong?" he says.

"What?" I'm so surprised that Andrew remembers something I said in therapy that it takes me a second to remember what he's talking about. "You mean the cognitive distortions?"

"Yeah," Andrew says. "Do you think this is one of those?"

"Andrew," I say. "I *told* you it was one of those. Yes. Yes, *Jesus*, this is absolutely one of those."

"I just— I *want* to believe you," Andrew whispers. His voice cracks. His eyes are still closed.

I swallow hard. "I want you to believe me, too," I say.

CLARISA

Dear Mom,

Of course I wrote you! You only made me promise approximately fifty times before we left for camp. Plus, you know just as well as I do that once that first letter was sent, another six were going to follow. On that note, it's been a really good week. I'm still counting—things like trees and steps and breaths when we hike, and sentences, of course—but I'm not so focused on the numbers that it feels like I can't talk to anyone else or do anything else, and it only feels like I'm suffocating twenty percent of the time, as opposed to eighty-five percent when camp started. Actually, I'm starting to think that maybe part of it is that the Zoloft is working, because I can't remember the last time I felt this good for such a long period of time. I'm nervous about even putting that in this letter, because I don't want to jinx it, but I'm keeping my fingers crossed.

I'm writing in the middle of "Art by the Fire Fridays," which is an activity they make us do every Friday night at nine. There's a microphone set up in front of a campfire and everyone who wants to goes up and shares something "creative." I've never done it, of course, because getting up and reciting something I've written in front of a crowd of a hundred teenagers in the middle of the night actually sounds like my worst nightmare. And even promising to you that I'll try to do it by the end of camp seems a bit ambitious. In fact, the only person who ever does Art by the Fire from our block is Andrew. But, anyway, I wanted to tell you that I've made progress on other things while here. Things that you might be happy to hear about even if I'm not tearing the place down with deep poetry every Friday night.

I think I'm starting to make progress with Stella. To be fair, I'm not sure if it's because Stella has gotten better or if it's because I've gotten used to her. I actually like her, which might sound weird, because of everything I've told you about her. But I think everyone else likes her, too. I think she means well, and maybe that's what matters. The other night she actually talked to me for a whole hour before we went to sleep—which might not sound like a lot if you're comparing it to your times at camp, but means a lot because it's, well, Stella. It almost feels like we're normal roommates.

Mason hasn't changed at all. I kind of yelled at him yesterday, which doesn't sound like something to be proud of, but I'm definitely a little proud. You would understand if you'd met him. He just sits around and reads Doctor Faustus, by Thomas Mann, and sometimes looks up and looks around with this really smug expression on his face, as if reading a thousand-page book while he's at summer camp is a good thing. It's insufferable. The only problem with Mason is that he is pretty good-looking, so sometimes I forget that I'm supposed to hate him. But don't worry—about five seconds after he starts talking, I usually remember again.

Andrew is up at the podium now and he's one of those people you have to meet to really get, Mom. Not even to "get," because I mean, I don't know if I "get" him, but he's really difficult to describe. Andrew is pretty shy, has no fashion sense, is awkward, has terrible self-esteem, and weighs approximately one hundred pounds less than what he should weigh, but you forget all of that when he starts playing the guitar, because he's just so, so good. Right now, he's up at the mic playing some song that he wrote this past week. It's giving me chills and I'm not even sure why. His voice isn't incredible, and nothing he writes seems that complicated, but still—you can tell everyone's really into it whenever he starts playing. I have to remember to ask him what the name of his band is so I can look them up when I get home.

In other news, I think I am currently in the middle of a, um, "camp romance" with Ben. I think I've been waiting this entire letter to tell you this, because this is everything you've ever wanted me to do at camp, right? Find some nice guy at camp and exercise my long-atrophied social skills? CONGRATULATIONS, MOM, YOUR SIXTEEN YEARS OF BEGGING HAVE FINALLY WORKED. Ben and I have been talking a lot, and I like talking to Ben a lot. Other than that, I try not to think too much about it. Otherwise, I get panicky and flustered, and as you know, those are the feelings I've been working on avoiding!

Okay, well, Andrew just finished his song, and Art by the Fire is over, so I have to go now. Plus, my hand is cramping, and I think Mason is trying to read over my shoulder. I'll

write you again soon. Write me back! Say hi to Ashley for me! And please don't get crazy about this Ben thing! I'm supposed to be the crazy one, remember?
Love,
Clarisa

BEN

THERE'S A FAMOUS SCENE in *(500) Days of Summer* in which Tom dances through the streets of Los Angeles to the tune of "You Make My Dreams" by Hall & Oates, grinning madly at strangers and frolicking with birds and prancing around fountains because he's just had sex with the girl of his dreams, and that, apparently, is worth an entire five-minute choreographed musical number.

Personally, I didn't love that scene that much. I mean, it was fine, sure, and it was fun to watch, I guess, but I didn't really get why the post-sleeping-with-Summer scene required that much fanfare. Zooey Deschanel is cute, but worthy of Hall & Oates and fluttering cartoon birds? I wasn't sold.

Three years, one more viewing, and two weeks of wilderness therapy camp later, and I think I'm starting to get it. I mean, I haven't gone blabbing to everyone about how in love with Clarisa I am, mostly because there's not really anyone to blab to. And it's not like we've had sex, or even gotten remotely close. Clarisa and I aren't Tom and Summer, except for the part where I also cry every time I watch *The Graduate*. But I think I feel the way Tom does in that scene when I spend time with her. Or even when I just look at her, reading or writing or talking to someone else. And when I say that I feel the way Tom does in that scene, I mean I feel all of it, even the ridiculous, absurdly over-the-top parts—the urge to start dancing even though I have no idea how to dance, to run through the streets grinning like a maniac, to lip-sync to '80s pop music.

I ask Clarisa if she wants to meet at The Ridge after lights-out tonight, because I think I might explode if I don't talk to her about all this, and also because that feeling I was talking about earlier is kind of addicting.

"You're sneaking out again?" Andrew says when I start throwing clothes back on after the first bed check.

"It's been a week!" I say defensively.

"Do you want a condom?" Mason asks. "Because I don't think the world needs any more people with your genes, sorry."

"No, I don't want a *condom*," I say. "Wait a second, you brought *condoms* to camp?"

"It's always best to be prepared," Mason says, turning a page of the *Playboy* in his hands. "Plus, I didn't know you were going to get on Clarisa right away and that the only other girl in our group was going to be—well, you know. God, if only they had put me in 3R—have you *seen* the blonde girl at their table at lunch? She's so hot that I'd—"

"Okay," I say, lacing my sneakers. "Okay, I am fleeing this conversation, because it's breaking my camp rule #1."

"What's your camp rule #1?" Andrew asks.

"My life is not *Wet Hot American Summer*," I say. "And if it starts to resemble *Wet Hot American Summer*, or anything of the 'summer camp filled with debauchery and shenanigans' variety, then something is going terribly wrong. Later, Andrew. Enjoy bonding with Mason."

"What's wrong with debauchery and shenanigans?" I hear Mason say as I shut the door.

The walk to The Ridge is shorter than I remember it, maybe because the path is so familiar at this point, or maybe because I'm so lost in my thoughts as we're walking. It's one of those cloudless, starry nights that's so clear it doesn't seem real. You can see beams of light slanting through the trees, and every airplane could be a shooting star, and everything on the ground looks almost like it's glowing. Clarisa's hair is gleaming in the moonlight and she smiles at me as we walk and I can feel all of the good chemicals in my brain firing at once, making me stupid, obscene, dangerous levels of happy. And then I think about how happy I am, and it makes me even happier, and then I think about how easy it is to be happy right now, here in this forest with this girl in this life, and *that* makes me even happier, and by the time we get to The Ridge, I'm grinning so widely that I can feel my face starting to hurt. I want to jump off the edge of the clearing. I want to jump off holding Clarisa's hand and float together over the forest and into the sky, into the expanses of space between the constellations that she loves so much, because that's the kind of thing that happens when you feel like this, because it has to be, it just has to.

"Wanna make a fire?" Clarisa says, turning to look at me. "I stole Stella's lighter before I— What's so funny?"

"Nothing's funny," I say. And then I laugh, which makes Clarisa look adorably confused for a few seconds. There are so many words and thoughts and feelings in my brain clamoring to get out that I can't actually get any of them out, certainly not in the beautiful and poetic and eloquent way that she deserves to hear them. "I'm just... I'm just so *happy.*"

Clarisa smiles. "I'm glad you're happy, Ben," she says. "I'm happy, too. Do you want to sit down?"

"Can't sit right now," I say. "I want to move. Let's collect wood." I still feel like I might explode, but in a glorious, beautiful sort of way. There's something different about the mania this time. I'm used to the exploding feeling—I felt it on the hike, I've felt it plenty of times before—like a supernova exploding in a bright white room, a blinding flash of light, brilliance suspended in the air for a few seconds. But I feel like that could last forever now. Like that supernova will never burn out, like my brain is combusting and my soul is glowing and my body is filled with energy. Before I know it, I'm running around the clearing, collecting wood and twigs and grinning madly as I do it.

"I think this looks good," Clarisa says after five minutes or ten minutes or maybe an hour or maybe more. "I'm gonna light it, okay?"

I walk over to one of the logs and sit down. We could jump into the fire, I think as she moves the lighter to the first branch and it catches. The flame spreads across the first branch and then leaps to the next, and then the next, and then the next, and then the entire thing is blazing. Clarisa sits down next to me and I can't tell which is warmer, the heat of the flame or her skin. We could jump into the fire, and we would become one with the flame, and we would blaze through the darkness of the night, and we would become one with the air pressing at us from all sides, and we would reach land and sea and mountain and valley and sky.

I slip my arm around her, and Clarisa turns to face me, looking surprised. "How bold," she says, and then smiles.

"Was it?" I say.

"Yeah," she says. "Well, no. Well, maybe? I don't know," she says, and then she laughs, and I imagine the sound waves from her voice meeting the sound waves from my voice and exploding into sparks.

"You're really quiet tonight," Clarisa says. "What are you thinking about?" And I wish I could project my thoughts onto a screen, onto the ground, onto the sky, onto the flames, into the air, somewhere, and show her, instead of trying to speak, and speaking too slow, or thinking too fast, and losing the thought, or losing my mind, or losing the vision, or losing the feeling, or losing it all. I wish I could show her moon rays gliding through the dark, flames torching the air, the distance between our hands right now, infinite and infinitesimal—show her that everything we are is made of waves, running into each other and bursting into split-second sparks inside our brains and inside our bodies.

"I'm thinking about everything," I say, even though it's been five minutes or ten minutes or maybe an hour or maybe more since she asked the question; "I'm thinking about the glimmer of light rays in the dark," because I want to try to explain, anyway; "I'm thinking about fire dancing through the air and leaving it singed, burned," because she is smiling at me again; "I'm thinking about how something as empty as distance can feel so full," because it's the truth; "I'm thinking about us," because I want her to know.

"That's a lot of things to think about," Clarisa says softly.

"What are you thinking about?" I ask.

"Not everything," she replies. She laughs. "But a few things."

"What things?" I say. I picture the sparks in her mind dancing around each other, colliding, forming pictures in the darkness.

"I don't know," she says. "Silly, nonprofound things. Like how it's so nice out, but also really humid, but also how the humidity here is different from the humidity in the city. And how I should be freaking out, because I'm so close to you, but I'm not. And how, in general, my mind has been so much calmer lately, and I don't know if it's because of the surround-ings and the peace and quiet or if it's because of the Zoloft or what. And how my psychologist, Ashley, told me that the meds and the camp would work together to 'enrich my life' or something like that, and I totally thought that all I needed were the meds, because what was 'wilderness therapy camp' going to do on top of that, and how I was just totally wrong." She laughs. "I'm sorry," she adds. "That's not very poetic."

"God, Clarisa," I say.

"I'm not a very theatrical person," she says.

"I am a very theatrical person," I say.

"So I've noticed."

And so Boy and Girl meet under moonlight. And so Boy and Girl trace constellations with pointed fingers and wide eyes. And so Boy and Girl share glances and stories and dreams.

"Clarisa," I say, "I really want to kiss you right now."

And so Boy confesses desire. And so Girl turns to look at Boy, eyes wide, smile tugging at the corner of her lips like oxygen tugs at fire. "Me, too," she says. And so Boy and Girl kiss illuminated by moonlight and next to a flame and pressed together by darkness, and so Boy and Girl grasp hands and share breath and make sparks and—

"Wait, okay," Clarisa gasps, pulling away. "Wait, okay, hi, sorry, okay."

"Are you okay?" I say.

"Yeah," she says. She's laughing now, which is good, be-cause I was starting to panic about her panicking. "I just, I counted to fourteen, and then I thought, oh, gosh, what if we don't make it to twenty-one? And then I thought, well, of course we'll make it to twenty-one if you just keep going, Clarisa, God, that's how kissing works, isn't it? But then I got so wrapped up in my thoughts that I didn't know what I was doing anymore, and then I freaked out because I figured it was probably bad, and so then, yeah," she says.

"Shut up," I say. "Shut up, Clarisa. How could you even think it was bad, goddamn," and then I'm trying to kiss her again but she's laughing and then I'm laughing, too, and we're falling all over each other, not quite kissing and not quite hugging and maybe not quite sane, either. And then we actually are kissing again, and it's all there is, all I can think about, all that's real, and there's nothing in my head other than energy and heat and the push and pull of waves sparking in my brain and in my body.

"Ben," she says after five minutes or ten minutes or maybe an hour or maybe more. "Ben, we should go back."

"Let's not," I say. "What's the worst thing that can happen? Let's just stay out here for another hour, or five hours, or forever." *Run away with me*, I want to add.

Clarisa laughs, stands up. She tugs my hand so that I'm standing up, too, and I fall into step next to her almost automatically. "Sounds like a great movie," she says. "But the part where we then slowly go crazy because of desperation and lack of food and then eventually die of dehydration and no one ever finds our bodies might be kind of hard to direct."

"Psychological horror," I say. "Very Polanski. I like it."

The walk back to The Hull goes by even more quickly than the walk out, but that's all right, because Clarisa's got my hand in hers and there is moonlight falling all around us and I'm going to make that movie one day and dedicate it to her and, I swear, it's going to top the box office and break records. As we walk, I can almost see cartoon birds appearing out of thin air, fluttering in front of my head and around Clarisa's shoulders. I imagine taking her by the hands, dancing through the forest, through the night. In the back of my mind, I can hear Hall & Oates playing.

WEEK THREE

STELLA

"AS WE MOVE into the third week of camp," Josh says, "I'd like for us to turn our attention to the third guiding principle of Camp Ugunduzi. We've talked about understanding our past. We've talked about forming authentic relationships. We know the importance of respecting ourselves, and of respecting each other. Now I want us to focus on something that allows us to make those two things habits in our daily lives, instead of just things we talk about but forget to practice. This final principle is the key to having healthy relationships with other people, and it's also the key, perhaps more importantly, to having a healthy relationship with ourselves. Can anyone tell me what this third principle is?"

It's Tuesday evening, and for our group therapy session, Josh has dragged us all out to this pond about a mile and a half off the main grounds. We're sitting in a circle on the grass next to the water. I keep waiting for Josh to make us hold hands and sing "Kumbaya," at which point I will have no choice but to tie rocks to my ankles and run into the water.

Josh insists that moving off the main grounds is for the purpose of "taking in all that nature has to offer us" and "appreciating a change of scenery," but I'm fairly sure it's to make it more difficult for us to run away halfway through the session, which is becoming increasingly uncomfortable every time he opens his mouth. It's a shame, too, because it really is a beautiful pond, especially when the sun is setting in the distance and you can see colors in the sky reflected in the water. I'd forgotten how much I liked this place when Josh dragged us all out here last year. Funnily enough, I *do* remember waking up the next morning with fifty mosquito bites. Just further evidence that memories of beauty are fleeting and memories of pain are forever.

"So?" Josh prompts. He grins at us. "Come on, did *anyone* read the camp brochure?"

I slap a mosquito away from my shoulder, which Josh mistakes for a raised hand. "Stella!" he exclaims.

"I was just—" I start, but it's no use.

"I knew we could count on you, Stella," Josh says, which is just a false statement. It's not even a reasonable attempt at a true statement. This has to violate some sort of rule of medical ethics or something.

"I really don't remember," I say.

"Give us your best guess," Josh says.

"Something..." I say. "Something...about...celebrating."

"That's good," Josh says, nodding approvingly. "But what are we celebrating?"

"I don't know," I say. "Birthdays. Christmas. Columbus Day, even though he was an asshole."

"Close!" Josh says. "Very close. The third principle of Camp Ugunduzi is learning how to celebrate our successes. Thank you, Stella."

"That wasn't close at all," Andrew says.

"'Celebrating our successes,'" Josh repeats. "What does that mean?"

"Isn't it…kind of your job to tell us?" Andrew says.

"Well," Josh says. "The phrase, like anything we use language to express, can mean something different to everyone. So I suppose what I'm really asking is what the phrase means to *you*. How do you all celebrate your successes? Do you? How do you reward the soul? Honor the motor that drives your life? Cultivate a garden of self-love?"

"I don't know about you guys," Andrew says, disregarding the latter half of Josh's tirade, "but I totally celebrate my successes. We threw a party and invited the entire school after we booked our first paid gig. And after we released our first EP… Well, I don't think Aidan's ever forgiven us for what we did to Amber that night."

"Who's Amber?" Clarisa says, looking alarmed.

"Oh, Amber is Aidan's cat," Andrew explains. He pauses, looking contrite, and shakes his head. "But we didn't know what we were doing—we were blazed as fuck." I look over at Clarisa, who is now mouthing the words *blazed…as…fuck* over and over again and frowning. "And after we finished our last tour, Jake's parents were out of town and we invited the two other bands we were touring with to a party at his place, and, dude, we got *wrecked*. Well, I got wrecked. I think everyone else got wrecked, too, but I don't really remember the night past eleven."

"I don't think that's the kind of celebrating Josh is talking about," Ben says.

"What?" Andrew says. "What could be more celebrational—celebratatory—*whatever*—than getting wrecked and spray painting a cat?"

"You spray painted a cat?" Clarisa says. The injustice has shaken her out of her "blazed as fuck"–induced reverie, as she sounds about ready to report Andrew's band to PETA.

"Yes," Andrew says. "The theme colors of our tour. Black and blue."

"That's awful!" Clarisa says.

"The point is," Ben says, "I think Josh meant more celebrating our successes in a kind of, you know, metaphysical way. Like, with a journal or something."

"Oh, yes," I say. "I forgot about that Nietzsche quote. The one about journaling being the pinnacle of metaphysics. 'I stared into the abyss of my Five Star spiral-bound notebook that I bought at Walmart for $5.99, and the abyss, which appeared to be rectangular and college-ruled, stared back.'"

"That's not what I meant," Ben says.

"That's not what he meant," Clarisa adds.

"What I meant," Ben says, "is that Josh was probably talking about something a little more self-aware and a little less hedonistic."

"The fuck is 'hedonistic'?" Andrew says.

"Literally every single thing you just described," I say, "is hedonistic."

"*Hedonism,*" Clarisa says, "is when you do things for the pursuit of pleasure, as opposed to actual enrichment. So, like celebrating by getting so *blazed* that you don't even remember what you're celebrating in the first place. As opposed to meditating every day, repeating some phrase like, 'We are talented and successful and I am a large contributing factor to that talent and success,' or writing it down fifty times until you've internalized it."

Clarisa is going to put Josh out of his job, I swear to God.

"That doesn't sound as fun as getting blazed and spray painting a cat," Andrew says.

"I mean, Clarisa's just saying that you shouldn't think that the only valid way of celebrating is getting really drunk."

"I don't think that's the only valid way of celebrating!" Andrew says. "We just did it because it was fun."

"Fun," Clarisa repeats. She looks skeptical.

"Clarisa, have you ever done a hit out of a gravity bong?"

"No," she says.

"Well, that explains it. Come to a show sometime," Andrew says. "Or to a pregame, or to an after party…"

"Um, *back off*," Ben says.

"I didn't mean it like that!" Andrew says. "You can come, too."

"This is a cute plan and all," Clarisa says, "but I have no interest in a gravity bong, or spray painting a cat, or wrecking a car."

"Getting *wrecked*," Andrew corrects.

"Either way," Mason interrupts, "it is definitely of significantly more therapeutic value to celebrate your successes by recognizing your own importance verbally or in writing, even though people will think you're self-important and pretentious, than to celebrate your successes by getting drunk and spray painting your friend's cat."

I spin around to look at Mason. It's the first thing he's said all session, and a part of me can't believe that he's actually said something…somewhat legitimate? Part of me expects him to burst out laughing and start calling us "irrational," Mason's favorite buzzword. Part of me wants to punch him out of sheer force of habit, "valuable" contribution to the group sessions aside.

"Are you feeling okay?" I ask Mason. He makes his best *who, me?* face, which just makes me feel more suspicious.

"Well, that's stupid," Andrew says. "They're both equally legitimate."

"No, they're not!" Clarisa says. "One is cognitive progress and one is just…wasting your brain cells!"

"Writing the same thing fifty times on a sheet of paper isn't wasting your brain cells?" Andrew demands.

"This argument is a waste of brain cells," I say.

"Well, let's ask Josh," Clarisa says. "Wouldn't you say that, you know, mindfulness and journaling are better ways of celebrating than indulging in frivolous, gratuitous, hedonistic indulgences?"

"Those are big words," Andrew says, "but she's wrong."

Josh takes a minute to look around the circle at each of us, smiling widely. Everyone stares back at him, waiting for an answer. They haven't learned that expecting concrete answers out of therapists is like standing in the middle of the Sahara with an empty bucket and waiting for rain. "Ah," Josh says. "What an interesting conversation. But, you see… I don't care."

Everyone stares at him, silent, for a moment, while I try my best to turn my snicker into a cough. "What do you mean," Mason says slowly, "you don't care?"

"I mean, I don't care!" Josh says. He spreads his arms to both sides. I watch two mosquitos land on one of them immediately, only to take off as he starts waving them around. *Poor mosquitos*, I think. And then I retract my sympathy, because at least they have the power to fly away. "The important thing is not how you celebrate your successes, but *that* you celebrate your successes, and you all seem to recognize the importance of that. It's not my job to sermonize to you about the proper ways of congratulating yourselves. Although, Andrew," he adds, "I would advise you to look into some of the health effects of regular marijuana usage and make a fully educated decision about whether you think it's worth the risks."

"You can't possibly— You can't honestly be recognizing and I quote 'getting blazed' as a legitimate means of self-recognition. You're a therapist!" Clarisa exclaims.

"*Dude*," Andrew says.

"My job," Josh says, "is to help you build healthy relation-ships with yourselves and with each other. You've already rec-ognized the most important part of that—not letting other people's judgments deter you from what you feel makes you the most fulfilled. Excellent observation on that point, Ben. From that point on—well, I say, explore. Test the waters. See what works. Maybe you, Clarisa, will find that it's journal-ing, and you, Ben, will find that it's enjoying a movie, and you, Mason, will find that it's curating a blog devoted to the delights of Thomas Mann, and you, Andrew, will find that it's enjoying a few beers with your band mates, and you, Stella, will find that it's making self-deprecating comments and staunchly denying anyone who attempts to tell you oth-erwise. Entirely hypothetical, of course," he adds, winking at me. "Find what you want to reward yourselves with when you deserve reward, and take the time to do it."

"That is ludicrous!" Clarisa says. She looks even more horri-fied than she usually looks, which is saying something. There's not even that much at stake here—just a few of our brain cells, and it's not like our brain cells are doing us much good as they are now, anyway.

Clarisa makes a sound as if she's going to start speaking again, and then seems to think better of it. A few seconds pass. "I mean," she says, apparently unable to keep the words con-tained, "I just honestly find it absurd that you could advocate for such potentially destructive behavior!"

"Gravity bong," Andrew advises. "Seriously, dude. You need it."

BEN

"HERE," CLARISA SAYS. "Spot me, okay?"

"Okay," I say. A thousand metaphors fill my head, about being afraid to fall and letting yourself fall, anyway, and the promise you make when you say you'll catch someone when they do. *Because it's a promise*, I think. *It's a promise that when they take the wrong step and slip, you're going to pull them back, that when they forget the reason they're walking the line in the first place, you'll be there to remind them, that if they fall off completely, you'll jump, too, and pray not to be too damaged to put them back together.*

"Is that crooked?" Clarisa says. She's stepped onto the chair next to us and pulled the fabric of the curtain onto the rod hanging over the window. She peers down at me.

"Uh," I say. *Focus, Ben*, I tell myself. I don't know how Clarisa does it. We've been alone in the cabin putting up the curtains for half an hour now. And all I want to do is pull her onto the couch and look at her and stay there forever, Safe Space be damned. From outside the cabin, I can hear Stella yelling at Mason to "shut the fuck up and go help Ben and Clarisa!"

"Language, Stella!" Jessie says, right on cue.

"Well," Clarisa says. She smiles, and, I swear, I get dizzy for a second. "I'd say we're doing better than they are."

"Yeah," I say. I step back and take one quick look at the curtain before my gaze slides back to Clarisa's face. "It doesn't look crooked to me," I say.

"Great," Clarisa says. She hops off the chair and looks around the room at the two curtains we've already put up. Then she pulls the one we just put up to the side, so that sunlight is falling through the window again, illuminating the room. Our shadows stretch out across the floor, diagonal and elongated and somehow gorgeous. *Shadows*, I think, *vary in length by the time of day and the angle of the sun. But they are always there, feet bound to yours.* Light, I think, might be the most amazing thing that the universe has ever created.

"Well, that's it, then," Clarisa says. "Good work, team."

She holds up her hand for me to high-five it, but I grab it and pull her toward the couch instead. She laughs. "Ben, what are you doing?" she says. "We should go see if Mason and Andrew and Stella need any help. Which, from the sound of it, they definitely—"

"Shh," I say. I pull her down next to me.

"—do," she finishes, but the word slips out of her mouth as an afterthought, leftover from a sentence that I've already forgotten she started.

"God," I say. "Look at the window. Look at the light. It's so beautiful, isn't it? The curtains are beautiful. Today is beautiful. You're so beautiful. It's all so beautiful."

"Thanks, Ben," she says softly. She looks at me for a second, brushes her hair behind her ear, smiles. I lean in to kiss her and she laughs as she moves in to meet me halfway. For a few seconds, everything in my head is gone again, blank, empty. I'm back in that endless white room, the one with the supernova inside of it. Floating. Glowing. Eternal.

"We should go," Clarisa says. She pulls away from me.

"Let's not," I say.

"Come on," Clarisa says. She's smiling, but she stands up and starts tugging on my hand. "Someone's going to come in here in a couple of minutes, anyway, and I don't want to—"

"No one's going to come in here," I say, still sitting. Her pulling is adorably ineffective. "They're preoccupied."

We listen for a second, just in time to hear Mason shout, "Goddamn it, Andrew, enough about the guitar already! It was voted down!"

"See?" I say. "Preoccupied. C'mon, I want to sit with you."

"I want to sit with you, too, Ben," she says. But she frowns. "But I really feel like it's weird for us to be in here all alone."

"Aren't you *happy*?" I say. I don't understand how Clarisa could possibly want to rejoin everyone else when everything that's good and right is in this room, right now, the way our laughs sound together, the way our hands meet, the way we kiss. *God.*

"Of course I'm happy," Clarisa says. "I'm quite happy actually. I feel nice, Ben."

"Nice?" I say. "You feel 'nice'? Clarisa, this feeling is *beautiful*. It might be the most beautiful feeling in the world. Do you know how many movies have been written about this feeling? How many musical albums? How many books? Hell, if Andrew felt this way, he'd never feel short on inspiration *again*. Clarisa, you do get that, don't you? This feeling is— I mean, it's why people live."

Clarisa laughs. "Christ, Ben. You really mean all that, don't you?"

I stare at her, shocked. "Of course I mean all that! Do you— Do you not?"

"Do I not what?" Clarisa says.

"Do you not feel that way?"

"I mean," Clarisa says. "I *like* you, obviously I do, but I don't know. I guess I don't think of it as dramatically as you do—"

"It's not dramatic!" I say. All of a sudden, there are black spots appearing in my beautiful white room, trying to drown out the light. *She doesn't get it*, I think. *She really doesn't, oh, my God.* "It's the truth, it's how things *are*, it's—"

"'It's why people *live*?'" Clarisa repeats. She smiles, but it's not the same anymore. "Come on, don't you think that's a bit much?"

"What do you mean 'a bit much'?" I say. "You mean all this time, when I told you stuff like that, about how I felt, you thought it was just, like, nonsense?"

"Well, I didn't think it was *nonsense*," Clarisa says. "I thought it was nice, if slightly overwrought, but nevertheless, I appreciated the sentiment."

"You *appreciated* the *sentiment*?" I repeat. I can feel my brain flooding with dark. I know this feeling, and I don't like it. I want to scream, I want to throw something across the room and watch it shatter, *I* want to shatter. I don't know how to make it stop. Clarisa pulls her hand out of mine to put her hair up, and I lean back and massage my temples with my thumbs.

"No, no, no, *no*," I say. I close my eyes and try to bring back the room, the white room, with the bright light, but the darkness is getting darker and pulsating and I can feel it rising in my stomach, threatening to explode. "We can't fight right now," I say. "The pacing is all wrong, this isn't right, everything was so good two days ago, fifteen minutes ago, there wasn't any foreshadowing, this is all wrong in the first act, I can't—"

"Life isn't a movie, Ben," Clarisa says, exasperated. "And besides, we don't *have* to be fighting right now—I don't know why you're so upset."

"It could've been! With you, and with me—it could have

been a movie! It could be," I say. I'm trying not to shout now, but it's so hard when my head is screaming, *This was all wrong, everything was all wrong, she's all wrong, you're all wrong—*

"Ben," she says. She puts her hand on my shoulder, rubs it with the pad of her thumb. "I like you a lot, and I hate seeing you like this, and feeling like I said something wrong and screwed up something really good. All I said was just that sometimes you're a little dramatic and, you know, unnecessarily *cosmic* and I don't know that that's necessarily entirely justified given the fact that, you know, we've known each other for two weeks, but that doesn't invalidate—"

"You always do this," I say. It used to be cute, charming, but now she does it and I can feel the darkness inside my brain roaring, swelling. "You always start using these really big words that don't do anything but make you sound really smart and...and really heartless."

"I said that I like you!" Clarisa says.

"You don't mean it."

"Why would I lie about that?"

"You don't mean it like I mean it, Clarisa," I say, and that's just it. Clarisa pulls her hand off my shoulder and undoes her ponytail, puts it back up again, pulls it over her shoulder. She didn't mean any of it, I think. Everything was wrong, and fake, and unreal, and I hate all of it for not being what I wanted it to be, and I hate all of it for being anything at all, and I hate myself for always wanting everything to be something it isn't.

"Are you guys clothed? Jessie wants to know how much progress you've—" Mason says, walking into the room, only to stop abruptly as he sees the two of us. "What's going on?" he says cautiously.

And so Boy and Girl fight, I think. *And so Boy realizes that every scene he has lived has been scripted to end this way, and he's simply been too foolish to see it coming.*

"Hello?" Mason says when neither of us replies. "I still have condoms, if that's—"

"Get out of the goddamn room, Mason!" I shout.

Mason raises his eyebrows and walks backward out of the room, slowly. *I hate him*, I think. *I hate him and his stupid novels and his stupid* Playboys *and his stupid condoms and his stupid fucking narcissism. And I hate myself for not being that type of person, and for fucking this up, and for always fucking it up, and for feeling this way, and for not being able to keep myself from feeling this way. I feel—*

"Ben," Clarisa says. She takes a deep breath and looks like she's about to cry. I don't care. I hate her, too. "Could you please not yell? It really stresses me out."

"Fine," I say, and stand up. "Fine, let's go see if they need any help. Apparently Jessie wants to talk to us, anyway."

"I don't want you to be upset," Clarisa says quietly.

"I don't want me to be upset, either," I say, turning around. "So it looks like neither of us are particularly fulfilled right now."

"Ben," she says, catching my hand in hers. The contact actually, physically hurts. But then if I told her that, she'd probably just think I was being dramatic and—what was it?— "unnecessarily *cosmic*." I want to burn something down. Like this stupid cabin, or the whole camp, or myself.

"Ben," Clarisa continues, "can we just forget about this? There's less than two weeks of camp left and I don't want to be fighting."

There was a time when the sound of her voice made me so high I could hardly think straight. But I feel like a different person now—one drowning in my own thoughts instead of floating over them, one with a crumbling, black room that suffocates any spark of light. A black hole, I think. I am a black hole.

"We're not fighting," I say. "We're not anything, Clarisa."

And I walk out of the room.

CLARISA

Dear Clarisa,

I'm so glad to hear that you're having a good time at camp, and that the medication is starting to work. I told Ashley what you wrote in your last letter, and she was very relieved to hear it, as well. Are you experiencing any negative side effects? She mentioned that drowsiness might be a problem. But we can finalize the dosage when you come back home.

All your news makes me so excited for you! My days at camp were some of my favorites. So happy that you and Stella are getting along. Mason is very lucky that I'm not at camp to keep him in line. And what's this I hear about a boy? So exciting! I trust you, but make sure you're careful, okay? But also, please don't be too careful. Remember to have fun! Wow, I never thought I'd be saying that to my daughter!

I'm so proud of you, & love,
Mom

It's a nice letter, and I can practically see my mother dying of excitement while writing it, but now I regret telling her about Ben in the first place. How am I supposed to explain what happened when I don't even understand it? One minute Ben and I were great, and then I said something about him being dramatic, and then he just went crazy. I figured this was one of those things where he would be really upset, and then sleep on it, and then be fine by morning. But then he spent all of today loudly talking to Mason about how "giving someone control over your emotions" is "tantamount to handing them a gun and guiding their hand to your head." Every time I tried to talk to him, he either flat out ignored me or moved away. The one time I did get him to say something to me—after I asked him over breakfast whether we could talk later—he just said, "I've said all that I have to say, Clarisa, and your lack of reciprocation means more than anything you could ever say." //

"This is ridiculous," I mutter to myself. Disbelief managed to override sadness for most of the day, but now that I'm back in my room, and Ben is still mad at me, and I still have no idea how to fix things, I feel awful. Being with Ben really did make me happy, even if he doesn't believe it, and knowing that he might very well ignore me for the rest of camp—and then for the rest of, well, forever—is making me want to cry. *Don't be ridiculous*, I think to myself. *You're not going to cry about this, Clarisa, you barely even know the guy. But you could have*, a voice in the back of my head adds. *You could have gotten to know each other and maybe had something wonderful, and then you went and ruined it, and you don't even know what you did.* //

"Oh, no," I say. I moan and bury my head in my hands. "If you're trying to get me to ask you what's wrong, it's not going to work," Stella says from her bed. I grit my teeth and look up at her. "Actually, I wasn't," I say. "I'd almost forgotten that you were there. But hey, thanks for the reminder." //

"It's what I'm here for," she says, sitting up in bed. "But actually, are you all right? You haven't done anything other than stare at that piece of paper and make weird noises for half an hour, and I don't think I'll be able to sleep if you do that all night." "How considerate of you," I reply. "I'll be fine, but..." I trail off, and Stella raises an eyebrow at me inquisitively. "Well, it's about Ben." //

"Oh." Stella flops back down onto her bed, sounding disappointed. "It's about Ben," she repeats glumly. "Is there something wrong with that?" I ask her. Leave it to Stella to ask me about my problems, and then make me feel like they're the wrong problems to have. "No, there's nothing wrong with that," Stella says. "And it was pretty obvious that you were fighting all day." //

"But..." I prompt. "But," Stella says, "what did you really expect to happen? Didn't I tell you it was a bad idea?" "You didn't know this was going to happen," I snap. "No one knew that this was going to happen. Because it wasn't going to happen, until it did." "Clarisa," Stella says, "this was *always what was going to happen*." //

"How can you say that?" I say. "I mean, I know you're all cynical and hopeless and whatnot, but you can't possibly believe that all romances end disastrously, can you? Because that's just sad, Stella, that's really just sad." "I don't think all romances end disastrously," Stella says. "Although thank you, I guess, for your compelling personality analysis. Some romances end passably, with both parties deluding themselves into thinking that they're happy." She pauses for a moment. //

"But that's not the point," she says slowly. "What's the point, then?" I demand. "The point is..." she says, and then hesitates again. "Look, I don't want to make you more upset than you—" "Just tell me, Stella!" I hiss. "Fine," Stella says. "The point is, Clarisa, that people who meet at *wilderness fucking therapy camp* don't usually make for good love stories—or, at least, good love stories with happy endings, anyway." //

It takes a second for what she says to sink in. And then I get angry. Really angry, because first of all, who is she to talk as if Ben and I are somehow broken beyond repair? And second, if every romance between two less-than-one-hundred-percent mentally healthy individuals ended poorly, there would never be any successful romances because *news flash, Stella, everyone is depressed these days.* "That's absolutely ludicrous," I say. "Our issues have nothing to do with how we feel about each other—or felt, maybe, I don't know. But the point is, he could really be in love with me, and I could really be—" //

"Are you joking right now?" Stella says. She climbs out of bed and slides into her chair, next to mine, just so she can yell a little bit closer to my face, I guess. "Are you joking?" "Are *you* joking?" I say. I get out of my chair and climb into my bed. Stella wheels around in her chair to face me again. "And can you please stop yelling?" //

"Oh, my God, Clarisa. Ben is not in love with you. You are not in love with Ben. You don't even *know* Ben!" Stella says. Her tone of voice makes me feel like I'm going to implode. I am not going to miss Stella, I decide. I am not going to miss Stella at all. //

"But he *could* be," I reply, "one day. And *I* could be, too, if I hadn't—" "You two were never going to be in love with each other!" Stella says. She gets up out of the chair and flops, facedown, onto her bed. She sounds almost as upset as I do, I think, a fact for which I immediately resent her. Who is she to be upset about this? It's not like she had her burgeoning romance collapse in on her in the past twenty-four hours. //

Stella flips around so that she's staring at the ceiling and takes three deep breaths. "You two were never going to be in love with each other," she repeats, and suddenly she sounds calm. "Clarisa, Ben was only ever going to be in love with some version of you he made up in his head, at least until he

224

figured out how to separate reality from fantasy, which he clearly still can't fucking do. You think he likes you? Do you honestly think he even knows who you really are? You're just some cute girl at camp he's projected his own fantasy onto, something nice and dramatic that he can turn into a movie if he ever manages to stay stable enough to finish writing a damn script. And that's fine, Clarisa, that's fine—it's not his fault and he probably doesn't even know what he's doing, but it never would have *worked* because you were never going to be able to be the person he made up inside his head because *that's not who you are!* //

"And you—Jesus Christ, Clarisa. 'One day I could be in love with him'? Do you honestly think you even *like* Ben right now? Because I think what you really like is the idea that being with him—that meeting in the middle of the woods to prance around a campfire and make out or whatever it is you guys do—makes you normal. A normal person doing normal things with another normal person at a normal summer camp like your mother wants you to be. And, you know, I get it, Clarisa. I really, really do. //

"Because it's nice to think that there's something that would just make us normal. That would make all our problems go away, that would mean that we were definitely going to be happy in the end, and that that something is as great as finding someone you honestly, really could be in love with. But the thing is—it's not. And it won't. You and Ben being together won't automatically make you a healthy, functional person in a healthy, functional relationship. You're still OCD and depressed and he's still manic-depressive. And being in love isn't a Get Out of Your Own Head free card and that's just how it is." //

"Why are you saying all this?" I say. The tears are starting to bubble up now, and even after I squeeze my eyes shut I can feel them seeping out from underneath my eyelashes. "Isn't it better to know?" Stella says. "You're not *right*," I say angrily. I hear Stella sigh and get off the bed. A couple seconds later, something hard hits my arm. I look up to find that Stella's thrown a box of tissues onto my bed. //

"I think," I say, "that you're just saying stuff to upset me because you can't handle the idea of being the only person who finishes camp unhappy. You're so depressed that you want everyone else to be depressed, too, just so you feel a little less alone and pathetic and sa—" "If I really wanted you to be unhappy, I would never have told you all this," Stella interrupts. But there's no venom in her voice, either. "Clarisa, I don't want to fight, or deal with you crying all night because of some boy who honestly doesn't deserve you. If I *really* wanted you to be unhappy, I wouldn't have bothered with all this—I would have let you and Ben have your stupid little fight and kiss and make up one week from now and maybe try to keep the romance going outside of camp, and I would let you fail, six months from now, and feel even more miserable then, when you realized everything I just told you, but on your own, after spending six months trying to make something work that was never, ever going to work. If I really wanted you to be as depressed as I was, Clarisa, I would let this ridiculous thing you have going with Ben crash and burn on its own, because that's what happened to me." //

At these last words, she pulls her pillow over her head so I can't see her face. "I thought you said Kevin wasn't a big deal," I say, so surprised that I forget to sound angry. "I thought you guys just…just made out a few times last semester. Isn't that what you said?" Stella laughs, her voice muffled. "Yeah, I guess I did say that, didn't I? Maybe I forgot to mention some of the details." //

"So what actually happened?" I say. "I already told you,"

Stella says, staring straight ahead at the wall as she speaks, saying the words slowly, evenly, emotionlessly. "Crashed and burned. He was angry, which made me depressed, I was depressed, which made him angrier, and we couldn't make it through a day without yelling at each other. We broke up, we got back together, we broke up, we got back together. We couldn't live without each other, being together made us both infinitely more miserable. Last time I saw him, he was in a depressive episode and I—well, you know how I am—and we fought and I broke his laptop screen and he threw a vase at my head and we haven't talked since." //

"What? You told me you just *made out a few times!*" I say again. I close my eyes and massage my temples. It's a stupid thing to say again, I know, but I can't think of anything else. Stella snorts and doesn't reply. By the time I open my eyes again, she's climbed out of her bed and walked into the bathroom. I listen to the faucet running as she brushes her teeth and stare at my mother's letter, still on my table, feeling oddly numb with understanding. //

MASON

"LET'S TALK ABOUT FORGIVENESS," Josh says.

It's Thursday night, and we're back at the pond, talking about each other's problems and providing a feast for the mosquitos. But Josh looks confused, an expression that I don't think I've ever seen on Josh's face before. I suppose this is the first time the wise gnome living in his beard hasn't been able to clarify a situation for him. "Why don't we all get in our usual therapy circle?"

I snort. We're not in our usual therapy circle because recent events have made sitting in a circle the equivalent of an ex-cruciatingly annoying SAT question. *If you have five campers at Camp Ugunduzi, the Northeast's premier wilderness therapy camp, and Ben and Clarisa can't sit next to each other because of a lovers' quarrel, and Clarisa and Stella can't sit next to each other because one is in denial about the nature of said lovers' quarrel, and Mason and Stella can't sit next to each other because of the eighty-five percent chance that they will rip each other's throats out, how many minutes will it take for them to arrive at a suitable seating plan?*

What has ensued is an odd sort of game of musical chairs: Ben and Clarisa arrive at the pond and stand next to each other out of habit, only to panic when they remember that they hate each other now. Everyone else has already sat down by the time they realize this, though, leaving us now in this terribly awkward lump shape. All further evidence, I think, that irrationality is what dooms all relationships between fundamentally and irrevocably irrational people. I can't say this, of course, because doing so would be breaking my newly acquired camp resolution to appease everyone so that I get out of the next week alive. But I sure as hell think it.

"Okay," Josh says. "Well, Mason, why don't you shift over a little bit to make room for Clarisa, and, Ben, why don't you shift over to Stella's side a little more—there you go. Perfect. It's almost Friday, guys, you can make it."

"Can we, though?" Stella mutters. I have to suffocate my desire to say something sarcastic back.

"Let's talk about forgiveness," Josh repeats. "We've been taught, throughout our lives, of the importance of forgiveness. We forgive our family for their careless moments in raising us, we forgive our friends for our fights, we forgive lovers for their indiscretions. We've been conditioned to forgive everyone, it seems, except for ourselves."

Andrew, next to me, is scribbling furiously into a notebook as Josh talks. *It's all useless!* I want to tell him. *Stop writing it down and just go do some push-ups or something!*

"But if we don't forgive ourselves," Josh continues, "how can we hope to move on? And if we cannot hope to move on, how can we hope to get better?"

"Hoping to get better is overrated," Stella says. "I prefer disdainful resignation, you know?"

Andrew freezes, midscribble, and looks up at Stella, confused, as if she hasn't been making snide comments like this all camp. Ah, the unfortunate by-product of Andrew's intense earnestness: stupidity.

"Why do you guys think it's so difficult to forgive our-selves?" Josh asks.

"Well, for starters, because forgiving yourself requires that you actually admit you did something wrong," Ben says. "And people prefer not to do that." He shoots an extremely unsubtle look at Clarisa, who turns scarlet.

"Sometimes people actually didn't do anything wrong!" she fires back. "And so there's no reason for them to forgive themselves."

"Those are both really interesting statements," Josh says while Clarisa and Ben glower at each other. "Do you think forgiving yourself is restricted to situations in which you've done something wrong?" Josh says.

"Um," Andrew says. "Well, if you hadn't done anything wrong, why would you need to forgive yourself? Isn't that kind of, like, the definition of forgiveness? Like, if you hurt someone—or spray paint their cat, or something—you should admit that you fucked up, ask for forgiveness, and forgive your-self. But if you haven't, then what's there to forgive?"

"Don't be ridiculous, Andrew," Stella says. "That would make too much sense. Haven't you noticed that we're in ther-apy?"

"You know, Andrew," Josh says, running a hand through his beard, "I think that applies well to straightforward things, like your relationship with the law, or even your relationship with other people. But what about your relationship with *yourself*?"

My relationship with myself, I think. I picture the words said over some sweeping, string-laden score interspersed with video clips of flower petals blowing away in the wind, or a single sailboat in a vast expanse of ocean, or some really old woman's eyes crinkling as she smiles, like in those Apple commercials that have nothing to do with actual Apple products.

"Sometimes," Josh says, now in full-out hippie mode, "we make certain decisions, and they don't lead to the conclusion we thought they would lead to, even though there was nothing morally wrong with that decision, and we need to forgive ourselves for that." He holds his hands in front of him with his palms facing up, as if wisdom is a physical thing that he can actually, physically, offer to us. "Other times, we need to forgive ourselves for setting certain goals that maybe didn't turn out to be the best for us. And other times, we resent ourselves for feeling certain things—even if there's no such thing as a wrong feeling!—and we need to forgive ourselves for that, too.

"And Ben is right," Josh continues. "In that sometimes the reason we can't forgive ourselves is because we don't want to acknowledge feelings we're uncomfortable with, or decisions we've made, or desires we have. We're afraid to," Josh says. "And that fear is often what keeps us from finding peace."

Andrew makes a noise somewhere between a whine and a groan. "Nnnnnnguh," he says.

"Deep," Stella says.

"Nnnnnnnnguhhhhhhh," Andrew says again.

"Andrew," I say before I can stop myself. "It's okay. Some people's vocabularies just aren't as good as other people's vocabularies. But I forgive you, and you should forgive yourself—"

"I was in the hospital," Andrew says. He suddenly sits up and looks around the circle. He looks crazy—eyes wide, taking long, deep breaths, hands fidgeting.

"Ah," Josh says, looking pleased with himself.

There's a brief pause as everyone takes in the revelation.

What's the big deal? I think. *Half of the people in this circle have probably been hospitalized. And the other half probably still should be.*

But—a testament to my superior powers of self-control—I keep my mouth shut.

"Hey, look," Stella says. "That's okay, Andrew! Normal

people actually think it's really cool when you've been in a psych ward. It's like telling them that you took a vacation to a really exotic country. Like, you know, visiting North Korea or something. Major street cred. Chicks will dig it."

"I wasn't in a psych ward," Andrew says quietly.

"Oh," Stella says. "So, then—"

"I had—" Andrew says, and then cuts off. He takes a deep breath. "I had a heart attack. Oops," he adds, smiling weakly.

Everyone stares at him, shocked.

"Oops?" Clarisa says.

"*Oops?*" Ben says.

"Not really an 'oops' kind of situation," I say.

"Well, I don't really know what else to say about it," Andrew says. He's finally put the notebook and pen down. "I don't even— I don't know. I don't know anything."

"How about saying what happened?" Clarisa says.

"I don't know," Andrew repeats. "We were playing a show, and we had just finished a song, and I just passed out. Doctors kept asking me if I felt anything strange in the hours leading up to the show, or during the show itself, but—dude, we were *playing a show*. I didn't feel anything other than, you know, nerves and adrenaline and all that. But I passed out, and so obviously the guys called me an ambulance, although I told them they really should've finished out the set—"

"You told them *what*?" Clarisa says.

"—and I went to the hospital, and it turned out that I'd had a heart attack. Something about prolonged calorie restriction, and weakening of the aortic something-or-others, and—"

"Oh, my God, Andrew," Stella says.

"I try not to think about it too much," Andrew says. "Or, you know. At all. I kind of hate myself for it," he adds quietly.

The rest of us fall into silence. What is there for us to say? Do I think Andrew is an idiot for letting that happen to him?

Uh, yeah. But am I going to bring that up right now, in the middle of a bunch of emotional vultures? I've learned my lesson.

"Like, who has a fucking heart attack?" Andrew says. "At sixteen? Who gets to that point? Girls diet all the time, and they don't have heart attacks. Half of my high school chain-smoked cigarettes, and they didn't have heart attacks. Lots of people are in bands, and they don't make their bands cancel the rest of their tour by *having a fucking heart attack. Who has heart attacks?*" he repeats, voice getting louder with every word.

"An eating disorder," Stella says, "is not a diet. Just like *hallucinating* is not a fucking *daydream*. No one goes to the hospital for schizophrenia and says, 'Oh, tons of people daydream, why'd I end up in the hospital?' *You weren't eating anything, Andrew! That's not a diet!"*

"I just hate myself," Andrew says.

"Goddamn it, Andrew," Stella says. She looks far more distraught than she has any right to be. *Probably has some ridiculous crush on him*, I think, because Stella is just the type of girl who pretends to be all hard and impossible to touch but goes to pieces at the first sign of a cute guy.

"I shouldn't, right?" Andrew whispers.

"You shouldn't," Clarisa says gently. She moves over so that she's sitting right next to Andrew and puts her hand on his shoulder. Ben rolls his eyes. "Andrew, I understand why you feel guilty. You feel like you let people you cared about down. But it's not your fault. If your parents were planning on taking you to Disney or something for vacation, but then your mom came down with strep throat, would you want her to hate herself for not being healthy enough to go?"

"It's not the same," Andrew says.

"Andrew," Clarisa says. I'm trying to figure out what exactly it is about her voice that makes people feel so much better—that makes people listen to her, that makes people *like* her. Is it the tone? The quietness? The length of the pauses between each sentence? "Please don't hate yourself for this. You were sick. It's not your fault. Your band wants you to be healthy. That's what you should want, too."

"I gained four pounds," Andrew moans.

"Since you got here?" Clarisa says. "Well, that's...that's great, Andrew—"

"No," Andrew says. He laughs, slow and watery. "No, dude, no. I gained five pounds just last week. Ask Josh, I wasn't thrilled."

Josh inclines his head slightly toward us, and Andrew chuckles. "No, just this week. Gained another four."

"That's nothing to be ashamed of," I say, trying to imitate Clarisa's lilt. I pause the way she does, feeling stupid. "Nothing to be ashamed of at all."

"Are you okay, Mason?" Clarisa says. "You sound kind of constipated. And...weirdly human." She frowns.

"Well, that's *really* good, Andrew," Stella says, thankfully stealing Clarisa's attention before she can notice that my face has broken into a completely inappropriate smile.

Stella moves over so that she's sitting right in front of him. What I want, more than anything else in that moment, is to run however many miles it is from camp to the nearest airport and fly back to Bethesda.

"I'm trying to believe that," Andrew says. He shuts his eyes again, presses his hands against his face so that when he pulls them away, his fingertips come away glistening. "But it's really—"

His voice catches, and he takes a breath.

"But it's really, really hard," he finishes.

"I know," Stella says.

Look at us, I think. All gathered around some idiot who

decided a crappy pop punk band was worth starving himself half to death for.

There's one week left, I think to myself. I close my eyes and take a deep breath. One week until my return home, and to reading in the morning and jogging in the evening and being around people who are often unreasonable, yes, but not downright insane, and how much worse can camp possibly get over the course of one week?

STELLA

BY THE TIME we make it back to The Hull the night of Andrew's revelation, I honestly can't even process how I feel. Andrew, with his blend of naiveté and self-loathing that really shouldn't be possible, has actually made me care about him, and caring about people is always just a recipe for misery. But there's something else. I keep thinking about the end of that session, when Clarisa came over and gave him this whole talk about why he shouldn't hate himself and how he was sick and how everyone just wants him to get better. And that's fine, because out of all of us, Clarisa is the one who's going to grow up and become a therapist and say things like, "Let's talk about our relationships with ourselves," in complete earnest. But I can't shake this ridiculous feeling that it should've been me giving him that talk, with my hand on his shoulder, trying to make him feel better. Because I *get* him, I really do, in a way that I don't think anyone else really does, and I should be able to make him *get* this—why gaining all this weight is a good thing, why his band is going to be great even if he doesn't weigh 120 pounds. And then I realize that that's a stupid way to feel, because first of all, I don't know that no one else can do that, and second of all, who cares?

"Are you okay?" I ask Andrew later that night. Ben and Mason are playing pool a couple feet away, and Clarisa is watching them with an enthusiasm that I, quite frankly, would find embarrassing, but Andrew is just sitting on the couch all alone, staring off into space.

It seems to take him a moment to realize that I'm there. "I'm okay," he says. "You know. I've obviously been better. But it is what it is."

"I'm sorry that all that happened to you," I say.

"I'm over it," Andrew says gruffly. He stands up. "Gonna go to bed."

"Are you?" I ask. Every part of me is screaming not to get involved, to let him be, that there's nothing I can do to help him, anyway, and that if there were, it would have worked by now. But I can't keep the words from slipping out.

"Am I gonna go to bed? Yeah…" he says.

"No. Are you really over it?"

"I'm fine," Andrew says. "Thanks, Stella."

Then he leaves.

And I am weirdly, inexplicably devastated. I don't understand how. I don't understand why. I don't even understand where it comes from. Andrew, I tell myself, is fine. And it's not my responsibility to keep him happy. In fact, Andrew should be *thankful* that I'm not doing a better job of making him happy, because relying on me for emotional wellness would be like relying on an alcoholic to preach temperance in middle school health class.

There's no such thing as a wrong feeling, I hear Josh saying when I'm lying in bed trying to sleep and still can't get the look on Andrew's face as he left the common room out of my head.

And the fact that Josh's stupid therapy slogans have gotten stuck in my head is so irritating that I can barely get to sleep the entire night.

ANDREW

I'VE BEEN HAVING NIGHTMARES.

I used to wish more than anything that I could go back home and see the guys again, that I could just be back in Aidan's basement making up riffs and lyrics and throwing out ideas for our LP title. But now I'm having nightmares about it, about when Josh isn't going to be around to remind me that what I'm feeling doesn't make sense, and Clarisa isn't there to tell me that having a heart attack because my body is weak as shit isn't my fault, and Stella's not going to be able to tell me why I feel how I feel before I've even figured it out. I keep waking up in the middle of the night, dreaming that I'm back in Washington and Jake and the other guys are pretending to be happy for me but actually think that I've ruined the band. I have dreams where Epic or Epigraph or one of the record labels we've been dreaming about for years says they dig our EPs, and then we fly out to New York or Hollywood, and they tell us that we don't fit the "image" of what they're looking for, or that they don't think that we match their "brand," and everyone knows it's all my fault. They say that bands live and die by their lead singer. I keep having this dream that I've been playing in an empty room by myself for so long that my hands are bleeding, only the guitar I'm holding turns into a rejection letter, and then the rejection letter turns into Aidan, who's yelling at me and trying to put me in a choke hold. I wake up at 3:00 a.m., panting, drenched in sweat, begging Aidan to understand but knowing that he won't, knowing that he shouldn't.

The thing is, it doesn't get much better after I've woken up. At least in the nightmares, I know that what I've done is wrong, and I know what would be right, and I know how I could fix it. I feel like I'm going crazy every morning when I get up and leave the room, because even after everything everyone has said about forgiveness, and forgiving myself, and how gaining all this weight back is not even anything that needs to be forgiven, I still can't do it. I still can't forgive myself. I don't know what I hate myself for more: gaining the weight back, or not being able to let myself do that without hating myself like everyone keeps telling me I need to do.

After Art by the Fire on Friday, I go back to my room, because maybe I just need to be alone. Maybe I just need to get one good night of sleep, and then tomorrow will be better. Maybe I just need to play some Nirvana and try to keep my thoughts from going out of control and wait until lights-out and go to bed.

Stella walks into our room at half past eleven. "Hey, assholes," she says, and then cuts off, wrinkling her nose. "Jesus, it's a mess in here. How do you live like this? No one let Clarisa in, she'll lose her mind. Anyway, come over after midnight, okay? We have to celebrate."

"What on Earth," Mason says, "is there to celebrate?"

I don't think I've agreed with Mason in the three weeks we've been at camp, but I feel myself nod in agreement.

"Do you guys know what day it is?" Stella says.

"A shitty day," I say. "Just like all the other days."

"Okay, Andrew," Stella says. "What you need is a drink."

"What I need is to get out of my *fucking head*," I say, and by the end of the sentence, my voice has risen to a shout.

"Right," Stella says. "That's what I said. A drink."

"Whoa, there," Mason says. "No need to shout. Here, this'll help." He tosses me one of the *Playboy*s he has lying next to his bed. *The Lingerie Issue*, the cover says in big curly lettering. There's some chick lying in a bathtub in her underwear on the cover. "She's not my type," I say, throwing the magazine back on Mason's bed.

"How can she not be your type?" Mason says, outraged. "Look at her!"

Stella walks over to Mason, picks up the magazine, and throws it into the trash. "It's the fourth, guys," she says.

"The...fourth..." Ben repeats. "The...fourth?"

"The Fourth of *July*, Ben. It's America's birthday! And we can't have a barbecue, because, you know, we're at crazy-people camp, and we can't set off fireworks, because we're at crazy-people camp, and we can't do anything fucking else, because we're at crazy-people camp, so we might as well get drunk. Meet me in our room after the check, okay?"

She gives us all one last annoyed look before walking out of the room. Mason retrieves the *Playboy* from the trash, scowling. "She is fucking insane," he mutters.

I don't know what makes me go over to the girls' side with Ben and Mason. I don't even want to drink, to be honest, and I turn down the shot glass Stella offers me even though she looks at me like I'm crazy when I do it. "I can't right now," I say.

"Andrew, if this is about the calories, I swear to—"

"It's not," I say. The last time I drank when I was sad I ended up puking in Sam's bathroom until 5:00 a.m., passing out on the bathroom floor, getting up at 1:00 p.m, and puking again until 5:00 p.m while Sam and the rest of my band mates tried to decide whether or not they needed to call an ambulance. I remember thinking to myself, while lying on the ground waiting for the room to stop spinning and for the nausea to go away, that at least I went the entire day without feeling hungry. A part of me wants to tell Stella that story, because she would have something to say about it, but for some reason I can't bring myself to. Stella just wants to drink and have a fun time, and I don't want to ruin it by telling a dumb story about this one time I drank too much because I was depressed.

"To America," Stella says. "The land of the free, except for when you're a depressed teenager, I guess."

"Cheers," Ben says, and everyone except me takes a shot.

I can't stop thinking about the fact that camp is basically almost over. Thinking about going back to Washington gives me that hollow, drowning, desperate feeling that you'll do anything to make go away. Part of me wants to grab the vodka bottle off the table and start chugging it. *It's going to be your fault*, I think. I picture Sam, and Aidan, and Jake, waiting for me at the airport, faces falling into disappointment instead of happiness when they see me. *It's going to be your fault, and everyone is going to hate you, and you're never going to be successful, and it's going to be your fault, and—*

"Andrew!" Mason shouts. I look around the room—1:15, the clock reads. How has it been an hour already? If this is how quickly the rest of camp is going to go by, I don't think I can handle it. I can't, I really can't, and now it actually starts to feel like I'm drowning. I can't handle anything apparently. Dieting. Recovering from dieting. Ending my recovery from dieting and going home. Mason comes over and throws an arm around my shoulders, like we're best friends or something. "Andrew. Bro."

"How much have you had to drink, Mason?" I say.

"Eh. Three. Maybe four. Possibly five. It's all the same at that point, isn't it?" Mason says. He grins broadly at me.

"Yeah, dude, totally," I say.

"Good," he says. "And Stella is fucking insane. Kind of in a hot way, though, do you know what I mean?" he adds in a whisper. He stumbles and almost falls on top of me, and I reflexively push him away.

"Oh, my God," Mason says. "Did you just try to fight me? Dude!" he says, laughing. He punches me in the arm in fake anger. I'm going to explode, I think. I'm going to explode or disintegrate, definitely one of the two, and either will be better than what I'm feeling now. "Everyone!" Mason calls gleefully. "Andrew just tried to fight me!"

"Good," Stella says. "It was about time someone did."

"Stella!" Mason calls. He stumbles over to her and puts his arm around her.

"Ugh, Mason," Stella says, shrugging him off. "Get *off* me, I swear to God."

"Stella," Mason repeats.

Clarisa walks over to me. "What is going on?" she says. "Why is everyone shouting?"

"Drunk," I reply.

"Well, why aren't you?"

"Too depressed."

Clarisa looks at me.

"What?" I say. The silence is unbearable. Clarisa is judging me just like everyone else: just like my band mates, just like my parents, just like my fans, thinking how stupid they were to have invested this much in someone so desperately pathetic. I can see it in her face, I know I can.

"Andrew, you know this is *good* for you, right?" Clarisa says. "Camp, and eating normally, and gaining weight."

"You're right," I say. "Even the fact that I'm depressed is stupid. That's probably why the guys are all sick of—"

"That is *not* what I meant," Clarisa says sharply.

"Oh, whatever, Clarisa," I say.

"Andrew, that's really—"

But Clarisa's attempts to make me feel better are cut off because Mason has grabbed the water bottle of liquor off Stella's table and is pounding it against the table as he talks, gesticulating wildly. "You mean to tell me," he says to Stella, "that this entire time, you've felt *no* sexual tension between us?"

"Exactly none," Stella says calmly. She takes the water bottle out of Mason's hand and puts it back down on the table after missing twice.

"I think you're lying," Mason says.

"I think you're an idiot," Stella replies.

"I'm truly offended," Mason says. "I'm so offended that I'm going back to my room, because you've done nothing but insult me and deny your obvious and palpable attraction to me. Bye, Stella. I hope you miss me as much as I'll miss you."

"I honestly think that he might be the worst person I've ever met in my life," Stella says after he leaves the room.

"I'm going to go back, too," Ben says. "It's almost quarter of, anyway."

"See you," Stella says.

"Night, Ben," I say.

Ben turns to look at Clarisa, who is staring at a part of the wall somewhere above Ben's head. She doesn't say anything. "Ugh," Ben says, rolling his eyes, and then leaves.

"Ugh," Clarisa says. She looks furious. She takes two steps forward and then freezes. Then she takes two steps back and freezes again. Finally, she seems to make up her mind and storms out of the room, too.

"Oh, fuck," Stella says. "I think she's actually going to try to talk to him."

I collapse onto the nearest surface, which happens to be Stella's bed. I can't take it anymore. I can't do it. These thoughts. I'm not ever going to be able to play music, ever again, and people aren't ever going to want to spend time with me, ever again, and I AM NEVER GOING TO BE HAPPY EVER AGAIN. It feels like all of the thoughts in my brain have turned into capital letters, getting bigger and bigger, storming around my head until I can't think and I can't speak and I can't do anything to try to make them stop.

"I can't do this," I say to Stella, and the words come out in this half-choked whisper. YOU ARE PATHETIC, the capital letters in my brain say. YOU ARE PATHETIC AND EVERYONE KNOWS IT. "I can't do this," I say again. What the fuck do I even want Stella to do? Stella can't do anything about this, Stella doesn't know how I'm feeling, Stella probably thinks the same thing, STELLA IS NOT GOING TO BE ABLE TO FIX YOU BECAUSE NO ONE CAN, ANDREW, NOT A FUCKING PERSON IN THE UNIVERSE IS GOING TO BE ABLE TO MAKE YOU BETTER. NOT JAKE NOT SAM NOT AIDAN NOT YOUR PARENTS DEFINITELY NOT YOURSELF BECAUSE YOU. ARE. PATHETIC.

"Andrew," Stella says. She walks over so that she's standing in front of me, almost trips onto me, and then steadies herself, laughing. "Listen to me. Look, I'm not saying this just because I'm drunk, okay?"

"Okay," I whisper, and I want to tell her that every time I have a nightmare, it feels like I'm drowning, except then it's like there's no oxygen in the air that I'm breathing when I wake up. And I want to add that all I want to do is get out of my own head, but I can't even write music anymore, because every time I touch the guitar I think of the band, and I miss them so much, and, God, I'm so afraid that they're going to hate me. I want to tell her that I keep dreaming of that day on the hike, when I passed out, except when I regain consciousness I'm in the hospital and not on the ground and the doctors are telling me that my body has sustained permanent damage, that I'm never going to play music again, that it's all over and it's all my fault. But I can't say anything because then my head is screaming again: OF COURSE THEY'RE GOING TO HATE YOU BECAUSE YOU FUCKED IT UP, ANDREW. YOU FUCKED IT UP.

"Andrew," Stella says, and almost falls again. She laughs and places one hand onto each of my shoulders to help her keep her balance. "Sorry, I'm just— I'm so dizzy. And—well, never mind. Anyway. You know everyone loves you, right?"

"They don't—"

"Shut up. Yes, they do. Well, I don't know about Mason, but who gives a shit about Mason—he's an asshole. People. Like. You," she says again. "And it has nothing to do with how skinny you are, or how successful your band is, or…or how tight your jeans are. Okay?" Stella says.

Everyone likes me, Stella says. And I guess I know that. People think I'm nice and interesting and good at singing and that's why the guys wanted to be in a band with me and that's why chicks flirt with me after shows and that's why people at camp talk to me and everyone likes me, but they have no idea that THEY SHOULDN'T, SHOULD THEY, ANDREW? YOU CANNOT POSSIBLY LIVE UP TO ALL THE REASONS THEY LIKE YOU BECAUSE YOU ARE NOT THAT GOOD A SINGER AND YOU ARE FUCKING TERRIBLE IN INTERVIEWS AND YOU CAN'T EVEN KEEP YOUR WEIGHT BELOW 125 FOR THE ONE THING IN THE WORLD THAT MATTERS

THE MOST TO YOU AND YOU ARE GOING TO LET
ALL OF THEM DOWN.

"I can't—" I say.

But I can't keep going and Stella says, "Shh," really softly, like she knows what I'm thinking and like it's okay and she throws me a box of tissues and I blow my nose and walk out of the room and when she says my name again from her bed I pretend not to hear her because there is no point in letting her down, too.

BEN

INT. CABIN COMMON ROOM—NIGHT
  Clarisa, a few steps outside of the girls'
room, on the verge of tears. And then there's
me, a few steps outside of the guys' room,
oddly unaffected. The common room between us,
but isn't there really so much more?

CLARISA

I don't know why I ran after you.

BEN

I don't, either.

CLARISA

I feel like we should talk.

BEN

So talk.

CLARISA

I mean—I haven't thought this through. I just— I want to— I don't know, Ben.

I shrug and turn around.

BEN (V.O.)

If Clarisa doesn't even know what she wants to talk about, it can wait until she's figured it out.

CLARISA

Ben, just…just wait. Can we meet after the bed check? At The Ridge. Please, just one last time. If you never want to talk to me again after that, that's fine. I just want to talk.

BEN

I don't have anything to say.

CLARISA

But I do. Please, Ben.

BEN (V.O.)

So, Clarisa's clearly drunk—her cheeks are flushed and her hair is disheveled and she doesn't have that reserved look in her eyes she always has when she's thinking about numbers. But she's also clearly anxious—rocking back and forth on her heels, taking uneven breaths. I haven't seen her like this since the first week of camp, I realize, and for some reason, something about that fact gets to me.

BEN

Okay. Sure, Clarisa, we'll talk. Should I meet you outside the cabin?

CLARISA

Yeah, that sounds good. Thanks, Ben, I promi—

Clarisa cuts off as Andrew walks into the room, A TOTAL MESS. He's sobbing. Eyes red, body shaking, struggling to breathe, the whole works.

ANDREW

Wh-why are you guys still up?

CLARISA

Oh, my gosh, Andrew—are you okay?

Andrew wipes his face with his hands and starts walking across the room, refusing to look at either me or Clarisa. He takes a few shaky breaths.

ANDREW

I'm fine. I'm going to bed.

CLARISA

Andrew, if you want to talk…

BEN

Not so desperate to meet at The Ridge now, are you?

CLARISA

Ben! What is wrong with you? Look at him!

ANDREW

No, don't. I'm fine. I'll be fine. Go have your talk. I'm going to bed.

Andrew walks by me into the guys' room. Clarisa looks after him, clearly unconvinced.

CLARISA

What do you think happened to him?

BEN

I don't know. Ask him yourself. Are we meeting outside or not?

CLARISA

We are! We are. I'll meet you.

I take one last look at Clarisa and then follow Andrew into the room.

INT. THE BOYS' ROOM—NIGHT
The clock on Mason's desk reads 2:03 a.m. in
red, spidery numbers. Mason is lying on his
back, breathing deeply. Andrew is on his side,
turned away from me, but I doubt he's asleep.
I keep flipping from one position to another,
impatient.
The door cracks open and Josh enters, looking around the room. A sliver of light slants
into the room, across the floor in a perfect,
diagonal line. Josh makes a few notes on a
clipboard he's holding and then exits. It's completely dark again, except for the light from
Mason's digital clock.
I throw off the covers and start putting on
my shoes.

BEN (V.O.)

The thing is, I really don't care. I'll go to
The Ridge with Clarisa and sit next to her on
a log—maybe even the same one I sat with her
on when Stella dragged us all to The Ridge on
the second night of camp, or maybe the same one
I sat with her on when I kissed her last week,
or maybe the third one, the last one, the only

one we haven't shared yet, just because there's a sense of dramatic finality about that, and isn't that my kind of thing? I'll watch myself tell her that it wasn't actually real, and I wasn't actually upset, and I don't actually hate her. I just don't care.

EXT. THE RIDGE—NIGHT
We sit on the third log. Well, I sit on the third log, because it feels right, and Clarisa follows me onto it. Neither of us speaks for a few minutes. I look over at Clarisa a couple of times, but she's staring into the distance and doesn't meet my gaze.

BEN (V.O.)

No one says anything about starting a fire, or about what a beautiful night it is, or about how there are so many *stories* written into the constellations in the sky. This is it. The Moment It All Falls Apart. And I feel totally, totally calm.

Clarisa finally turns to look at me.

CLARISA

You just got really mad at me and stopped talking to me.

BEN

Yeah.

CLARISA

I don't even really get what I did wrong.

BEN

You didn't do anything wrong.

CLARISA

What?

BEN

You didn't do anything wrong. I shouldn't have gotten mad at you. Not *that* mad at least.

CLARISA

If you know that, then why did you? Was it just some stupid game, Ben? So you could feel dramatic and powerful and—

BEN

It wasn't a game. I just felt like I had invested all of this emotional energy into this— you know, *thing*—and you…didn't really care that much.

CLARISA

I told you that I cared! I still—

BEN

No, you didn't. Not in the way I did.

CLARISA

So that's it, then. You just… You got mad because you felt like I didn't care about you as much as you cared about me. And then this entire week—this *entire week*—you just ignored me. You totally blocked me out. You talked to Mason before you would talk to me! Because you were mad that I didn't care about you as much as you cared about me? That's *it*?

BEN

Yep. That's it.

A beat of silence.

CLARISA

That is the stupidest thing I have ever heard.

BEN

You're right. I shouldn't have gotten so upset.

Clarisa's pissed. Her voice lowers into a hiss and she starts talking really quickly, like the shy, bullied girl in every high school movie ever made when she's Finally Had Enough. I'd probably be freaked out, if I weren't so—well, you know.

CLARISA

And now what? Now what, Ben? Now that I've gone and been depressed the whole week and cried to Stella about it—to Stella, Ben, *Stella*—and gotten drunk over you and begged you to come talk to me, that's enough? That's proof that I care about you enough for you to talk to me, is that it? Now that I've been miserable for a week, you're ready to start talking to me again?

BEN

It's not that complex, Clarisa.

CLARISA

What is it, then?

BEN

Clarisa, I just— I don't...care anymore. I don't even know if I'm really sitting here right now, on this log with you, in the middle of fucking nowhere, in some bullshit camp in upstate New York. Did we kiss here? Did we play Never Have I Ever and stare at the constellations here? Did we light a fire here? Did I fall in love with you here? I appear to be sitting here, in the same place that I did all of those things. But I don't feel it. I feel like…nothing. I feel nothing. I feel like I'm drifting through this endless purgatory that happens to look, right now, like the middle of the woods in up-state New York under a clear sky next to a pretty girl who maybe I started to learn the stars with, once, in another life, and maybe I kissed, once, in another time, and maybe I fell in love with, once, in another universe.

BEN (V.O.)

Which is a pretty great speech, if I do say so myself. But evidently Clarisa doesn't think so, because—

CLARISA

Well, that's just great, Ben. That's really great. You don't know. You don't even know if you're here or not. You don't know what you really felt, and you don't know if any of it was real—

BEN

If I felt it because I was fucked up, does it make it less real?

CLARISA

I don't know, Ben. But I felt it even though I wasn't, and to me, that makes it more real.

BEN

You're not fucked up?

CLARISA

I don't like that phrase. I don't swear.

BEN

Well, there you go, ladies and gentlemen. She *doesn't swear*. Irrevocable proof that she is one hundred percent, beyond a reasonable doubt, not fucked up.

Clarisa looks shocked. On the verge of tears. Takes a deep breath.

BEN (V.O.)

So, it wasn't the nicest thing to say. But I was just being honest. I don't even really feel bad about it, until Clarisa pulls herself together and points out, in the kind of voice that you can practically see slicing through the air and slapping me in the face—

CLARISA

You sound like Mason.

BEN

I'm sorry. I don't mean to. God, I hate Mason.

★ ★ ★

Another beat of silence in a conversation that makes a very good argument for the proposition that real life would be infinitely less awkward with a soundtrack.

CLARISA

Stella says it never would have worked out, anyway.

BEN

She's probably right.

CLARISA

Would you have felt sad, Ben? If we had tried, and it didn't work?

BEN

If I was like this that day?

CLARISA

Yeah.

BEN

No.

Clarisa nods slowly and then drops her head

into her hands. She pulls her hair into a ponytail and takes a deep breath.

                    BEN

  I would have been sad, though. Even if I
didn't feel it.

  Clarisa nods again. She stands up and laughs,
although I'm not sure why.

                  CLARISA

  You would have been sad. But not felt sad.
Why do I feel like that shouldn't make me feel
better?

                    BEN

  I'm sorry.

                  CLARISA

  It's okay. Let's go back.

                    BEN

  You know, every other time you've said that
to me, I've argued.

  Clarisa smiles. And the moment deserves violins, even if I can't feel it.

CLARISA

Yeah?

BEN

Let's stay.

I pull her hand into mine, thread my fingers through hers.

CLARISA

Ben…

BEN

Just a couple more minutes. Find me Lyra.

CLARISA

Lyra.

Clarisa looks around the sky for a couple of seconds and then points upward with her other hand, the one that's not in mine.

CLARISA

Okay, see that star? The really bright one, right there? That's Vega, the fifth bright-est star in the night sky. There's this folk-tale about a princess and a cowherd who fell

in love, but her father— Okay, wait, that's be-
side the point. I'll tell you that story some
other time. You'll cry, I promise. Anyway, below
Vega there's kind of this rhombus shape—there,
do you see it? Um, and then it's just kind of
a triangle up top—*there*, and that's it. That's
Lyra.

BEN

That's…Lyra.

CLARISA

Yep.

BEN

That's supposed to be an eagle?

CLARISA

An eagle carrying a lyre. Hence, you know,
Lyra.

BEN

I don't see an eagle. I also don't see a lyre.

CLARISA

Yeah, it's not a very good eagle carrying a
lyre. But I mean, none of the constellations

really look like what they're supposed to look like. That's why the point is kind of just learning the stories, you know?

I'm silent. I don't know what to say, and I don't think Clarisa expects a reply, either. For a second, we're both just standing there, hand in hand, looking at the sky. At Lyra, the eagle carrying a lyre that just looks like a cardboard box that's been knocked over.

CLARISA

(quietly)
We should go back.

BEN

Okay.

BEN (V.O.)

Clarisa pulls her hand out of mine as we start walking back toward the main grounds, and a part of me knows, somehow, that this is going to be the last time we're together like this, probably forever. I'm glad I'm dissociated when I come to that realization, because thinking about how it would affect me normally is kind of frightening. That's it, that's all, that's over.
The Girl has pulled her hand out of yours for the last time. The next time you see her,

you will smile and pretend none of this ever happened. The eagle is really just a box having delusions of grandeur and none of the other constellations are much better, either. The stars filling these constellations no longer spell out your name, for her. Or hers, for you. But maybe tomorrow she'll tell you the story about the princess and the cowherd, the one she was so excited about. And maybe it'll be one of those days when a story like that will actually make you cry.

MASON

NO ONE REALLY wants to be the one who tells her.

"Sorry I'm late," Stella says as she walks out of the cabin. "I feel terrible this morning." She takes a quick look at Jessie, who taps her pen against her clipboard and bites her lip. "I feel terrible most days, of course, but today I feel particularly terrible, though it's entirely unclear why. Clarisa, you look pretty terrible, too, not going to lie. And, Mason, *you*— well, you just look normal, so, terrible, and Ben looks— Wait, where's Andrew?"

I look down at my oatmeal. *Kind of thin*, I think. *Probably should've used milk instead of water.*

"He got stuck in his jeans, didn't he?" Stella says. "Honestly, I'm surprised it didn't happen earlier. His jeans are so tight that they're probably hazardous. Like, does Andrew want kids when he's older? Because if he does—"

"Stella," Jessie says quietly. This will be the one moment of the summer when she earns her entire paycheck.

"—he should really consider going up a size, or maybe four sizes. And while he's at it, maybe buy a few new colors? I mean, black is in, but—"

"Stella," Jessie repeats. She puts the pen down on the clip-board and folds her hands in front of her. "There was an in-cident," she says, "last night, involving Andrew."

I've looked back at my oatmeal, but I count the seconds that Stella is silent. *One. Would coffee creamer substitute for milk when making oatmeal? Two. I probably should've just gotten toast; this is kind of disgusting. Three. Or a bagel. You can never go wrong*—

"Oh, my God," Stella says. I look up. She looks shocked, but shocked in an uncertain way—like she can't tell if this is real or not, like she's still trying to figure out whether or not it's a joke. "Oh, my God," she repeats. The uncertainty is draining out of her expression as she looks around at the rest of us. "Oh, my God, *don't* fucking tell me—"

"Stella, please watch your—"

"What is it with you and telling me to watch my fuck-ing language?" Stella snaps. "Are you *seriously* going to tell me to watch my language right now, Jessie? Right now, of all times? I can deal with it every other fucking day of camp, even though—news flash! Teenagers swear—but *right now*?"

"Stella, listen to me," Jessie says. "Andrew is *okay*."

"He's okay," Stella repeats.

"He's going to be okay," Jessie says.

"Well, which is it?" Stella says. Her breathing is starting to get uneven. The hysterics are coming now. I can sense hys-terics coming from a mile away, a skill picked up from years of living with my mother. "Is he okay, or is he going to be okay? And where the fuck is he?"

"He's in the hospital," Jessie says. At least she's given up on trying to keep Stella from swearing.

"He's in the hospital," Stella repeats. "He's. In. The. Hos-pital. Andrew is in the fucking hospital." She takes another long, jagged breath.

"Well, let's go, then," she says suddenly. "I want to go."

"Campers don't leave camp grounds over the duration of their stay," Jessie says. "Perhaps after camp ends next week, when your parents come and—"

"When my parents come and pick me up?" Stella says, voice low. "When my parents come and pick me up? Oh, you mean when we have a flight back to Connecticut to catch in an hour and a half and who knows if Andrew is even still *in* the hospital and *is he fine, or is he* going *to be fine, Jessie, because those are two very different things.*"

"Stella, I understand your frustration. But even I don't have a lot of information right now. The hospital is in communication with Director Palmer, who has promised to let the counselors know as soon as more information becomes available, and we'll let you know as soon as we know anything. But for now, you should get some breakfast."

Stella walks over to the table that I'm sitting at and falls onto the bench. She brings both hands over her mouth and looks up at the sky. "Jesus fucking Christ," she says, blinking rapidly. "Jesus. Fucking. Christ."

"Stella," I start, but she cuts me off.

"Don't even start, Mason. I can't talk to you right now."

"I haven't even *said* any—"

"Did you say something to him?" Stella demands. I almost start laughing. One thing goes wrong and obviously her first reaction is to blame me. No wonder it's so difficult to be "nice" and "understanding" to these people. "Did you say something to him last night? Mason, if you said something to him, I swear to—"

"I didn't say anything to him! Jesus, you are being insane right now, do you realize that? Stop taking your feelings out on everyone else for once and just calm the fuck down!"

"I'm not taking my feelings out on anyone," Stella says. She's breathing hard, trying to keep her voice steady. "I just asked if you had said anything to him, because that would be totally unsurprising because you are an asshole!" Her voice has doubled in volume by the end of the sentence.

"You think that you're the only person who feels shitty about this? We all feel shitty about this, but you're the only person trying to pick a fight right now, Stella. You are the only person trying to make this my fault, when—"

"Do you feel shitty about this?" Stella says. "Do you, Mason? Do you really give a shit? Because you know what? I don't really think you do. I don't think you give a flying fuck about Andrew. Or anyone else, for that matter. I don't think you care that he's in the hospital. I don't think you care that—"

And that's when I lose it. Stella bitching at me relentlessly all camp is one thing, Stella talking in that insufferable tone of voice when she's been sent to this camp not once but *twice*, Stella thinking that she's the only one suffering—all of that, I would endure to carry out the resolution I made this week. But this is too much, and I feel something inside me snap along with, I suppose, my hopes of making it out of camp well liked. But who *cares* about that, really? Who *actually cares* about being liked by a bunch of unstable, emotionally incapable teenagers? Josh can take his "understanding breeds understanding" and shove it right back where it came from.

"Fine," I say to Stella. "You know what? You're right. I don't care. That's right. I don't care about you and I don't care about anyone else and I *certainly* don't care that Andrew's in the hospital, because guess fucking what, it means that he's not here, at this stupid, ineffective camp filled with stupid, ineffective peo—"

"What the fuck is wrong with you?" Stella shouts, and I'm so taken back that I cut off into silence. For all her craziness, I don't think I've ever heard Stella shout before. Hiss, swear, condescend, lecture, sure. But shout? What's happening in

front of me seems almost surreal: Stella, shouting at the top of her lungs, gasping for air every few words, hands clenching and unclenching in front of her as she yells. *"What the fuck... is wrong...with you?"*

"Stella," Jessie says, but she's way too late on that one.

"You have *no right*," Stella shouts. "No *goddamn...fucking... right*—to say that. How fucking *dare* you? Do you know how badly Andrew wanted this, Mason? Do you know how hard he worked for this camp? Do you have any fucking *idea* how much this meant to him, Mason, do you? Out of any of us—and you don't even count, Mason, you never should've been here in the first place—out of *any of us*, he wanted this the most. He deserved this the fucking most and now he can't have it and *how...fucking...dare...you?*"

Stella covers her face with her hands, breathing hard.

"Stella, I think you need to go spend a few minutes in your room," Jessie says.

"Okay," Stella says, nodding with her face still in her hands. She looks up at Jessie and then up at the sky again. "Oh, my God," she says again, voice cracking, and I almost think, for a few seconds, that we're going to go through that entire thing again—that she's going to lose it completely and start swearing at Jessie and yelling at me all over. But then she exhales sharply and pushes herself up off the table. "Okay, okay, okay," she says. She walks back into the cabin.

Fucking hell, I think. Stella picks one person to get weepy over and it's *Andrew*, for fuck's sake.

WEEK
FOUR

CLARISA

I'VE NEVER REALLY lost anyone before. I mean, there's
my dad, I guess. From what I hear from my mother—or more
from what I *don't* hear from her, really—he wasn't that great
to her or to me, and the divorce was apparently this messy,
protracted affair that lasted two years and almost left both of
them bankrupt from legal fees. But I was so young that the
only thing I remember is that for part of my life, my dad was
kind of around, and then for the next part of my life, he wasn't
even that. It doesn't really hurt to think about. It's just kind
of a thing that happened that I suppose must have been somewhat unpleasant, like remembering a particularly bad cavity
filling or the first time I got a B on a report card. All of my
grandparents and relatives are still alive, and when I think
about my friends, I realize that I'm probably the one *they* lost,
as opposed to the other way around. //

It feels weird to talk about "losing" Andrew, because it's
not like he died, nor is he going to die. For the morning and
most of the afternoon, Jessie keeps telling us that while we
don't have very much information right now, we do know
that Andrew is "definitely" going to be "okay." But how okay

can "okay" really be when things like this happen, anyway? I can't picture him waking up in the hospital, smiling, and thinking to himself, "Thank God I'm okay!" I can't picture Andrew waking up in the hospital at all actually, but I guess I've just never had much of an imagination. I can't picture the fact that Andrew is not coming back to camp, and that he's going to fly from the hospital back to Washington in a few days, and that my mother is going to drive us back to the city in a few days, and Stella is going to fly back to Connecticut, and everyone else is going to leave, and we are never going to see each other again. We are never going to get to say good-bye, or to understand what happened, so when it really comes down to it, we all lost Andrew. //

For some reason, I always thought that when people were dealing with loss and grief, time slowed down for them. Isn't that what all the books say? *She sat in her chair and stared at the photograph in her hand for what felt like hours, but when she looked up at the clock, she found that only five minutes had passed*, or something like that. But the opposite happens to me—the entire day goes by in a numb, surreal blur. It's like I'm sitting at the breakfast table and Ben is telling me about what happened, and then I blink, and Stella is screaming and losing her mind, and then I blink, and there's a movie playing in front of us, and then I blink, and we're at dinner and no one has anything to say, and then I blink one more time, and I'm lying in my bed waiting for Stella to finish brushing her teeth so that we can go to bed. But the thing is, even though the day goes by so quickly, it still feels like I've been sad for a really long time. There's an ache in my chest and I feel heavy all over and it's like I can barely remember a time when I didn't feel this way. //

"Hey," Stella says as she walks out of the bathroom. The clock reads 11:15 p.m. I feel like I've watched her walk out of the bathroom a thousand times over the past few weeks, always around this time, on days when camp feels like the best place in the world, on days when it feels like I'll do anything to get out and go back home. And I don't understand how suddenly, this time, everything could be so different. "How are you?" she asks, climbing into her own bed and pulling her covers around her. "I feel pretty bad," I reply. "Yeah," she agrees, "this is all pretty shit." //

I laugh, because I'm pretty sure that that's how Stella has characterized every single situation we've been in at camp so far, and this time she might actually be right. Then I realize that that's not very funny at all, and I want to start crying. "I just don't know what to do," I say. "Because I feel really sad, and...and obviously something really sad happened, and... and I just don't know what I'm supposed to say or do to feel better, you know? Like, this is how it is, and it sucks, but it's just how it is." "You feel helpless," Stella says. She turns onto her side so that she's looking at me. //

"So, what?" I say. "It just feels like this forever? Because it's not like we're ever going to be able to change what happened, or even go back and ask why, or see him again. We're always going to think about him when we think about camp, this is always where that train of thought is going to end, and that's—I mean, is that just it?" "I don't know," Stella says. "It feels like this, and it's all you think about all the time, and then one day, in a few weeks or a few months or a few years, you realize that you haven't thought about it in a long time. And that even though when you do, it feels sad, it also feels— I don't know, removed, somehow." //

Removed, somehow. It's hard to imagine losing Andrew ever feeling like losing my dad, who I barely knew. I wonder if Ben and Mason are having this conversation at the same time, just across the cabin. Or maybe Mason is just reading Mann and

Ben is just lost in his own head. We could meet up, I think. We could invite them over and talk about it, an illegal midnight unofficial therapy session that the counselors would actually probably be proud of. Stella must be thinking about the same thing, because she asks, "How are you and Ben?" //

"Oh," I say. "Oh, we're fine. I mean, we talked about everything last night, and—I mean, I think we resolved it." I look at her. Stella looks kind right now. Sad, sure, but the sadness has wiped all the sarcasm out of her expression and she looks open, vulnerable, like any other seventeen-year-old girl whose camp experience has just gone terribly wrong. Stella looks like how I feel and something about that is reassuring. //

"You were right," I add. "About that whole thing. It wouldn't have worked out." Stella drops her gaze. "I'm sorry," she says. "No, it's fine," I reply. "There's no hard feelings or anything, and…we'll probably even keep in touch." //

"Okay," Stella says, and it takes me a second to realize that she's crying. Not hard, not like Andrew was last night—*God*, I think, and it almost feels like I might start crying, too—but there are tears streaked down her cheeks, and every time she breathes, her breath catches a little. "Stella, are you okay?" I say. "I didn't mean to make you feel bad! I mean, honestly, *I'm* not even that sad about Ben anymore, you know? Please don't be upset about it. It's just a thing that happened that ended and that's—" //

"No," she says. "No, it's not your fault. It's not even about that, really. It's just…" She trails off for a second and sits up so she can blow her nose. "It's just, it makes me think of Kevin, is all. And how we're not friends anymore, and that—" she takes a shaky breath "—*sucks.*" //

"Do you still have his number? Just text him, Stella. I'm *sure* he'll be glad to hear from you. It's never too late to be friends with someone, you know?" "It's not like that," Stella says. "We tried." "Well, you can still—" //

"No, we really can't," Stella says. "We did that for almost a year. Breaking up, getting back together, breaking up, hating each other, forgiving each other, promising we'd stay friends, realizing we still loved each other, getting back together only for it to fall apart again. Eventually we realized that we just couldn't. Be friends, I mean. There's too much there, you know? Sometimes there's just too much bitterness, I think, and too much history and you're not even staying friends with a person anymore—you're staying friends with a history and a version of yourself and all these memories that you just...just need to let go of." //

"Oh," I say again. *I hate today*, I decide. Today is full of sad things that I can't do anything about, and that I can't say anything about, and that I can't make go away. Today is a helpless day. "I mean, maybe one day, when it's more removed," Stella says, "and I can think about it without it hurting so much. But now it's still so...so—" "—raw," I finish. //

"Yeah," Stella murmurs. "It's still really raw." I think briefly again about inviting the guys over. None of us are getting to sleep for a while, anyway. But I'm so tired, and my entire body feels like it's made out of lead. I have nothing to say, anyway, so how can I expect anyone else to have anything to say, either? Ben's theatricality will just make everything feel more surreal and Mason's callousness will probably make me cry. //

"Good night," I say to Stella. "It's a little too late for that, no?" she replies. "But good night, Clarisa." "Maybe tomorrow will be better," I add. I hear her laugh, muffled under the covers. "Yeah," Stella says. "Maybe." //

STELLA

PALMER COMES TO the next 1L therapy session and makes everyone sit through another one of his long, boring, meaningless speeches, which is just so typical of him, honestly. Does he really think he's going to be able to make any of us feel better by prattling on for ten minutes about nothing? That hearing some asshole in a suit who didn't even *know* Andrew—not the way we did, not after we spent the last three weeks of camp *with* him and he spent the last three weeks of camp sitting in some gray office churning out emails about a camp he only ever sees on the first day—tell us how to feel could possibly be a good idea?

"I'm sure all of you know what happened this weekend," Dr. Palmer says. They've collected us all by the picnic tables after breakfast and canceled our usual hike. *And for what?* I think. I would almost rather hike. Pain, I've learned, can be the easiest way to numb the pain.

"I have no intentions of wasting your time by dancing around the subject, nor by plying you with unnecessary information that only serves to distract. In the predawn hours of Saturday morning, Andrew tried to commit suicide. We can be nothing but thankful and relieved that he did not succeed, but are deeply saddened by the circumstances that precipitated the event in the first place. We at Camp Ugunduzi are working closely with doctors at the hospital Andrew is currently at to better understand how this occurred. In the meantime, you should know that Andrew is expected to make a full recovery, after which he will return home with his parents, who have been notified and are flying to New York right this moment. Camp will proceed according to schedule after lunch today. Until then, the counselors will be leading a session to help you better understand the events of the past couple of days and begin the healing process.

"We understand that this must be a difficult time for the rest of you. We have all come to know and love Andrew during our time together. I'm sure you are all feeling a wide range of emotions, which may range from shock to sadness to anger to confusion. These emotions are normal. The importance of that statement cannot be overstated, so I will repeat it once more: *these emotions are normal*. Throughout the last four days of camp, our counselors will be working to help you start to process these feelings as we move through this difficult period together, and your parents have been notified and encouraged to make plans as necessary for the weeks after your return home.

"Finally, if there is one thing that I cannot stress enough, it is that we are all going through this together. Oftentimes, in the aftermath of a tragedy, it is all too easy to feel alone, isolated, misunderstood, lost. I hope that if and when you feel this way, you'll take a step back and realize that we are experiencing those things together, and that there is a group of people here at Camp Ugunduzi who can and want to help you in every way we can. Please remember that. And please, if at any point in the coming days, your feelings or thoughts become overwhelming or unmanageable, speak to a counselor. We're here for you, and you're here for each other. Are there any questions?"

This is Dr. Palmer's defining characteristic, I realize. That no matter how long he talks for or what he says, by the end it all sounds like a bunch of white noise.

"Wonderful," Dr. Palmer adds. I don't think his facial expression has changed the entire time he's been speaking. "I'll leave you to it, then. And again, please don't hesitate to reach out if you need any support, advice, or anything else. I hope you have a last week of camp that is—if not good, per se—helpful and enriching."

He appraises us all for one last moment before walking off the grass, back into the counselors' cabin.

"That was bullshit," I say immediately. "I am amazed by how much bullshit that was. That was incredible. He could teach lessons."

"Stella!" Jessie says. "Was that a productive comment?"

"Was *that* a productive comment?" I retort. I don't want to get into it right now with Jessie, I really don't, but the idea that *I'm* the one making unproductive comments here makes something inside me explode. "What about Palmer, going on and on for ten minutes about who's been notified of what and who's going to help whom with what and who should be shoving what up their ass? Did no one bother to ask him if his entire speech was really a productive comment?"

"Stella," Josh says, "before we address your understandable anger—"

"I'm not angry, I'm stating a fact!"

"I'll give you a fact," Ben says. He sits down on the grass next to the tables. "I can't get Andrew out of my head. But I don't— It doesn't even *feel* like anything. I feel like I should—

well, I feel like I should *feel like* something, but I don't. I can't. I just keep seeing his face, over and over again."

"I feel like I don't even know what happened," Clarisa says. "I'm sad obviously, and I'm angry, but I almost feel more confused than anything else. Like…like I'm not processing that this is real yet. And my feelings haven't figured out what they're supposed to be."

"I feel shitty," I say. Because there's nothing more than that to say.

"Do you want to elaborate on that, Stella?" Jessie asks. "Like Ben and Clarisa did? Are you experiencing anything similar to what either of them described?"

"No," I reply. I don't want to elaborate on how I feel. I don't even want to *think* about how I feel. I say the next words slowly, forcefully, as if by doing so they'll magically become true. "I just feel shitty. And I…would like…to feel…better."

"Unfortunately," Jessie says, "we can't simply *will* ourselves to feel better. It's a nice idea, but the grieving process—and the healing process—can take weeks, months, yea—"

"Yeah, I know that," I snap. This is what I hate about therapy. The fact that all anyone can ever do is tell you the same things over and over and over again, and even when nothing they're saying works or makes sense or makes *anything at all better*, they're still saying those same fucking things. "Grief takes time, time heals all wounds, time, time, time, whatever. I'm just saying that I'm over it. I'm over grief taking time. I'm over wounds taking time to heal. I'm *over it.*"

"In times like these," Josh says, "it can be helpful to divide things into those that we can control, and those that we can't, and to devote our emotional energy into affecting things in the former category. Does anyone understand what I mean?"

"So basically," Mason says, "don't waste our time worrying about things we have no control over."

"Yes and no," Josh says. "Of course we'll worry about them. Of course we'll feel sad about them. We'll worry about Andrew getting better, and we'll feel sad that we didn't get to see him accomplish that, and perhaps we'll feel angry that we have so little control over the situation. That's all emotional energy, and that's all perfectly normal, and perfectly healthy. But at the end of the day, it's important to recognize that those are things we can't change. And so, while we accept our sadness and allow ourselves to worry and forgive ourselves the anger, it's also important to think of the things that we *can* control that can make for a healthier healing process. Can anyone give me any examples?" Josh asks.

"We can control how we cope," Clarisa says. "We can avoid ineffective coping mechanisms like blaming other people, or blaming ourselves, or, I don't know, alcohol." Clarisa's parents must be paying for one of those three-hundred-dollar-per-session Upper East Side shrinks, the way that rolls off her tongue. I can feel my sadness coiling up inside me and turning into white-hot rage, building and building and building until the force of it might kill me, I think, until it's so strong that I don't know whether I'm more angry or scared.

"Fine," I say. "FINE. I shouldn't blame other people, I shouldn't blame myself, and I shouldn't become an alcoholic. Really helpful. Totally needed Andr— Totally needed someone to get kicked out of camp for me to learn all those lessons, thanks. Meanwhile, no one can tell me what I *should* do."

"Well, that's different for everyone, Stella," Jessie replies gently. "Some people find that exercise makes them feel better, and some people find that writing about their feelings helps them move on, and most people find that talking with others who are undergoing similar experiences can be thera—"

"I'm not interested," I say, "in talking about my feelings, or in writing about my feelings, or in exercising. I'm. Not.

Interested. In. My. Feelings. I'm interested in making them go away."

I hear Clarisa take a breath in, as if she's going to respond, but then she seems to think better of it and exhales slowly.

"Why?" Josh finally says.

"What do you mean, 'why?'" I say.

"Why do you want to make your feelings go away?" Josh repeats. He looks around the circle at the rest of us. "And is there anyone else who feels similarly? Please, do share," he says.

"Why do I want to make my feelings go away?" I repeat slowly. I squeeze my eyes shut to tamp down the feelings, even knowing that it's no use.

"Why do I want to make my feelings go away?" I say again. No one responds.

This is it, I think. This is the point of no return. This is the moment at which I could count to ten slowly, I could snap a rubber band against my wrist, I could listen to soothing music, I could make lists of things I know to be true, I could call upon every single fucking coping mechanism I have learned from every single therapist I have ever been to, and it would still be useless. It would still be useless. Because this is everything that's happened in the past three weeks bubbling up inside me at once, filling my stomach and my chest and my head; this is the white-hot rage from five minutes ago exploding through my veins and my arteries and my body until I'm running on it, until I'm running on sadness and anger and fury.

"Because it fucking hurts!" I shout. "Because it fucking *hurts* to feel, and it fucking *hurts* to care, and because it's *pointless*, Josh, it's fucking pointless. There's no point. Maybe if you're some normal, happy, well-adjusted teenager living in a *Gossip Girl* novel preoccupied with what ridiculously priced handbag you're going to wear to school tomorrow and what ridiculously handsome boy you're going to fuck next—maybe *then*,

maybe when you know you're going to have a happy ending, maybe *then* there's a point. But for us? There is no point in caring about things and there is no point in caring about other people and there's *certainly* no fucking point in *hoping* for people, or for each other—or for *ourselves*, or—"

"I don't think that's true," Clarisa says quietly.

"THAT'S WHAT I'VE BEEN TRYING TO TELL YOU ALL FUCKING CAMP!" I say. "People like us don't have good things, Clarisa! People like me, who wouldn't be able to keep a good thing if it flew into my face and literally blinded me, and my parents, who literally can't even eat breakfast without breaking into a fight—THERE IS NO FAIRY TALE HERE. You get meds and you get good days and maybe, if you're lucky, you find someone who understands. But don't get attached because people…like…us…don't…have…good…things."

"Let's think about what you're saying for a moment, Stella," Jessie says, and the sound of her voice is enough to send me spiraling into rage all over again.

"AND THIS!" I shout before I can stop myself. Shouting at a counselor is grounds to get kicked out of camp, I know, but I don't care. I wish they'd kick me out, I really do. I wish they'd kick me out, I wish they'd kicked me out three fucking weeks ago, I wish I hadn't come in the first place, I wish, I wish, I wish, I wish, and it all dissolves into a rage that I direct in Jessie's face—

"THIS IS YOUR FAULT! NONE OF THIS WOULD HAVE HAPPENED IF YOU HADN'T MADE ME COME BACK THIS YEAR, JESSIE, NONE OF THIS WOULD HAVE HAPPENED IF YOU HAD JUST LET ME HAVE ONE FUCKING NORMAL SUMMER TO MYSELF—"

"I did not make you come back to Ugunduzi," Jessie says. Her voice is clipped. She almost looks sad, a fact which somehow makes me *more* angry. Who is she to feel sad right now? What right does she have? "I merely advised your parents that—"

"YOU ADVISED MY PARENTS THAT I WOULD BENEFIT FROM ANOTHER SUMMER HERE! WHAT THE FUCK WERE THEY GOING TO DO AFTER YOU SAID THAT, JESSIE? YOU DID THIS, YOU FUCKING—"

"Stella," Jessie interrupts. "Please lower your voice."

I stop yelling. Not because Jessie asks me to—no, that literally could not fucking matter less to me right now, not after everything she's put me through—but because I realize with a shock after I cut off that I've actually run out of things to shout. I realize with a start that I'm actually crying, that the anger has dissipated into an overwhelming sense of exhaustion, that what I really want is to just go home and go to bed and never, ever emerge.

"Yes," Jessie says. "I did advise your parents to send you back to Ugunduzi. Because I thought you needed it, Stella. You made tremendous progress last summer, but there were still so many ways in which I wanted the privilege of seeing you grow."

That's the other thing I fucking hate about Jessie. I can never tell if what she's saying is supposed to be nice or not.

"This summer has been difficult for you, I know," Jessie says. "But I'm proud of you."

"What?" I say.

"What?" Ben says.

Clarisa flops onto the grass and covers her eyes, as if to say, *Well, that's that, then.*

"I'm proud of you for letting yourself care, Stella," Jessie says.

"But I don't want to care," I retort.

"But you let yourself," Jessie says. "About Andrew. About

Andrew's well-being. About his happiness. You cared about him. And now you can't fight it off with a sarcastic comment or a snide remark, and that's *difficult*, Stella, but that's *good*."

"I'd like to un–let myself care," I say stupidly, ignoring the rest of her comment. My brain doesn't know how to process it, I think. I am physically incapable of comprehending her words.

"Do you?" Jessie says. "Do you really?"

I stare at her, at a loss. *Yes*, I tell myself to say. *YES*, I want to scream. *YES, I DO. I WANT TO TAKE IT BACK. I WANT TO START OVER. I WANT TO NOT CARE*. But I can't say the words.

"I don't know," Josh says pleasantly when my silence has stretched on for a solid minute. "I— Well." He looks serious for a moment. "I, too, am quite hurt right now. I've had the privilege of working with Andrew pretty extensively in individual therapy over the course of these weeks and found him wonderful in group, of course, and I grew to like and care for him, just as I've grown to like and care for each of you, and just as you've grown to like and care for each other. Losing Andrew is painful for me, just as I imagine it's painful for all of you. It's slightly different, of course—I haven't bonded with him in the same way that you all have—but the pain is there. When I think of Andrew, I feel helpless, and when I think of how I wasn't able to keep this from happening, I feel angry, and when I think of the fact that I will likely never see him again, I feel deeply, deeply sad. And yet.

"I am so happy," he says, "to have met Andrew. I am so happy to have been able to work with him, and watch him in his moments of progress, and watch him help you all through your moments of progress. Andrew was remarkable," Josh continues. "I'm sure many of you agree with me there. He was kind, and open, and caring. He was always willing to talk and never—not once—belittled someone else's problems. It was truly inspiring, to care about someone like that. Now, of course, we forget the joy, because we are hurt. Because we could not get him to see what we saw in him, because we may never have the opportunity to be with him again, because we don't know what to make of the feelings he's left us with. Those are all awful, awful emotions. I wonder, though, if we appreciate that our sadness, our anger, our confusion, are rooted in the same thing as the happiness Andrew brought us, at the hope he made us feel. Would I rid myself of this sadness, knowing that it would also mean giving up the joy of working with Andrew and really, truly, coming to care for him? I don't think I would."

And now I finally start to understand what Ben was talking about at the beginning of the session. Because as Josh is talking, I can see him. I can see Andrew in a thousand different images in a thousand different places: sitting on the floor of our bedroom, guitar cradled in his arms; lying on the grass, eyes shut and face peaceful; sitting in a circle at the pond, trying to explain the appeal of a gravity bong to Clarisa. He's talking about his band and he's laughing at something I said to Mason and he's squeezing his eyes shut, hoping desperately to get better.

I look over at Clarisa, sitting next to me. "Yeah," she says, and I wonder if she's remembering Andrew in all of the ways that I am. She must be, I conclude, because what she says next sends me into tears all over again even after I tell myself that I don't agree with her, that I can't, that Clarisa has never been more wrong.

"Yeah," Clarisa says. "I don't think any of us would, either."

The days after emotional breakdowns are always difficult to understand. Everything feels weirdly dulled and far away; I'm always sad, of course, because sadness doesn't go away that easily, but not in the sharp, piercing way that I'm used to. Instead, I'm sad in a dull, throbbing sort of way. An emotional hangover, I've always called it, and the fact that I've experienced it so many times to have a term for it almost makes me laugh.

I do okay through breakfast on Tuesday, because I refuse to talk to anyone and focus really hard on applying an even layer of cream cheese onto the cinnamon raisin bagel that I'm eating. Things get harder when we walk into our stupid Safe Space Cabin to put up the Christmas lights Clarisa guilted us into getting. I can't stop thinking about every other time we've gone into the cabin together, with Andrew, and tried to figure out how to design the damn thing, with Andrew, and painted the stupid walls, all with Andrew.

We all take a quarter of the ceiling of the main room and step on and off one of those step-up booster things, sticking little hooks to the ceiling and then stringing the Christmas lights across. I try to focus on my physical movements, and nothing other than my physical movements—pressing the stick-on hook to the ceiling, applying even pressure for ten seconds, taking one step down and then another step onto the floor off the ladder. I memorize the sequence of the colors of the individual bulbs on the string of Christmas lights as I pull it across the room—*red, blue, green, red, pink, yellow, blue, red, green, pink, yellow*—and try not to think about things like how, if Andrew were here, he would definitely have something to say, and he would say it, even if no one else seemed remotely interested in talking, something about his band and the time *they* put up Christmas lights together a year ago and how by the end there was a gravity bong involved, and then I'm smiling but also trying not to cry, because those stories were honestly so stupid, but the way he told them somehow made them endearing and *damn it, Stella, get ahold of yourself and focus*. I step back onto the ladder and look at the lights in front of me. *Red. Green. Yellow. Green. Pink. Blue. Yellow. Loop it over the hook. Step back down. Grab a hook off the ground and step back up. Do not think of him do not think of him do not think of*—

"Shit," Ben says, and his voice rings oddly loud in the silence.

"Language, Ben," Jessie murmurs from the corner. I turn around to look at him as he walks over to the wall on his side, where the guitar decal has come unstuck and fallen off the wall. He picks it up, smooths it out, and sticks it back.

The guitar decal, I think, and I swallow hard. *It's like he's haunting us. Focus, Stella*, I think again. I press the hook onto the ceiling and watch the nail of my thumb turn white as I push. I grab the string of Christmas lights from my other hand—*Pink. Yellow. Green. Blue. Yellow. Red. Green. Red. Pink. Blue.*

Blue.

The memory comes rushing back a second after the word registers in my brain: *blue*, one of the colors of Andrew's band, one of the colors that he spray painted that poor cat, *blue*, and I told him that it was a terrible color in that conversation and he didn't even say anything; he just kept on talking about... about— I don't know, what was he even talking about that session? Something about feeling bad that he was gaining weight and not being able to stop it and I should have known, God, why didn't I say something and *Jesus Christ, Stella, STOP THINKING ABOUT IT for the love of fucking God.*

"Fuck," I mutter. I pull the Christmas lights onto the hook and step back down, breathing hard. I turn around to make sure Jessie hasn't heard and see instead that the stupid decal has fallen off the wall *again*. Before I can stop myself, I walk over to it. It's a terrible decoration, I think. The guitar on it is an electric, when he probably would have wanted an acoustic, like the one he has, and it's cartoonish and kitschy and there's nothing remotely glamorous about it. I press it back against the wall, anyway, because I can't just leave it lying on the ground, first moving my hands around the edges and then pressing the center into place, thinking about how it's all wrong and how Andrew would've hated it and how Andrew hated the idea of getting it in the first place, and then I'm basically beating the stupid fucking decal into the wall, the stupid electric guitar that's all we have left of that stupid fucking boy, and all of a sudden I can't take it anymore. "Goddamn it," I say out loud, and my voice comes out twice as loud as Ben's when he broke the silence earlier. Everyone looks up from what they're doing, and I see Jessie take a breath, no doubt ready to tell me to watch my language. But I don't care anymore. "Goddamn it," I say again, and I must look insane, bent into the wall like this, both hands still pressed into the middle of the decal, trying to get the stupid thing to stay on the wall or maybe just trying to get it to stay out of my head. I pull my hands back, take two steps away, and watch as—of course—it falls back onto the ground.

Something inside me explodes, and it hurts. It really, really hurts. *If this is confronting my problems head-on*, I think, *then I was right all along. I want no part of this, none at all.* But the decal is on the floor and in my head and lodging itself inside my stomach like shrapnel and I don't know how to make it go away.

I turn around to face Jessie.

"Stella," she starts softly. *She's going to lecture me about language*, I think. *She's going to lecture me about language, and* then *she's going to lecture me about all the terrible things I said about her yesterday that for some reason she hasn't yelled at me about yet.*

But Jessie doesn't do either of those things. She just looks at me: inquisitive, waiting.

"Aren't you going to tell me not to swear?" I demand.

"Stella," she says softly. "You are an intelligent young

woman. I believe you should ask yourself if it was ever really about the swearing."

And *that* leaves me so taken aback that I almost forget what I wanted to bring up in the first place. "I think," I say evenly after a few moments, "that we should get a guitar. An acoustic. To put here."

I don't say "for Andrew," and I don't say "because that's what he deserves," and I don't say anything else stupid and corny, either. I don't have to. Everyone is thinking it, anyway.

For a minute, no one says anything. Out of the corner of my eye, I see Mason bury his head in his hands and Clarisa run her hands through her hair, taking deep breaths. But I keep my gaze on Jessie, who looks back at me, unreadable. "He wanted a guitar," I say, and I can feel my eyes filling with tears.

"Okay," Jessie finally says. I don't realize how tightly I'm holding the string of Christmas lights until I loosen my grip and realize that my palm is stinging from where my fingernails were digging into the skin. "I'll see if we can get it here by Thursday."

MASON

NOT TO SOUND like a complete asshole or anything, but I've pretty much checked out.

Camp has turned into Getting Over Andrew 101, as if we're all traumatized children and he's the father we lost in a terrible car accident or something. All of our therapy sessions are now focused around "managing our grief" and "moving on together" and "making sure we're in a good place when camp ends." But I don't need to manage my grief, because I don't really have any, and I don't need to move on from anything, since I'm not really behind. I don't know if I'll be in a good place when camp ends, but if I'm not, it won't be because Andrew went and tried to off himself. Even our conversations outside of therapy are always about Andrew now. Everyone spends one day brainstorming crazy ideas to get to the hospital where Andrew is—"maybe if we steal one of the counselors' cars?"—and another day recovering from the fact that none of those plans could ever, ever work. I feel like I'm stuck at a weeklong funeral for someone who hasn't even died.

It's not that I'm not sad that Andrew tried to kill himself. That's obviously a very sad thing, because it means that Andrew thought that his life wasn't worth living, just because he was 130 pounds, and that's ridiculous. Just the fact that he thought he looked better when he was severely underweight is appalling. That's just life, though, and I'll deal with Andrew the same way I deal with almost all of the other people in the world who are bad at understanding reality: by accepting it as an unfortunate fact of life and moving on.

There's a part of me that wonders, though, about how things would have been if Andrew hadn't done it. If Andrew had gotten up with the rest of us that morning, dragged his skinny ass to breakfast, and stared miserably into his oatmeal for half an hour the way he did every single other morning. Then Stella never would have started screaming, and I never would have tried to help her, and she never would have lost her temper at me for no reason at all. It doesn't really matter, of course, because camp is basically over and we're all leaving and soon all of Stella's misdirected anger will be nothing more than a distant memory.

But still. I can't keep myself from wondering.

On Wednesday, we go for our last hike of the summer. It's the same trail we did for the first hike, because doing the same hike twice is apparently supposed to demonstrate something about how much stronger we've become and how much our perspectives have changed over the last four weeks at camp.

They're right about that first part. I remember getting winded the first time we did this trail, but this time, the effort barely registers. No one else looks particularly tired, either, and Clarisa and Ben actually end up racing the last half mile. This leaves me and Stella walking behind them, a fact that Jessie seems to find alarming. She's a couple of feet in front of us but keeps turning around every few minutes, presumably to make sure that neither of us has pushed the other off the mountain.

"You don't have to worry, you know," Stella says after five minutes of relentless suspicion. "He's not worth life in prison."

Jessie and I laugh at the same time. "You can never be too careful with the two of you," she says.

"The two of us?" I say, feigning outrage even though she's probably right. "We're saints!"

"Angels," Stella says. "We are angels." It feels weird to hear her sarcasm being deployed on my side for once, but then I remember that, really, she's just on her own side.

"That so?" Jessie says. She falls back a few steps so that she's walking in line with the two of us. I've never liked Jessie. This entire camp, she's been such a control freak, always telling us that we need to stop swearing and be respectful and all that other bullshit. But she looks relaxed today for some reason.

The end of camp, I think. It's filled everyone with this lazy good mood, this affection for everyone else that doesn't make any logical sense.

"How's heaven these days?" Jessie asks.

"Beautiful, of course," I reply. "But a little boring, to be honest. Things have really slowed down in the last millennia. Ever since Lucifer got kicked out, things just haven't been the same, you know?"

"Things do get a little dry without someone to stir up trouble," Jessie agrees. "That's why we keep inviting Stella back."

Stella turns to look at Jessie, shocked. "Shots fired," she says.

"As if you haven't been the one firing them all camp," I say.

Stella laughs, looks down at the ground. "Yeah, that's fair," she murmurs. "But seriously," she adds, "I'm not coming back."

"Yeah?" Jessie says.

"Yeah. I'm gonna have a good year. I'm over this." We're coming up in the final stretch now—I can see the turn where the trees disappear and the cliff lies, just out of sight. "Then again," Stella adds, "I said that last year, and look what happened with that…"

"You're a different person now, Stella," Jessie says. "You know that as well as I do."

"She must have been pretty damn bad last year, then," I say.

Stella elbows me in the side. "Yeah, I probably *actually* would have pushed you off the mountain."

"Because you were tough enough to make it through jail last year?" I ask.

Stella snorts. "Because I didn't care what happened to my life last year."

"Oh."

Empathy, I think. *This is one of those situations when I am supposed to have empathy.* But what does she want from me, really? If she had no self-respect, that was her problem. I try to think of something to say—something that won't make Stella hate me, but something that isn't a meaningless platitude.

"It's fine, Mason," Stella says, smirking. "And besides, here we are. Same place we were the first time we hiked together. God, do you remember that? Josh was leading it and you were fucking exhausted. It was pathet—"

Now it's my turn to elbow her in the side, and she cuts off, laughing. Ben and Clarisa are sitting together on the rocks already. It's so windy that it's hard to hear what they're saying to each other, but every now and then, one of their laughs comes floating through the air to where Stella, Jessie, and I are.

"Watch your language," Jessie says, but she's smiling.

"You're always going to be there to nag me about that, aren't you?" Stella says. But she's smiling, too.

"Yes," Jessie says. There's a moment's pause when they look at each other. And then she adds softly, "Think of it as another reason not to come back."

"Yeah," Stella says. She hesitates. It almost looks like she's about to say something else sappy and emotional and dumb, but then she snaps out of it. "Well, aren't you going to make us get in a circle and talk about how much we've learned, and how much we've changed, and how it's the *same mountain* but looks *totally different* given the *newfound perspectives* that we've developed over the course of the past four weeks?" Stella says. She rolls her eyes so many times while saying that one sentence that I feel a little dizzy by the time she's done.

"Hmm," Jessie says. "No."

"What do you mean, 'no'?" Stella says.

Jessie laughs. "Well, you guys can talk about that if you want," she says. "But I don't think you all need me to facilitate this discussion. You can do it yourselves if you really want to."

"Do it *ourselves*?" Stella says. "Are they paying you to let us *do things ourselves*?"

"Stella, you all only have two days left with each other. I'm not going to take that away from you."

Stella looks from Jessie to Ben and Clarisa to me, and then at the ground. "Two days, huh?" she says.

"Two days," I repeat. "Thank God," I add.

She looks up at me and laughs. "Yeah," she repeats softly. "Thank God. Well, we might as well go sit with Ben and Clarisa and pester them while we can."

Stella walks over to Ben and Clarisa and sits down next to them, but I hang back for a second and look out at the sky. They were wrong, of course, on that whole perspective thing. Nothing's changed since the last time we were here. It's actually amazing how exactly the same it looks. The same red tape across the dirt a few feet away from the ledge, the same drop-off, the same expanse of treetops below and endless sky above.

"Hey," I say to Jessie, who has gone back to writing notes on her clipboard.

"Hmm?" she says.

"I don't think anyone here is that great," I start, and she looks up at me, eyebrows raised. "I didn't mean that in a mean way. I just meant that I feel like I have different goals and priorities and problems from most of the other people here," I explain.

"Okay," she says. "And that's fine, Mason."

"A really important skill when it comes to getting what you want and being successful in life," I continue, "is being able to make other people who have different values and priorities like you."

"Well, I don't know that that's *necessarily*—"

"It is," I say. "So how do you think I did?"

"What?" Jessie says.

"Like, if this were the real world, and they were the various different people I needed to get on my side. How would I have done?"

Jessie looks incredulous, which *I* feel incredulous about because it's a perfectly valid question. "You're asking me if they *like* you?" Jessie says. "Why don't you just go over and ask them yourself?"

"They're all emotionally confused," I reply. "It's useless trying to get a straight answer out of any of them. So I'm asking your professional opinion."

"You're asking my professional opinion on whether or not Stella, Clarisa, and Ben like you," Jessie repeats. There's a smile spreading across her face that I don't like.

"Never mind," I say. "Forget it."

"All right," Jessie says, now making no effort to disguise her smirk.

"It is all right," I say. "Because I am going to be back in Bethesda in forty-eight hours and I will never, ever have to come back."

"You know," Jessie adds, ignoring my comment, "it was a perfectly legitimate concern."

"It's not a legitimate concern. I mean, it is a legitimate concern to the extent that whether or not people like you allows you to do things in life and whatnot, but it's not a legitimate concern in that whether or not crazy people like you is—not— important." I shrug, and walk over to Clarisa and Ben and Stella. When I look back a few minutes later, Jessie is writing on her clipboard again.

"What were you two talking about?" Stella asks.

"Oh," I say. "Just some bullshit about perspective and changing and how it all looks now."

"Rough," Stella says. "What's the conclusion?"

"Looks the exact damn same," I reply.

"Sounds about right," Stella says. And she smiles.

On Thursday, the wall mount and guitar Andrew wanted comes in.

We take turns hammering two nails into the wall, each taking a swing and then passing the hammer to the next person. It's poetic and symbolic, I guess, but also a completely inefficient usage of our time.

After we've gotten the wall mount secured, Stella picks up the guitar and hangs it up on the mount. And then that's it. That's the closure everyone's been looking for. That's the way we've chosen to preserve Andrew's memory, or whatever it is they all think we're doing.

We all take a step back and look at the guitar. *It looks really, really dumb*, I think. It looks like a team of rookie interior decorators went mad and decided to stick a guitar on a wall between two movie posters in a sea of Christmas lights, because that's basically what happened. Still, though, it's what

Andrew would have wanted, and what Andrew would have wanted is apparently now what everyone else wants.

"Well," Stella says uncertainly, "I guess we're done, then."

Clarisa is crying again for some reason. She rests her head on Stella's shoulder, and Ben slides his arm around her.

"Yep," I say.

BEN

EXT. CAMP UGUNDUZI MAIN GROUNDS—NIGHT

The fire is blazing. The s'mores are on the table. The mic is set up. All the groups are sitting at their picnic tables with the counselors, and even Dr. Palmer—who's hovering in the back like an eagle, clad in a gray suit once again—has made an appearance.

BEN (V.O.)

This is the last night of camp.

Jessie's at the microphone, giving a speech about how much she's enjoyed working with us, and how honored she is, and how she hopes we always remember that emotional health is something maintained, not simply won. I wonder if closing speeches always feel this dramatic at Camp Ugunduzi, or if maybe that's just me.

There's something really nice and poetic about tonight. I spent the entire first day of camp feeling like I was walking into a movie, and now I'm spending the last night of camp feeling like I'm walking out of a movie, and maybe, when I look back on it, everything that happened in between will feel like a movie, too. Maybe even one that's better than *Wet Hot American Summer*.

JESSIE

And now I'd like to invite Clarisa from the 1L block to the microphone for her first Art by the Fire performance. Clarisa, I know how much bravery this is taking for you, and believe me when I say that I am so proud.

BEN (V.O.)

Clarisa walks from the picnic tables to the microphone looking calm, peaceful, and at some point between the time when she smiles at me before getting up and the time when she makes it to the other side of the fire where the mic stands, something in my brain explodes and all of a sudden there's a montage playing in front of my eyes, violins swelling and piano embellishments going off in the background and one mournful, sweeping cello underneath it all—

INT. CAMP UGUNDUZI MAIN GROUNDS—DAY—FLASH-BACK

The FIRST DAY OF CAMP. We're sprawled out

across the grass in front of Jessie and Josh, introducing ourselves, everyone glancing around at everyone else to try to figure out what they should be doing. Clarisa looks petrified.

CLARISA

Clarisa, sixteen. I'm from the city. New York, I mean. New York City. Um, I like— I like the countryside, and Romantic poetry—Romantic as in the time period, not as a general adjective—and reading, and stargazing, and, uh, the color green, and the spring, and numbers. Sorry, that was a lot, but it had to be seven, and, oh, yeah, OCD and anxiety. And—yeah, that's it.

EXT. THE RIDGE—NIGHT—FLASHBACK

The SECOND NIGHT OF CAMP. We're at The Ridge for the first time, and the sleep deprivation from the night before combined with the thrill of sneaking out has left us all buzzed, inordinately social. Clarisa, Andrew, and I are sitting on a log by the campfire. Andrew's frazzled, in the process of walking away, when he says—

ANDREW

I just want to think for a bit.

—and leaves the two of us.

BEN

Guess it's just us, then.

CLARISA

Yep.

The two of us fall silent, each turning to stare into the flames.

BEN (V.O.)

I should say something. I know I should say something. This is one of those situations where I should definitely have something to say, and I *would* have something to say, if only lack of practice hadn't left me absolutely incapable of social interaction. Oh, God, would it be normal to ask her what her favorite movie is? Is that a normal question to ask someone in this situation?

BEN

So what's your favorite movie?

Clarisa doesn't look away from the fire, or move at all, for that matter.

BEN (V.O.)

Shit. That was a weird thing to say, wasn't it? Jesus Christ, Ben, what a—

CLARISA

Oh, God, sorry. Did you say something? Sometimes I just get really lost in my own head, you know? Like, people are talking around me, and I'm just— I'm totally in my own thoughts. It's kind of a problem.

BEN (V.O.)

I have watched upward of a hundred romantic comedies over the course of my short and pathetic life and not one of them has featured a meet-cute like this. I have lost the ability to talk. Clarisa is staring at me now like she's worried that *she's* crazy and I have actually *lost the ability to talk* and, BEN, YOU NEED TO SAY SOMETH—

BEN

I...I totally understand what you're saying.

CLARISA

Yeah?

BEN

Yeah.

INT. SAFE SPACE CABIN—DAY—FLASHBACK

Stella is holding a sheet of paper and a pen, looking at Clarisa expectantly. Clarisa looks at me, an expression of the deepest longing on her face. From the desperation on her face, you'd think we were arguing over the best way to save a dying child, as opposed to whether or not Christmas lights will look good in a cabin we'll never see again after the end of the summer.

CLARISA

Come *on*, Ben, think about how, you know, moody and ambient and atmospheric they are. Please?

I raise my hand.

EXT. THE RIDGE—NIGHT—FLASHBACK

The STARS above. The EARTH below. CLARISA lying next to me and we are definitely, *definitely*, not supposed to be here right now, but when Clarisa turns her head, there's not a single doubt left in my mind.

CLARISA

Do you want to go back?

BEN

We can go back. Or we can stay. It's really up to you.

The hint of a smile plays at the corner of her lips. I can see myself reflected in her eyes.

CLARISA

Okay.

INT. SAFE SPACE CABIN—FLASHBACK
The SECOND WEEK OF CAMP, and the days are all starting to blend together into one. I'm arguing with Mason—who at this point has revealed himself to be an INSUFFERABLE PRAT—in the middle of the room.

MASON

There are four walls, and four people other than me. Why do I have to help, Ben?

BEN

You have to help because...because—

CLARISA

Because Ben and I are going to paint the front wall together.

Clarisa stands up and walks over to Mason and me, one hand on her hip, the other pointing at the wall. She looks evenly at Mason.

CLARISA

And it's totally fair, because that wall is basically twice the size of Stella's.

BEN

Oh, shit.

EXT. THE RIDGE—NIGHT—FLASHBACK
We are kissing.
INT. BOYS' CABIN—NIGHT—FLASHBACK

BEN

SHE BASICALLY SAID THAT SHE DIDN'T CARE ABOUT ME AT ALL!

ANDREW

Ben, I don't think that's what she said.

MASON

But it's probably what she meant. Girls suck, dude. You just gotta hit it and quit it.

BEN

Hit it and quit it? *Hit it* and *quit it*? That sounds like the kind of thing that lands you in *jail*, Mason.

EXT. CAMP UGUNDUZI MAIN GROUNDS—DAY—FLASHBACK
It all still feels like a dream. Clarisa places her bagel onto the table and sits down next to me.

CLARISA

Hey. You look exhausted.

BEN

Clarisa…

CLARISA

I'm exhausted, too, honestly. We were out so late last night, but I'm glad.

BEN

Clarisa…

CLARISA

What? Ben, are you okay?

BEN

(all in one breath)
Last night after we got back I think Andrew
tried to kill himself I don't know what happened but when I woke up he wasn't there and
Jessie wouldn't give me any specifics but he's
still not here and I just keep remembering how
he wouldn't stop crying and oh my God Clarisa
what if—

CLARISA

Hey. Breathe. It's gonna be okay, all right?

She puts her hand on my shoulder and squeezes
it.

BEN

I— All right.
EXT. MOUNTAINTOP—DAY—FLASHBACK
It is THE BEGINNING OF THE END. Stella and
Mason are standing with Jessie, a few feet away.
There is so much to see in front of us. We are
so small. I look out at the trees and the sky,
and then back at Clarisa, and then back at the
trees and the sky.

BEN (V.O.)

This is the last time I will take in this view. This is the last time I will see these trees and this sky with this girl sitting next to me and this is the last time I will sit on this small piece of Earth and pray for the clock to stop, for time to freeze, for the universe to stop expanding for a second and just let me have this small moment to myself for a little bit longer. This sky. These trees. Clarisa.

BEN

This is it, isn't it?

Out of my peripheral vision, I see Clarisa turn to look at me and smile.

CLARISA

Yeah, Ben. This is it.

EXT. CAMP UGUNDUZI MAIN GROUNDS—NIGHT—END FLASHBACKS
Clarisa is standing at the microphone.

CLARISA

I have this poem that I really want to share with you guys. I didn't write it, unfortunately, because—well, I have no writing talent. So there's that. But it's a really nice poem, written by Lord Byron, who, for all his, um, ill-advised and reckless love affairs, was actually quite talented.

Clarisa catches my eye and winks.

CLARISA

Anyway, before I start reading the poem, I wanted to talk for a few seconds about something. I didn't actually prepare anything, so I'm just going to kind of ramble—sorry—but I do want to say thank you to everyone.

I've never been really social. When my mom told me that she was making me come here this summer, I had a panic attack. She—well, I always thought that what my mom wanted more than anything was for me to just have normal experiences, and be a normal teenager, and have normal teenage problems, you know? Things like finishing my algebra homework on time, and whether or not the cute guy in geography would text me back, and all that stuff. I figured that she wanted me to live the same awesome teenage years that she got to live, which I just—well, I've just never been able to do that. And I always felt bad, because I felt like I was letting her down a lot.

So when she told me she was sending me here, I felt like it was bound to be just another situation in which she wanted me to be normal and I just couldn't do it, because I'm just not normal.

So, anyway, I thought it was going to be awful. And it was, at first. But then I talked to a few people, and I got to know everyone, and maybe the Zoloft kicked in somewhere in the middle there, too, and I started to really… have…fun. Which sounds incredibly stupid, now that I'm saying it out loud. But—I don't know. I came to really love Ben's stupid monologues, and Stella's sarcasm, and Mason's bluntness, and Andrew's…Andrew's— Jesus, one second.

Sorry, it's still— It's still hard. And Andrew's *music*. And I loved who I was around it all.

And I guess I just want to thank you all for that. I didn't have a normal camp experience, and I didn't become a normal teenager, but I've been really happy. And I figure maybe that's what my mom really wanted all along.

Clarisa looks down at the sheet of paper she's holding and wipes a few tears away, laughing.

CLARISA

Okay, I'm just going to read the poem now. It's called "So We'll Go No More a Roving." I hope you guys like it.
(a beat)
So, we'll go no more a roving.
So late into the night.

Though the heart be still as loving.
And the moon be still as bright.
For the sword outwears its sheath,
And the soul wears out the breast,
And the heart must pause to breathe,
And love itself have rest.

Though the night was made for loving,
And the day returns too soon,
Yet we'll go no more a roving.
By the light of the moon.

Clarisa stops reading. Clarisa starts crying. Clarisa must know that I didn't understand a single word of the poem she just read, but goddamn was it beautiful.

CLARISA

And that's it. Thanks, guys. Really. Thank you so much.

BEN (V.O.)

And that's it. The music is louder than ever as she reads her poem, strings swirling in a mad crescendo so intense that I can barely register the words she's saying at the microphone. But by the time she's back at the table, sitting next to me, blowing her nose, mumbling about how ridiculous that was, and laughing to herself all the while, the strings have faded into silence and the piano melody has trailed away and my head is the kind of silent that rings in the air. If this were a movie, this right here would be the end of the third act, this right here would be the moment when the waterworks start, because the only thing meant to tug harder at the heartstrings than sweeping violin crescendos and repeated piano melodies in minor keys is when they burn away and there is nothing left of all that splendor but silence.

CLARISA

Wow, that bad, huh?

BEN

You were great, Clarisa.

CLARISA

Really? Because I feel like I read everything too fast, and I didn't say at least three of the things I actually wanted to say in the introduction, and then I definitely repeated the same things I did say over and over and over again, and I feel like—

BEN

Clarisa, it was really nice.

CLARISA

Thanks, Ben.

BEN (V.O.)

We're just friends, I know. We're just friends, and it's for the better, and even if it weren't, this is how we've arrived at page one hundred and twenty of the screenplay and that's just how it is. But now Clarisa is looking at me, and I'm looking at her, and maybe we hold the eye contact for a few seconds too long, because Stella is making quiet vomiting noises that neither of us are acknowledging and it's all too easy to wish that there could be a fourth act on the other side of this scene.

JESSIE

Stella! You're up!

Stella walks up to the microphone and makes a face, like she's being forced to jump into a cold pond in the middle of winter, or chug a gallon of orange juice after brushing her teeth, or one of those other stupid things that kids who are bored at home do for the sake of getting famous on YouTube.

STELLA

I want to talk about Andrew.

I'm not usually the type of person who wants to talk about things, especially not things that make me upset. I prefer to just never think about them and hope they go away, which is actually about the same way that I deal with things like homework I haven't done or life ambitions I'll never achieve.

The problem is, I couldn't stop thinking about it. Andrew, I mean. I would close my eyes and picture him talking to me, telling me about how badly he wanted to tour the Northeast. I would open my eyes and wish he was there, standing in front of me with his guitar tossed over his shoulder. It's like being in love, except even worse, because you can't just project your feelings onto someone else. Saturday was like that. Sunday was like that. Monday was like that. Tuesday was—well, you get the idea. And all this time, I just kept asking myself, *Why do you care so much, Stella? Why?*

Well, it's been almost a week now, and I think I'm starting to understand why losing Andrew was so hard for me. It's because— It's because—

Stella bites her lip, turns away from the microphone for a second. When she turns back, she's taking long, shaky breaths.

STELLA

It's because I have to believe that Andrew is going to be okay. I have to. I have to believe that Andrew is going to realize that he is an amazing musician, and his band is so lucky to have him, and that it doesn't matter how much he weighs, and that he's so great a person that it wouldn't matter, *anyway*, honestly, and I just have to believe that he's going to be okay, someday, someday soon, yesterday, preferably, but since that didn't happen, just soon. I have to believe that Ben is going to finish his movie script and make it big in Hollywood and come to be known as some crazy-yet-brilliant director who is miserable to work with because you never know whether he's talking to you or talking to himself, and I have to believe that Clarisa is going to realize that she's right about everything she's said about me, that I'm bitchy and moody and jealous of other people's happiness, and, Clarisa, I have to believe that you'll never let yourself become that person, become who I am, and...and I have to believe that Mason is going to, I don't know, become a better person, somehow, and that he's going to be okay, too. I have to believe that you're all going to be okay, because I have to believe that I...am going to be...okay.

Stunned silence.

STELLA

And that's it. That's it. Thanks. Sorry. Thanks.

CLARISA

I think you're okay, Stella.

I nod vigorously as Stella walks back to the picnic table.

BEN

Better than okay. O-K-*plus*. O-K-*plus*-plus.

Stella's choked up, trying to keep it together. We watch as she takes a deep breath and finally manages to laugh. Another deep breath, no doubt gearing up to express how touched she is at our glowing testimonial to her character—

STELLA

God, shut the fuck up.

DR. PALMER (O.S.)

If I may?

As she looks up to see Palmer standing at the front, tapping on the microphone and smil-

ing at us like we're a collection of lab rats
that have won him a Nobel—

STELLA

("fuck off" sweetly)
Of course you may.

DR. PALMER

Wow. Wow. What incredible performances, from
everyone. What astounding, disarming honesty.
What stellar writing. What courage. I am so, so
impressed by all of you. Truly. You know how I
know when I've watched something amazing? When
I step away from it and I realize that it's not
just that I've learned something about Andrew,
or Britney, or Camille, or Mason. I've learned
something about myself. I've learned something
about the way...

BEN (V.O.)

Dr. Palmer rambles on about how amazing we
are, but everyone's zoned out by the third sentence. Stella whispers something about how she
heard this all last year, and rolls her eyes so
hard I feel tempted to tell her that her face
might get stuck that way. Clarisa is tying her
hair into a long, neat braid. Mason is digging
into his tenth s'more of the evening. And I'm

just— I'm just looking around at everyone, trying to take it all in.

Maybe I should pay attention. Everything Palmer says sounds like it comes straight out of a monologue, and there's something cinematic about how he looks right now in his gray suit, standing on the other side of the dying flames. If camp were a movie, Palmer's speech would play over the last scene as the camera swept upward over the night sky and the violins swelled one last time and the audience started crying all over again.

Camera follows Ben's narration—over the fire, the campers, the sky—and we FADE TO BLACK.

BEN (V.O.)

But then again, maybe that's not the point.

CLARISA

"HOW ARE YOU FEELING?" my mother asks me, the moment she steps on the gas, and the question is so astonishingly *normal* that I burst out laughing. My mother looks at me like I've lost it. "Sorry," I say. "That question is just so…standard, you know?" "And standard has become a bad thing?" she replies, sounding faintly amused. "Not bad," I reply. "It's just—well, all of camp felt so surreal, and thinking back on it even now feels so surreal, and so to hear a question like that is just kind of, I don't know, amusing." //

I watch the last of the camp grounds disappear from view behind us as my mom turns onto the ramp to the highway. *That's it*, I think. It feels like the millionth time I've thought that phrase in the past twenty-four hours. But this time, it really is. It really is all over. "I'm feeling okay," I say to my mother. "A little sad, though." //

"I'm sorry, honey," she says. "Is it because of—you know—*the boy*?" She lowers her voice to a whisper as she says the last two words, as if Ben will magically materialize in the backseat if she mentions him too loudly. "Oh, Ben?" I say. "No, not really. I mean, I'll miss him, of course. But it's about everyone else, too." //

"You never did tell me what ended up happening with Ben," she says. Outside my window, the miles are starting to fly by, exit numbers dropping rapidly as we drive south. The trees are thinning out on both sides of the highway, leaving towering stacks of boulders in their place. Soon those will disappear, too, and be replaced by scattered houses. And then those will be replaced by skyscrapers, and then—well, then I'll be home. "I didn't, did I?" I say, feeling a pang of guilt. The last week of camp was so hectic that I completely forgot to write her. //

"No," my mom says. "Or how living with Stella was in the last few days, or how you're feeling about Andrew..." She trails off. *What happened with Ben?* I think. *And how was living with Stella? And how am I feeling about Andrew?* I don't know the answer to those questions, much less how to explain them to someone else. //

I should tell her about the fight, I decide. I should tell her about the fight, and then how we made up, and I should tell her that we decided to just be friends, and how I think that's the right decision, I really do, even though when I think of that now, something inside me still aches like I've lost something. But if I tell her all that, then I'll have to tell her about the sneaking out. She might not be thrilled about that part. But on the other hand, I doubt she'll be too angry. My mother's been to summer camp, and who goes to summer camp without sneaking out at night? And if I tell her about the sneaking out, I might as well tell her about that first night with Ben, too, out at The Ridge, underneath the stars, and how being with him was like discovering something new and magical, like the first time I looked upward and traced the constellations with my eyes. //

And after I tell her about Ben, I should tell her about Stella, and how even after four weeks of living with her and fighting with her and—toward the end—crying with her, I'm still not entirely sure where Stella and I stand, or where we ever stood. I should tell her about Stella's speech and how she said that she hoped that I would never become her, and how that didn't make any sense to me, because Stella is one of the strongest people I've ever met. I should tell her about how I wanted to tell her that, this morning, when I said goodbye to her, but I was afraid to, I guess—afraid that she'd just end up throwing something at my head and telling me to "get the f★★★ out of the cabin already" or something like that. And so I just said, "Bye, Stella—text me when you land, okay?" and she just said, "Yeah, will do—have a safe trip," and then I left. I should tell her about how I regret that now, in the way you always regret not saying things the moment it becomes too late to say them. *But maybe it's not too late*, I think, feeling my phone in my pocket. Maybe I'll text her or something, now that I'm out of target practice range. //

And then after *that*, I guess I'll tell her about Andrew. Saving Andrew for last seems like the right decision, because I'll probably be crying too hard when I'm done with that to say much more. Where do I even start with Andrew? I can tell her about how beautiful his music was, of course, but that won't bring it back. And I can tell her about how desperately he tried to get better, but that won't make it easier for him to succeed. And I can tell her about how much I miss him. But that'll do the least out of any of those. //

In the end, I decide to just tell her all of those things. And maybe then I'll bring up my father, which we've never really talked about. Maybe I'll ask her if losing him ever felt like she was racing against time to stop something that had already happened. I turn around and grab a bottle of water from the backseat. "A lot happened with Ben," I say. I don't realize how much time has passed since she asked the question in the first place until I see my mother raise her eyebrows, surprised that I've spoken. "So I might as well start from the beginning." //

STELLA

I'M THINKING OF Andrew's band as the plane takes off.

I don't know why. The memory comes out of nowhere, right as the plane's wheels leave the runway and it starts to climb. I guess it's like all the other repressed memories buried back there in the depths of my subconscious, waiting for the worst possible moment to pop up and make it impossible for me to move on.

What I'm remembering is from one of the very first days of camp, the day I took everyone out to The Ridge for the first time. I was trying to pass this note to Andrew telling him and the guys to come to our room after lights-out. All I needed was for him to say a few words to me so Jessie wasn't too suspicious and then take the damn piece of paper out of my hand.

But Andrew wouldn't shut up. I made the mistake of asking him about his band, and then he went on and on about how it was called The Eureka Moment, and how serious that name was, and how long it took them to come up with it. Eventually I just gave up, grabbed his hand, and forced the piece of paper into it. I swear, he looked almost as petrified as he looked that one morning when he was confronted with a bagel. It would have been amusing, if it weren't such a sad statement about how unapproachable I apparently am.

I never told Andrew this, but I think I get it. How he felt with his band when they couldn't come up with a name, I mean. I know what it feels like in those moments when you've been sitting in some basement trying to brainstorm for hours and hours, when you've tried every possible solution and still haven't found the one that actually works. You start Prozac. You go to wilderness therapy camp. You try to fall in love, and then you try to fall out of love. And you wait. You wait and you wait and you wait for the second when these things all come together in a flurry of sparks and sunlight and you magically transform into a happy, well-adjusted person who goes to school and has friends and doesn't spend half her days lying in bed trying to remember today's excuse to keep living. You wait so much that you forget that there are things that used to make you happy, that there are kinds of love that make you a better person, that life is worth living even if it really, really sucks.

I've spent a lot of my life waiting on that damn eureka moment, but what I'm starting to realize is that maybe it never comes. Maybe we go through our entire lives trying to find the right therapist and the right meds and the right people to surround ourselves with, and on some days it works, and on some days it doesn't, and that's just how it is. Maybe eureka moments, like the meaning of life and romances that end well, belong in Ben's melodramatic, half-finished screenplays, and not in real life. Maybe we never get that moment when the clouds part and the sun comes shining down and everything is suddenly clear and right and life is beautiful, grand, rich with meaning.

Maybe all we get are things like Clarisa and I making it through camp without killing each other, and Mason becoming a halfway (okay, quarter-way) decent person by the end of it all, and the fact that the rest of my life is waiting on the other side of this flight, far away from the endless beauty and the endless hikes and the endless rules of Camp Ugunduzi. And maybe, for now, that's good enough for me.

★ ★ ★ ★ ★

ACKNOWLEDGMENTS

BEFORE COMPLETING THE first draft of *Four Weeks, Five People* in my junior year of college, my most successful attempt to write a book came in the sixth grade, when my neighbor (hi, Cecilia) and I came up with an idea for a wild sci-fi novel that combined string theory, superpowers, and Christianity (I was a weird kid). I wrote seventy pages of *Warped* before abandoning it in favor of easier hobbies like playing outside, listening to the new All-American Rejects album on repeat, and coming up with ideas for other novels that were all eventually also abandoned. The only thing that separates the book that lies before you now from the countless half-finished novels buried in the depths of my hard drive are the following people:

Filippo Bulgarelli, who planted the idea for a camp story told from multiple perspectives in my head one hot August afternoon in Philadelphia.

Kathy DeMarco van Cleve, an incredible teacher and mentor, who guided me through the perilous first-draft journey with patience, kindness, and wisdom. Kathy, I have no qualifiers for my thanks to you.

My English 121 classmates—Gina, Laura, Megan, Ishita, Kirara, Hayley, Alex K., Allie, Daniel, Dan, Matt, Alex P., and Shelby—who read the very first scenes in a story called "Ugunduzi" and believed in it from the very start.

Christina Teodorescu and Sam Kaplan, who could not possibly have known that their decision to befriend a shy, bookish girl in the ninth grade would eventually lead to being emailed a new draft of a novel every two weeks and being asked, "So what are your thoughts? Is it boring yet?" each time.

Tori Coviello, my oldest friend and my very first writing partner. Thank you for being a part of my story.

Laura Dail, my agent, who invested in this novel as if it were her own, answered all of my frantic and/or nonsensical questions about publishing and beyond, and made my oldest, craziest, most unimaginable dream of becoming a published author a reality.

T. S. Ferguson and Natashya Wilson, my fantastic editors at Harlequin TEEN, as well as the *Seventeen* team, who believed that a messy, unpolished manuscript by a first-time author could become something great. Thank you for your guidance, your time, and your tireless energy.

Finally, my acknowledgments to Ms. Carolyn Given, Ms. Kristen Small, and Dr. Anders Lewis are long overdue. The earliest miracle of this novel (and there are so many) is that my writing dreams as a young girl—which could have been dashed so easily—were always nurtured by kind and inspiring and altogether incredible teachers.

*Find out what happened to Stella
between her first and second summer
at Camp Ugunduzi!*

*Turn the page for a look at
Jennifer Yu's next novel*

Imagine Us Happy

Everyone always wants to know how it ends. That's the best part of love stories, right? The part when the prince comes back to rescue the princess with a white horse and a sword that sparkles and a smile that sparkles even brighter. Or when the second suitor with the slicked-back hair who came out of nowhere turns out to be a total jerk, and our heroine's love triangle resolves itself in a beautiful, heart-rending reconciliation with Mr. Right in the pouring rain. Or, if it's not that kind of love story, it's the part where our main character is left waiting outside in the rain all alone, cursing her naiveté and wishing she'd realized sooner that "true love" is nothing but Disney's greatest, most profitable invention.

There are a thousand different love stories and a thousand different ways that each of them could end, and believe me, I know—there's nothing worse than reading three hundred pages or watching two hours of a whirlwind romance expecting rose petals and wedding streamers only to get heartbreak instead.

I guess that's why I'm starting at the end. I don't want anyone to be confused about the type of love story I'm about to tell, or where it's going, or what to expect. And I don't want to disappoint anyone in search of a happy ending. I'll say it from the start: this isn't that kind of story.

68. the last time

THE LAST TIME Kevin and I fight, it's the second week of April. A week straight of seventy-plus-degree temperatures have finally coaxed the trees in my backyard into full bloom. I'm watching the leaves of the old oak tree sway as Kevin shouts at me for the last time.

"Goddamn it, Stella," he says. "You can't even look at me, can you?"

He's wrong. It would be easy to look at him. It always has been. It would be easy to turn away from the window, to walk to where he stands across the room, to take his hands in mine and look him square in the eye. But then I would start crying, I know, and he would soften in the way he always does when he's burned down the anger inside him and doesn't have the energy to shout anymore, and then I would forget in the way *I* always do that it's only a matter of time before something reignites it and we start all over again.

"Stella," Kevin says. His voice cracks, and the sound of that is almost—*almost*—enough to break me. Even after all this time, after everything we've been through, after Jeremy and Columbia and the party in March, after *all that*, Kevin is still the only person who says my name like that. Like the key to something beautiful and secret is tucked between the syllables.

"I think you were right," I respond quietly. "This isn't going to work."

"Come *on*, Stella, you know that I didn't mean that," Kevin says. And all of a sudden, he's pissed again. I can hear it in the quickening of his breath, in the way his words start tumbling out of his mouth all at once, sharp like knives. "You're really going to give up on this? On *us*? Over some stupid thing that I said? Stella, you know I only said that because you ditched me to hang out with half the football team and didn't even tell me about it!"

It's 4:05 in the afternoon. My mother will be home from the grocery store soon, and Kevin will have to leave.

It's only a matter of time.

"Talk to me, Stella, *please*, come on," Kevin says. And then, when I don't: "You know what? Fine. I'm leaving. I'm not going to stay here and beg for something you obviously don't give a shit about."

Kevin pushes his chair back so violently that it falls over and hits the floor as he stands.

"I fucking love you," he says loudly. "I'm sorry if that's not enough for you."

He grabs his backpack off my bed, knocking half of my books off my desk in the process. I suppose I should be thankful that no one has thrown anything yet, unlike when we fought a couple of weeks ago and shattered my window in the process. I hear him stomp across the room and pause in my doorway. He's looking at me, I know. Waiting.

"You're being a coward. You know that? You're just fucking scared."

I barely register the words. The wind outside has picked up again and I'm watching the branches of the oak tree arch gracefully in the wind, leaves fluttering into each other. By the time Kevin swears one last time, storms down the stairs and slams the front door shut behind him, it feels like I'm listening from a place very, very far away, where none of this really matters.

The last time Kevin and I fight, there's a profound sense of anticlimax about the whole deal. The emotional pyrotechnics will come later, I know, but in the moment I am surprisingly calm. I do not yell. I do not cry. I do not run back into his arms and let myself fall headfirst, foolishly back in love with a mirage.

The last time Kevin and I fight, it is the second week of April. It's seventy-five and perfect outside, and the afternoon sun makes every particle of dust drifting through my room look like a tiny speck of gold. I have known Kevin for eight months, have sworn up and down that I love him for five, have fought with and fought for and fought because of him so many times the mere thought of it exhausts me.

The last time that Kevin and I fight, I sit back and stare out the window and let him go. Because yes, I am scared, and yes, I am being a fucking coward. But there is nothing left here worth being brave for.

0. a memory

WHEN WE FIRST moved from Hartford to Wethersfield, my dad hung a tire swing from one of the branches of the old oak tree. To my six-year-old self, that swing was magic. A way of escaping gravity that the scientists, cooped up in their offices and boring laboratories, somehow missed. I would have sworn that I went faster on that swing than cars moved on the highway.

One afternoon, I fell off the swing and broke my arm. It hurt like hell, but what hurt more was getting back from the hospital and seeing that my dad had cut the tire swing down. I didn't care that I had to wear a splint for two months, or that all the kids at school started making fun of me for being clumsy, or that I had to learn to write left-handed to take my spelling tests. I forgot the excruciating pain of hitting the ground with my arm bent the wrong way and the sickening *crack* of bone giving way underneath my weight the moment I saw that the swing was gone. Who cared about the pain? I just wanted to feel that magic again.

Sometimes I think of Kevin and all I can remember is that last fight. Kevin, calling me a coward and storming out of my house. And me, refusing to talk to or even look at him in a moment when the desperation in his voice could wring water from the desert. I remember that fight, and I wonder how two people who loved each other could grow to be so deliberately, vindictively cruel.

But I guess that to understand what happened that last day, you have to understand who Kevin and I were before—before he became a boy screaming at the girl he swore he loved, and before I became the girl loving him right back even though I knew I couldn't. You have to understand everything that happened to us between August of 2016 and that day in April. You have to start at the beginning, to when that boy just wanted to read his copy of Modern Philosophy: An Anthology *and get into Columbia and the girl was just trying to survive junior year with minimal emotional fallout. Back to the first day of school, to our first class with Dr. Mulland, to the first time I met Kevin.*

1. resolutions for junior year

FIND SOMEWHERE TO hang out with Lin and Katie in this town that ISN'T Porky's Pizza, the roller rink or, for fuck's sake, THE MALL.

Get an 1800 on the SATs, or whatever it takes to get into a school on the opposite side of this country.

Break twenty minutes in the 5K by our last cross-country meet of the season.

Convince Mom and Dad that if they're going to scream at each other all the time, the least they can do is get me some nice speakers for Christmas.

Spend more time in therapy listening to Karen talk, and less time coming up with unlikely escape routes from her office.

Ditch Homecoming, on account of the fact that it is a glorified high school mating ritual.

Ditch prom, on account of the fact that it is a glorified high school mating ritual.

Convince Katie to ditch Ashley Kurtzmann's house parties, on account of the fact that they are ALL GLORIFIED HIGH SCHOOL MATING RITUALS.

Hate people less, despite their unreasonable obsession with glorified high school mating rituals.

2.

LIN, IN TYPICAL Lin fashion, arrives at my house on the first day of school at 7:15 a.m. sharp.

I, in typical Stella fashion, spend fifteen minutes lying in bed after my alarm goes off trying to work up the motivation to get dressed instead of actually doing it, and don't make it out the front door until 7:22 a.m.

Lin is wearing a black T-shirt that says:

THINGS ADO:
1. Nothing

Her long, brown hair is pulled into a high ponytail, and I notice as I clamber into shotgun that she's put on eyeliner today, which is about as much makeup as Lin ever wears. That's how I know that Lin is taking the first day of school Very Seriously.

"Stella!" Lin says, and wraps me in a hug. "God, it feels like it's been forever. How *are* you?"

I can feel the grin spreading across my face before I even know why I'm smiling. Maybe it's the fact that Lin looks so happy to see me that she doesn't even say anything about how late I am. Maybe it's that she's forgotten to put the car in Park before reaching over to hug me, and we start rolling down the hill before she goes, "oh, shit," and brakes hard. Maybe it's that it really does feel like it's been forever—it's been a long morning, and an even longer summer—but now that I'm sitting in Lin's car, half-terrified that her shitty 1996 Ford Taurus is going to roll right into my front porch, it also feels like nothing's changed at all.

"I'm good," I say automatically, because I've learned that responding to "How are you?" with any answer other than "Good" is a great way to find yourself trapped in conversations you don't want to be having with people you don't want to be having them with. Then I remember that Lin is one of my best friends—not my parents, not my therapist, not Ashley Kurtzmann making her best bid for Miss Congeniality—and I try to be a little bit more honest.

"Well, as good as anyone about to suffer through another year at Bridgemont could possibly be, anyway, which is maybe not-so-good," I say. "And my parents are at each other's throats, of course, but what else is new? What about you? How's the college application struggle?"

Lin rolls her eyes as she pulls out of my neighborhood and starts driving toward Katie's house. "I have written two hundred and fifty drafts of my supplementary essays for Brown," she announces, "and every single one of them is terrible. Don't even get me started on the common application essay."

"Bleak," I say. If Lin doesn't think she can get into a good school, then I might as well just mail it in and take a full-time job at McDonald's now.

"You know what I realized, Stella?" Lin continues. "There is not a single thing I have ever done in my high school career that's original. I mean, here I am, starting senior year, and not a single nonprofit, patent or international peace prize to my name. Not a single lousy Olympic medal!"

"Not *one* Olympic medal?" I ask, faux-outraged.

Lin parks the car in Katie's driveway and makes a face at me. "That's not funny, Stella. Wait 'til you and Katie go through this when you're seniors next year. Speaking of—holy shit. What has she done with her *hair*?"

I turn around to get a better look, but the only thing I manage to get a glimpse of before Katie climbs into the car behind us is a flash of bright, bright purple.

"I FUCKING MISSED YOU GUYS SO MUCH!" Katie shouts.

"Your hair," Lin says, as we both crane our heads around our seats to stare at Katie. "It's—wow."

"Do you guys *love* it?" Katie asks. And then, before either of us can respond: "I think it really says—", she pauses, then adopts a bossy, confrontational tone and rolls her blue eyes upward, "'—I know what I want and I don't give a shit what anyone else thinks.'"

"Oh, that's great," I say. "Seriously, Katie, everyone who's never had a conversation with you will be really convinced."

"Shut up, Stella," Katie says, laughing. "How was camp? How's *life*? I have so much to tell you guys."

The truth is, I am often completely bewildered as to how Katie and I are still friends. In the third grade, we were assigned to do a project on sequoia trees together, and I suppose the process of spending an entire afternoon drawing pictures of trees and pasting them onto a poster is the kind of lifelong bonding experience that's strong enough to withstand vastly divergent personalities and completely incompatible definitions of appropriate speaking volume. If it were anyone other than Katie, I would hate her—but the power of the sequoia, apparently, is mighty indeed.

"Let's not talk about camp," I say as Lin starts driving toward school. "I was having such a nice morning and I'd hate to ruin it. Even managed to get out of bed and everything."

"But was it amazing?" Katie says. "Did you discover yourself? Did you, you know, *meet anyone?*"

"Katie," I say, very seriously, because once Katie starts talking about boys, it's very important to rein her in before she goes off the wall. "I was at a camp for troubled teenagers. We were in therapy all day. Not exactly romantic circumstances."

"Don't call yourself a troubled teenager," Lin says. "You're not troubled. You're just—"

"Difficult? Emotionally disturbed? Had a complete meltdown in the middle of our American history final for no apparent reason and almost got kicked out of school?"

There's a beat of silence. "You," Lin finally says, "are going to have a killer common app essay."